THE
BUTTERFLY
GARDEN

Center Point
Large Print

**This Large Print Book carries the
Seal of Approval of N.A.V.H.**

THE
BUTTERFLY
GARDEN

DOT HUTCHISON

CENTER POINT LARGE PRINT
THORNDIKE, MAINE

The text of this Large Print edition is unabridged.
In other aspects, this book may vary
from the original edition.
Printed in the United States of America
on permanent paper.
Set in 16-point Times New Roman type.

ISBN: 978-1-68324-303-8

Library of Congress Cataloging-in-Publication Data

Names: Hutchison, Dot, author.
Title: The butterfly garden / Dot Hutchison.
Description: Center Point Large Print edition. | Thorndike, Maine :
Center Point Large Print, 2017.
Identifiers: LCCN 2016056202 | ISBN 9781683243038
    (hardcover : alk. paper)
Subjects: LCSH: Missing persons—Fiction. | Kidnapping—
Investigation—Fiction. | Large type books. | GSAFD: Suspense fiction.
Classification: LCC PS3608.U8594 B88 2017 | DDC 813/.6—dc23
LC record available at https://lccn.loc.gov/2016056202

To Mom and Deb
Because you were halfway through
answering the question before you realized
how deeply disturbing it was.
And because everything else.

THE
BUTTERFLY
GARDEN

I

The techs tell him the girl on the other side of the glass hasn't said a word since they brought her in. It doesn't surprise him at first, not with the traumas she's been through, but watching her now from behind the one-way mirror, he starts to question that assessment. She sits slumped in the hard metal chair, chin resting on one bandaged hand as the other traces nonsense symbols onto the surface of the stainless steel table. Her eyes are half-closed, deep shadows bruising the skin beneath, and her black hair is dull and unwashed, scraped back into a messy knot. She's exhausted, clearly.

But he wouldn't call her traumatized.

Sipping his coffee, FBI Special Agent Victor Hanoverian studies the girl and waits for his team members to arrive. At least his partner, anyway. The third core member of their team is at the hospital with the other girls, trying to get updates on their conditions and—when possible—their names and fingerprints. Other agents and techs are at the property, and what little he's heard from them makes him want to call home and talk to his

9

own daughters, make sure they're well. But he has a way with people, especially traumatized children, so it's the sensible choice for him to be here, waiting to go in and talk to this particular victim.

He can see the faint pink lines around her nose and mouth from an oxygen mask, smudges of dirt and soot across her face and borrowed clothing. Bandages wrap around her hands and her upper left arm, and he can trace the bulky line of others beneath the thin undershirt someone at the hospital gave her to wear. She shivers in the off-green scrub pants, her bare feet pulled away from the cold floor, but doesn't complain.

He doesn't even know her name.

He doesn't know the names of most of the girls they rescued, or the ones they were far, far too late to save. This one hasn't talked to anyone but the other girls, and even then there were no names, no information. Just . . . well, he can't really call it comfort. "You'll die or you won't, now relax for the doctors so they can work" wasn't exactly reassuring, but that's exactly how the other girls seemed to take it.

She sits up in the chair, her arms extending slowly over her head until her entire back is curved like a bowstring. The mics pick up the painful pop of vertebrae. Shaking her head, she slumps back over the table, her cheek pressed against the metal, her palms flat against the surface. She's facing away from the glass, away from him and the others she knows must be there, but the angle offers another piece of interest: the lines.

The hospital gave him a picture of it; he can see just the edges of those brilliant colors peeking out against the back of her shoulder. The rest of the design is harder to see, but the undershirt isn't thick enough to obscure it completely. He pulls the picture from his pocket and holds it up against the glass, looking between the glossy paper and what he can see of the design on the girl's back. It wouldn't be significant except that all but one of the girls have them. Different colors, different designs, but all the same in essentials.

"You think he did that to them, sir?" asks one of the techs, watching the girl on the monitor. That camera is aimed from the other side of the interview room, showing an enlarged view of her face, her eyes closed, her breaths slow and deep.

"I guess we'll find out." He doesn't like to make suppositions, especially when they know so little yet. This is one of the very few times in his career where what they found is so much worse than they could have envisioned. He's accustomed to thinking the worst. When a child goes missing, you work your ass off but don't expect to find the poor thing alive at the end of it. Maybe you hope. You don't expect. He's seen bodies so small it's a wonder there are even coffins to fit them, seen

11

children raped before they know the meaning of the word, but somehow this case is so unexpected he isn't quite sure where his footing is.

He doesn't even know how old she is. The doctors guessed sixteen to twenty-two, but that doesn't help him much. As young as sixteen, she should probably have a representative from child services, but they've already swarmed the hospital and made things difficult. They have valuable and necessary services to provide—but that doesn't get them out of his way. He tries to think of his daughters, what they would do if they were locked in a room like this girl, but none of them are this self-contained. Does that mean she's older? Or just that she's had more practice seeming unaffected?

"Have we heard more from Eddison or Ramirez yet?" he asks the techs, not taking his eyes off the girl.

"Eddison's on his way up; Ramirez is still at the hospital with the parents of the youngest girl," one of the women reports. Yvonne doesn't look at the girl in the room, not even at the monitors. She has an infant daughter at home. Victor wonders if he should pull her off—this is only her first day back—but decides she'll say something if she can't handle it.

"She was the one who triggered the search?"

"Only been gone a couple of days. Disappeared from the mall while shopping with her friends.

They said she went out of the dressing room area to switch sizes and never came back."

One less person to find.

They'd taken pictures at the hospital of all the girls, even the ones who'd died en route or on arrival, and were running them through the missing persons database. It will take time for results to come up, though. When agents or doctors asked the ones in better shape for their names, they turned to look at this girl, clearly a leader among them, and most said nothing. A few seemed to think about it before dissolving into sobs that brought the nurses running.

But not this girl in the interview room. When they asked her, she just turned away. As far as anyone can tell, this is one girl with no interest in being found.

Which makes some of them wonder if she's a victim at all.

Victor sighs and drains the last of his coffee, crushing the cup before tossing it in the trash bucket by the door. He'd prefer to wait for Ramirez; another female in the room is always helpful in circumstances like this. Can he wait for her? There's no telling how long she'll be with the parents, or if other parents will flock to the hospital once the photos are released to the media. *If* they're released to the media, he amends with a frown. He hates that part, hates plastering the pictures of victims across television screens and newspapers so there's never a way for them to forget what happened to them. At least they can wait until they get the missing persons data.

The door opens and slams shut again behind him. The room is soundproof but the glass rattles slightly and the girl sits up quickly, eyes narrowed at the mirror. And, presumably, the ones she has to know are behind it.

Victor doesn't turn around. No one slams a door quite like Brandon Eddison. "Anything?"

"They've matched a couple of fairly recent reports, and the parents are on their way. So far it's all East Coast."

Victor pulls the picture from the glass and puts it back into the pocket of his jacket. "Anything else on our girl?"

"Some of the others called her Maya after she was brought here. No last name."

"Real name?"

Eddison snorts. "Doubtful." He struggles to zip his jacket over his Redskins T-shirt. Once the response team found the survivors, Victor's team was called in from off duty to handle it. Given Eddison's tastes, Victor's mostly grateful there are no naked women on the shirt. "We've got a team going through the main house to see if the bastard kept anything personal."

"I think we can both agree that he kept some very personal things of theirs."

Perhaps remembering what he saw at the

property, Eddison doesn't argue. "Why this one?" he asks. "Ramirez says there are others not too badly injured. More frightened, maybe more willing to talk. This one looks like a tough nut."

"The other girls look to her. I want to know why. They must be desperate to get home, so why do they look at her and choose not to answer questions?"

"You think she might be part of this?"

"That's what we need to find out." Picking up the bottle of water from the counter, Victor takes a deep breath. "All right. Let's go talk to Maya."

She sits back in the chair when they walk into the interview room, gauze-covered fingers laced together across her stomach. It's not as defensive a posture as he would expect, and it's clear from his partner's scowl that he's thrown by it as well. Her eyes flick over them, taking in details and filing away thoughts, none of which show on her face.

"Thank you for coming with us," he greets her, glossing over the lack of choice she'd been given. "This is Special Agent Brandon Eddison, and I'm Special Agent in Charge Victor Hanoverian."

The corner of her mouth ticks upward in a fleeting movement he can't really call a smile. "Special Agent in Charge Victor Hanoverian," she repeats, her voice hoarse with smoke. "Quite a mouthful."

"Would you prefer Victor?"

"I don't really have a preference, but thank you."

He unscrews the cap and hands her the bottle of water, using the moment to adjust his strategy. Definitely not traumatized, and not shy either. "Usually there's another part to the introductions."

"The helpful tidbits?" she says. "You like to weave baskets and take long swims, and Eddison likes to walk the streets in heels and a mini?"

Eddison growls and slams a fist onto the table. "What is your name?"

"Don't be rude."

Victor bites his lip against the temptation to smile. It won't help the situation—certainly won't help his partner's state of mind—but the temptation is there just the same. "Would you please tell us your name?"

"Thank you, but no. I don't believe I care to share that."

"Some of the girls called you Maya."

"Then why did you bother to ask?"

He hears Eddison's sharp intake of breath, but ignores it. "We'd like to know who you are, how you came here. We'd like to help you get home."

"And if I said I don't need your help to get home?"

"I'd wonder why you didn't get home before this."

16

There's a not-quite smile, and a flicker of an eyebrow that might be approval. She's a beautiful girl, with golden-brown skin and pale brown, nearly amber eyes, but she's not soft. A smile will have to be earned. "I think we both know the answer to that. But I'm not in there anymore, am I? I can get home from here."

"And where is home?"

"I'm not sure if it's there anymore."

"This isn't a game," Eddison snaps.

The girl appraises him coolly. "No, of course not. People are dead, lives are ruined, and I'm sure you were very inconvenienced at having to leave your football game."

Eddison flushes, tugging the zipper up higher over his shirt.

"You don't seem all that nervous," Victor notes.

She shrugs and takes a sip of the water, holding the bottle gingerly in her bandaged hands. "Should I be?"

"Most people are when talking to the FBI."

"It's not that different from talking with—" She bites her chapped lower lip, winces at the beads of blood that seep through the cracked skin. She takes another sip.

"With?" he prompts gently.

"Him," she answers. "The Gardener."

"The man who held you—you talked with his gardener?"

She shakes her head. "He *was* the Gardener."

17

• • •

You have to understand, I didn't give him that name out of fear or reverence, or some misguided sense of propriety. I didn't give him that name at all. Like anything else in that place, it was made up out of the whole cloth of our ignorance. What wasn't known was created, what wasn't created eventually ceased to matter. It's a form of pragmatism, I suppose. Warm, loving people who desperately need approval from others fall victim to Stockholm syndrome, while the rest of us fall to pragmatism. Having seen both sides in others, I'm for pragmatism.

I heard the name my first day in the Garden.

I came to with a splitting headache, a hundred times worse than any hangover I'd ever experienced. I couldn't even open my eyes at first. Pain lanced through my skull with every breath, let alone movement. I must have made a sound because suddenly there was a cool, damp cloth over my forehead and eyes and a voice promising that it was only water.

I wasn't sure which unnerved me more: the fact that this was obviously a frequent concern for her, or the fact that it was a *her* at all. There'd been no woman in the pair that kidnapped me, of that much I was sure.

An arm slid behind my shoulders, gently pulling me upright, and a hand pressed a glass against my lips. "Just water, I promise," she said again.

I drank. It didn't really matter if it was "just water" or not.

"Can you swallow pills?"

"Yes," I whispered, and even that much sound drove another nail through my skull.

"Open up, then." When I obeyed, she placed two flat pills on my tongue and brought the water up again. I swallowed obediently, then tried not to vomit when she gently lowered me back to a cool sheet and a firm mattress. She didn't say anything else for a long time, not until the colored lights stopped dancing across the backs of my eyelids and I started to move of my own volition. Then she pulled away the cloth across my face, shielding my eyes from the overhead light until I could stop blinking.

"So you've done this a few times before," I croaked.

She handed me the glass of water.

Even folded over on herself, on a stool beside the bed, it was easy to see that she was tall. Tall and sinewy with long legs and lean muscles like an Amazon. Or a lioness, really, because she slumped bonelessly like a cat. Tawny gold hair was piled atop her head in some fancy nonsense, revealing a face with strong architecture and deep brown eyes with flecks of gold. She wore a silky, black dress that tied high around her neck.

She accepted my frank appraisal with something

like relief. I suppose it was better than shrieking hysterics, which she'd probably gotten before.

"I'm called Lyonette," she said when I'd looked my fill and given my attention back to the water. "Don't bother telling me your name because I won't be able to use it. Best to forget it, if you can."

"Where are we?"

"The Garden."

"The Garden?"

She shrugged, and even that was a fluid gesture, something graceful rather than inelegant. "It's as good a name for it as any. Do you want to see it?"

"I don't suppose you know a shortcut to a way out of here?"

She just looked at me.

Right. I swung my legs over the edge of the bed, planted my fists on the mattress, and realized I could see every bit of me there was to see. "Clothing?"

"Here." She handed me a piece of silky, black something that proved to be a slinky, knee-length dress that came high around the neck and low on the back. Really low. If I'd had dimples on my ass, she'd've been seeing them. She helped me tie the ropy sash around my hips, then gave me a gentle push toward the doorway.

The room was plain, severely so, with nothing in it but the bed and a small toilet and sink in one corner. In another corner was what seemed to be a tiny open shower. The walls were made of thick glass, with a doorway in place of a door, and there was a track on either side of the glass.

Lyonette saw me looking at the track marks and scowled. "Solid walls come down to keep us in our rooms and out of sight," she explained.

"Often?"

"Sometimes."

The doorway opened into a narrow hallway, running along to my right, but only a short way on my left before it hit a corner. Almost directly across from the doorway was another entryway with more of that tracking—it led into a cave, damp and cool. An open arch on the far side of the cave brought breezes running through the dark stone space, bits of light catching in the waterfall that babbled and churned just outside. Lyonette led me out from behind the curtain of water into a garden so beautiful it nearly hurt to look at it. Brilliant flowers of every conceivable color bloomed in a riotous profusion of leaves and trees, clouds of butterflies drifting through them. A man-made cliff rose above us, more greenery and trees alive on its flat top, and the trees on the edges just brushed the sides of the glass roof that loomed impossibly far away. I could see tall black walls through the lower-level greenery, too tall to see what was beyond, and little pockets of open space surrounded by vines. I thought they might be doorways to halls like the one we'd been in.

The atrium was massive, almost overwhelming in its sheer size before you even looked at the riot of color. The waterfall fed into a narrow stream that meandered down to a small pond decked in water lilies, white sand paths tracking through the greenery to those other doors.

The light through the ceiling was deep lavender and streaked through with rose and indigo— evening. It had been bright afternoon when I was taken, but somehow I didn't think it was the same day. I turned in a slow circle, trying to take it all in, but it was too much. My eyes couldn't see half of what was there, and my brain couldn't process half of what I saw.

"The fuck?"

Lyonette actually laughed, a hard sound that abruptly cut short as though she were afraid anyone might hear it. "We call him the Gardener," she said dryly. "Apt, no?"

"What is this place?"

"Welcome to the Butterfly Garden."

I turned to ask her what that meant, but then I saw it.

She takes a long sip of water, rolling the bottle across her palms. When she shows no signs of continuing, Victor gently taps the table to get her attention. "It?" he prompts.

She doesn't answer.

Victor pulls the photo from his jacket pocket, laying it on the table between them. "It?" he asks again.

"See, asking me questions to which you already know the answer doesn't make me inclined to trust you." But her shoulders relax and she leans back into the seat, on familiar footing.

"We're the FBI; usually people think we're the good guys."

"And Hitler thought he was evil?"

Eddison lurches to the very edge of his seat. "You're comparing the FBI to Hitler?"

"No, I'm engaging in a discussion about perspective and moral relativity."

When they got the call, Ramirez went straight to the hospital, and Victor came here to coordinate the deluge of incoming information. Eddison was the one to tour the property. Eddison always reacts to horror with temper. And with that thought, Victor flicks his eyes back to the girl on the other side of the table. "Did it hurt?"

"Like hell," she answers, tracing the lines on the photo.

"The hospital says it's a few years old?"

"You make that sound like a question."

"A statement seeking confirmation," he clarifies, and this time the smile creeps out.

Eddison scowls at him.

"Hospitals are many things, but completely

incompetent doesn't tend to be one of them."

"And what the hell does that mean?" snaps Eddison.

"Yes, it's a few years old."

He recognizes the patterns now from years of asking his daughters about report cards and tests and boyfriends. He lets the silence hang for a minute, then two, and watches the girl carefully flip the photo over. The shrinks on the larger team would probably have a thing or three to say about that. "Who did he have do it?"

"The one person in the world he could trust without reservation."

"Multi-talented man."

"Vic—"

Without taking his eyes from the girl, Victor kicks the leg of his partner's chair, jarring him. He's rewarded with that suggestion of a smile. Not the real thing, not even a ghost of it really, but something like it.

The girl peeks under the edge of the gauze taped around her fingers, fashioned like gloves rather than mitts. "The needles make a hell of a sound, don't they? When it's not what you choose? But it is a choice, because there *is* the alternative."

"Death," Victor guesses.

"Worse."

"Worse than death?"

But Eddison pales and the girl sees, and rather than mocking him for it, she gives him a solemn nod. "He knows. But then, you haven't been there, have you? Reading about it isn't the same."

"What's worse than death, Maya?"

She scrapes a nail under one of the fresh scabs on her index finger, peeling it away so dots of blood blossom against the gauze. "You'd be amazed at how easy it is to get tattoo equipment."

For the first week, there was something slipped into my dinner each night to make me docile. Lyonette stayed with me during the days, but the other girls—of which there were apparently more than a few—stayed away. This was normal, she told me when I remarked on it over lunch.

"The weeping thing stresses everyone out," she said around a mouthful of salad. Whatever else could be said of the mysterious Gardener, he provided excellent meals. "Most prefer to stay out of it until we know how a girl's going to settle in."

"Except for you."

"Someone has to do it. I can put up with the tears if I have to."

"Then how grateful you must be that I haven't provided you with any."

"About that." Lyonette stabbed a strip of grilled chicken and twirled her fork. "Have you cried at all?"

"Would there be a point to doing so?"

"I'm either going to love you or hate you."

25

"Let me know, I'll try to behave accordingly."

She gave me a fierce smile, all her teeth showing. "Keep that attitude, but don't do it with him."

"Why does he want me sleeping at night?"

"Precautionary measures. There's a cliff right outside, after all."

Which made me wonder how many girls had thrown themselves over before he implemented those precautionary measures. I tried to gauge the height of the man-made monstrosity. Twenty-five, maybe thirty feet? Was that high enough to kill someone on impact?

I'd grown accustomed to waking up in that empty room when the drugs wore off, Lyonette sitting on a stool beside the bed. But, at the end of the first week, I woke up on my stomach on a bench with hard padding and the astringent smell of antiseptic thick in the air. It was a different room, larger, with metal walls rather than glass.

And it had someone else in it.

I couldn't see at first, not with the drugged sleep still seaming my eyelids together, but I could feel someone else there. I kept my breathing slow and even, straining to hear, but a hand settled on my bare calf. "I know you're awake."

It was a man's voice, midrange and cultured with a Mid-Atlantic cast to it. A pleasant voice. The hand smoothed up my leg, over my ass, and along the curve of my back. Goose bumps prickled in its wake, despite the warmth of the room.

"I'd prefer for you to lie very still, otherwise we'll both have cause to regret it." When I tried to turn my head toward his voice, the hand moved to the back of my skull to keep me still. "I would prefer not to bind you for this; it ruins the line of the work. If you feel you cannot remain motionless, I will give you something that will guarantee it. Again, I would prefer not to. Can you be still?"

"For?" I asked, almost in a whisper.

He tucked a glossy-smooth piece of paper into my hand.

I tried to open my eyes but sleep meds always made them gunk up more than usual in the morning. "If you're not going to start *right* now, may I please sit up?"

The hand stroked my hair, the fingernails scraping lightly against my scalp. "You may," he said, sounding startled. He did, however, help me sit up on the bench. I rubbed the crystals from my eyes and looked down at the picture in my hand, aware of how his hand kept caressing my hair. I thought of Lyonette, of the other girls I'd seen from a distance, and I couldn't say I was surprised.

Creeped out, but not surprised.

He stood behind me, the air around him filled with a spicy cologne. Understated, probably pricy.

In front of me was a full tattooist's setup, the inks arrayed on a standing tray. "It won't be the full design today."

"Why do you mark us?"

"Because a garden must have its butterflies."

"Any chance we could leave that metaphorical?"

He laughed, a full, easy sound. This was a man who loved to laugh and didn't find as much cause to do it as he'd like, and was therefore always delighted by the opportunity. You learn things over time, and that was one of the biggest things I learned about him. He wanted to find more joy in life than he did. "Small wonder my Lyonette likes you. You are a fierce spirit, much like she is."

I didn't have an answer to that, nothing that made sense to say.

He carefully hooked his fingers through my hair, pulling it back over my shoulders, and picked up a brush. He worked it through my hair until there wasn't a single knot to be found, and even after. I think he enjoyed it as much as anything else, really. It's a simple pleasure, brushing someone else's hair. Being allowed to. Eventually he pulled it into a ponytail and wrapped it with an elastic, then coiled it into a heavy bun and secured it with a scrunchie and rubber-tipped pins.

"Back onto your stomach now, please."

I obeyed, and as he moved away I caught a glimpse of pressed khakis and a button-down shirt. He turned my head to face away from him, my cheek pressed against the black leather, and placed my arms loosely at my sides. It wasn't quite comfortable, but wasn't direly uncomfortable either. When I steeled myself not to jump or flinch, he lightly slapped my rear. "Relax," he instructed. "If you tense, it will hurt more and take longer to heal."

I took a deep breath and forced my muscles to unclench. I curled and uncurled my fists, and with each uncurl I released a bit more tension from my back. Sophia taught us that, mainly to keep Whitney from her periodic breakdowns, and—

"Sophia? Whitney? These are some of the girls?" Eddison interrupts.

"They're girls, yes. Well, Sophia probably counts as a woman." The girl takes another sip, eyes the quantity left in the bottle. "Actually, Whitney would too, I guess. So they're women."

"What do they look like? We can match their names to—"

"They're not from the Garden." It's hard to interpret the look she gives the younger agent, equal parts pity, amusement, and derision. "I had a life before, you know. Life didn't begin at the Garden. Well, not this Garden anyway."

Victor turns the photo over, trying to calculate how long such a thing must have taken. So large, so much detail.

"It wasn't all at once," the girl tells him,

following his eyes to the pattern. "He started with the outlines. Then he went back in over the course of two weeks to add in all the color and detail. And when it was done, there I was, just another one of the Butterflies in his Garden. God creating his own little world."

"Tell us about Sophia and Whitney," Victor says, content to leave the tattoo for a time. He has a feeling what happened when it was done, and he's willing to call himself a coward if it means not hearing it yet.

"I lived with them."

Eddison tugs the Moleskine from his pocket. "Where?"

"In our apartment."

"You need—"

Victor cuts him off. "Tell us about the apartment."

"Vic," Eddison protests. "She's not giving us anything!"

"She will," he answers. "When she's ready."

The girl watches them without comment, sliding the bottle from hand to hand like a hockey puck.

"Tell us about the apartment," he says again.

There were eight of us who lived there, all of us working together at the restaurant. It was a huge loft apartment, all one room, with beds and footlockers laid out like a barracks. Each bed had a hanging rack for clothing on one side, and rods for curtains on the other side and at the foot of the bed. It wasn't much for privacy but it worked well enough. Under normal circumstances rent would have been hellish, but it was a shit neighborhood and there were so many of us that you could make your rent in a night or two and call the rest of the month spending money.

Some even did.

We were a strange mix, students and hoydens and a retired hooker. Some wanted the freedom to be anyone they wanted, some of us wanted the freedom to be left alone. The only things we had in common were working at the restaurant and living together.

And honestly? It was kind of like heaven.

Sure, we clashed sometimes, there were arguments and fights and occasional pettiness, but for the most part those things blew over pretty quickly. Someone was always willing to loan you a dress or a pair of shoes or a book. There was work, classes for those who took them, but otherwise we had money and an entire city at our feet. Even for me, who grew up with minimal supervision, that kind of freedom was wonderful.

The fridge was kept stocked with bagels, booze, and bottled water, and there were always condoms and aspirin in the cabinets. Sometimes you could find leftover takeout in the fridge, and whenever social services came to visit Sophia, and see how she was improving, we made a grocery run and hid the booze and condoms. Mostly we ate out or had things delivered. Working around food every night, we generally avoided the apartment kitchen like the plague.

Oh, and the drunk guy. We were never sure if he actually lived in the building or not, but in the afternoons we'd see him drinking in the street and every night he'd pass out in front of our door. Not the building door—our door. He was a fucking pervert too, so when we came back after dark— which was pretty much every night—we took the stairs all the way up to the roof and then came down one floor on the fire escape to come in through the windows. Our landlord put a special lock on there for us because Sophia felt bad for the drunk pervert and didn't want to turn him over to the cops. Given her situation—retired hooker–drug addict cleaning up to try to get her kids back—the rest of us didn't push.

The girls were my first friends. I suppose I'd met people like them before but it was different. I could stay away from people and usually did. But I worked with the girls and then I lived with them, and it was just . . . different.

There was Sophia, who mothered everyone and had managed to be completely clean for over a year when I met her, and that was after two years of trying and slipping. She had the two most beautiful daughters, and they'd actually been kept together in the same foster home. Even better, the foster parents fully supported Sophia's goal of earning them back. They let her come see the girls pretty much whenever she wanted. Whenever things got rough, whenever the addiction started screaming again, one of us would stuff her in a taxi to see her girls and remind her what she was working so hard for.

There was Hope, and her little stooge Jessica. Hope was the one with the ideas, with the vivacity, and Jessica went along with everything she said and did. Hope filled the apartment with laughter and sex, and if Jessica used sex as a way to feel better about herself, at least Hope showed her how to have some fun with it. They were the babies, only sixteen and seventeen when I moved in.

Amber was also seventeen, but unlike the other two, she had a bit of a plan. She got herself declared an emancipated minor so she could get out of the foster system, took her GED, and was taking classes at a community college to get her AA until she could figure out a major. There was Kathryn, a couple of years older, who never, ever talked about life before the apartment. Or about much of anything, really. Kathryn could sometimes be prevailed upon to go with the rest of us to do something, but she never did anything on her own. If someone lined all eight of us against a wall and asked who was running from something or someone, a person would point to Kathryn every time. We didn't ask her, though. One of the basic rules of the apartment was that we didn't push on personal history. We all had baggage.

Whitney I mentioned, she of the periodic breakdowns. She was a grad student in psychology, but was so fucking high-strung. Not in a bad way, just in an "I don't react to stress well" kind of way. Between semesters she was fantastic. During semesters we all took turns getting her to chill the fuck out. Noémie was also a student, getting one of the most useless degrees known to man. Really, I think the only reason she was going to college was because she had scholarships and getting an English degree gave her an excuse to read a *lot*. Luckily, she was very generous in sharing her books.

Noémie was the one who mentioned the apartment to me my second week at the restaurant. It was my third week in the city and I was still living at a hostel, bringing all my worldly possessions to work with me every day. We were in the tiny staff room, changing out of our uniforms. I kept mine at the restaurant just in case my stuff got stolen while I was sleeping, so at least I'd still be able to work. Everyone else changed there because the uniform—a long dress and heels— just wasn't the sort of thing they pranced around in on their way home.

"So, um . . . you're pretty trustworthy, right?" she said with no preamble. "I mean, you don't stiff the busboys or hostess, you don't steal anyone's stuff from the staff room. You never smell of drugs or anything."

"Does this have a point?" I pulled on my bra and fastened the hooks behind me, rearranging my breasts to fit. Living in a hostel gave you a certain lack of modesty, one reinforced by the tiny staff room and the number of female employees who had to change there.

"Rebekah said you're just a step up from the street. You know a bunch of us live together, right? Well, we've got an extra bed."

"She's serious," called Whitney, fluffing her red-gold hair out of its braided bun. "It's a bed."

"And a footlocker," giggled Hope.

"But we've been talking about it and wondered if you'd like to move in. Rent would be three hundred a month, includes utilities."

I hadn't been in the city that long but even I knew that was impossible. "Three hundred? The hell you get for three hundred?"

"Rent is two thousand," Sophia corrected. "Share of rent would be three hundred. The extra is what covers the utilities."

That sounded about right, except . . . "How many of you live there?"

"You would make eight."

Which wouldn't make it that different from living in the hostel, really. "Can I stay with you tonight and see it, and decide tomorrow?"

"Sounds great!" Hope handed me a denim skirt that looked barely long enough to cover my underwear.

"That's not mine."

"I know, but I think it would look really cute on you." She was already one leg into my overlarge corduroys, so rather than argue, I shimmied into the skirt and decided to be very careful in bending over. Hope was curvy as hell, running a little to plump, so I could pull the skirt low on my hips for a little extra length.

The owner's eyes lit up when he saw me leaving *with* the girls. "You live with them now, yes? You be safe?"

"The customers are gone, Guilian."

He dropped the Italian accent and clapped me on the shoulder. "They're good girls. I'm glad you'll be with them."

His opinion went a long way toward convincing me even before I saw the apartment. My first impression of Guilian had been hard but fair, and he proved me right when he offered a trial week to a girl with a duffel bag and a suitcase beside her at the interview. He pretended to be native Italian because it made the customers somehow think the food was better, but he was a tall, heavyset ginger with thinning hair and a moustache that had eaten his upper lip and was now seeking to devour the rest of his face. He believed a person's work was a better judge than their words, and he appraised people accordingly. At the end of my first week, he simply handed me the schedule for the next week with my name inked in.

It was three in the morning when we left. I memorized the streets and the trains, and wasn't nearly as nervous as I should have been when we walked into their neighborhood. On feet aching from hours of high heels, we trudged up the many flights of stairs to the top floor and then to the roof, weaving through various patio furniture, covered grills, and what looked to be a flourishing marijuana garden in one corner, and down one flight on the fire escape to the large bank of windows. Sophia worked the key into the lock as Hope giggled her way through an explanation of the drunk pervert in the hallway.

We had a few of those at the hostel.

It was a huge space, open and clean, with four beds lining each sidewall and a group of couches clustered together in a square in the center. The kitchen had an island counter to separate it from the rest of the room and a door led off to the bathroom, which had a huge open shower with ten different heads facing different directions.

"We don't ask questions about the people who lived here before," Noémie said delicately when she showed it to me. "It's just a shower though, not an orgy."

"You convince maintenance of this?"

"Oh, no, we fuck with them all the time. That's half the fun."

I smiled in spite of myself. The girls were fun to work with, always tossing jokes and insults and compliments around the kitchen, venting about irritating customers or flirting with the cooks and dishwashers. I'd smiled more in the past two weeks than I could ever remember doing before. Everyone dropped purses and bags on their foot-lockers and many of them changed into pajamas or what passed for them, but sleep was a long way off yet. Whitney pulled out her psychology textbook while Amber pulled out twenty shot glasses and filled them with tequila. I reached for one but Noémie handed me a tumbler of vodka instead.

"The tequila is for studying."

So I sat on one of the couches and watched Kathryn read through Amber's practice test, one shot glass for each question. If Amber got the question wrong, she had to drink the shot. If she got it right, she could make someone else drink it. She handed the first one to me, and I tried not to choke on the nasty-as-shit mix of tequila and vodka.

We were still awake when daylight came, and Noémie, Amber, and Whitney all trundled off to class while the rest of us finally crashed. When we woke up early in the afternoon, I signed the agreement they had in place of a lease and paid my first month from the past two nights' tips. Just like that, I wasn't homeless anymore.

"You said this was your third week in the city?" Victor asks, running through a list of cities she might mean. Her voice is clean of larger dialect markers, no regionalisms that could help identify her origin. He's fairly sure that's on purpose.

"That's right."

"Where were you before that?"

She finishes off the water rather than answer. Carefully standing the empty bottle on one corner of the table, she sits back in the chair and slowly rubs her bandaged hands up and down her arms.

Victor stands and shrugs out of his jacket, walking around the table to drape it over her shoulders. She tenses as he walks near, but he takes care not to let his skin brush hers. When he returns to his side of the table, she relaxes enough to slide her arms through. It's large on her, draping in baggy folds, but her hands emerge comfortably from the cuffs.

New York City, he decides. Warehouse-style apartments, restaurants open extremely late. Plus she said trains instead of metro or subway—that meant something, didn't it? He makes a mental note to contact the New York office and see if they can find anything on the girl.

"Were you in school?"

"No. Just work."

A tap on the window sends Eddison out of the room. The girl watches him leave with some satisfaction, then turns a neutral expression back on Victor.

"What made you decide to go to the city?" he asks. "It doesn't sound like you knew anyone there, didn't have a plan for when you got there. Why go?"

"Why not? It's something new, right? Something different."

"Something distant?"

She arches an eyebrow.

"What is your name?"

"The Gardener called me Maya."

"But that wasn't what you were before."

"Sometimes it was easier to forget, you know?" She fidgets with the edge of the cuffs, rolling and unrolling them with quick motions. Probably not much different than rolling silverware sets when it came to it. "You were in there, no chance of escape, no way of going back to the life you knew, so why cling to it? Why cause yourself more pain by remembering what you don't get to have anymore?"

"Are you saying you forgot?"

"I'm saying he called me Maya."

I was mostly isolated from the other girls until my tattoo was finished, with the exception of Lyonette, who still came every day to talk with

40

me, to rub ointment over my raw back. She let me study her mark with no sign of shame or disgust. It was a part of her now, like breathing, like the unconscious grace of her movements. The level of detail was stunning and I wondered how much the intricacy suffered when it came time to refresh the brightness of the ink. Something kept me from asking, though. A good tattoo took years to fade enough that it needed to be touched up; I didn't want to think about what it would mean to be in the Garden for that long.

Or worse, what it could mean if I wasn't.

The drugs still appeared in my dinner, which Lyonette brought to me on a tray along with her own. Every few days I woke up, not in the bed, but on the hard leather bench, with the Gardener running his hands along the previously inked areas to test how they were healing, how sensitive they were. He never let me see him, and unlike my room with its semi-reflective glass everywhere, the dull metal walls gave me no hope of catching a glimpse.

He hummed as he worked, a sound that was somewhat lovely on its own but clashed horribly with the mechanical hum of the needles. Golden oldies, mostly: Elvis, Sinatra, Martin, Crosby, even some Andrews Sisters. It was a strange kind of pain, choosing to lie there under the needles and let him write his ownership into my skin. I didn't see that I had many options, though.

41

Lyonette said she stayed with each girl until the wings were done. I couldn't explore the Garden yet, couldn't look for a way out. I wasn't sure yet if Lyonette knew there was no way out or if she just didn't care anymore. So I let him put those damn wings on me. I never asked what would happen if I fought, if I refused.

I almost did, but Lyonette paled so I changed the question to something else.

I thought it had something to do with the way she never took me through the halls, only out into the Garden itself, through the cave behind the waterfall. Whatever she didn't want me to see— or didn't want to show me, which isn't the same thing at all—I could wait. Cowardly, I guess. Or pragmatic.

It was near the end of the third week in the Garden that he finished.

All morning he'd been more intense, more focused, had taken fewer and shorter breaks. The first day he'd inked along my spine and worked in the outline for the wings and the veins and the blocks of the larger patterns. After that, he'd started at the wing tips and worked his way back in toward my spine, rotating between the four quadrants of my back to keep any one area from getting unworkably raw. He was nothing if not meticulous.

Then the hum stopped and his breaths were short and fast as he wiped away the blood and excess ink. His hands trembled at their work where before they'd been nothing but steady. Cold, slick ointment came next, rubbed carefully into every inch of skin. "You're exquisite," he said hoarsely. "Absolutely flawless. Truly a worthy addition to my garden. And now . . . now you must have a name."

His thumbs stroked along my spine, where the first ink was done and the most healed, traveling up to the nape of my neck to tangle in my pulled-up hair. Greasy ointment clung to his hands, leaving my hair matted and heavy in his wake. Without warning, he pulled me down the bench until my feet were on the floor, my upper half still on the leather. I could hear him fumbling with his belt and zipper and I screwed my eyes tightly shut.

"Maya," he groaned, running his hands along my sides. "You are Maya now. Mine."

A hard knock on the door stops her from describing what came next, and she looks both startled and grateful.

Victor swears under his breath and lurches out of his chair to the door, jerking it open. Eddison motions him into the hallway. "What the hell is wrong with you?" he hisses. "She was actually talking."

"The team going through the suspect's office found something." He holds up a large evidence

43

bag filled with driver's licenses and identification cards. "Looks like he kept all of them."

"All of them that had one, anyway." He takes the bag—Christ, that's a lot of cards—and shakes it a little to see past the first layer of names and pictures. "Did you find hers?"

Eddison hands him a different bag, a small one holding a sole piece of plastic. It's a New York ID and he recognizes her immediately. A little younger, her face softer even if her expression isn't. "Inara Morrissey," he reads, but Eddison shakes his head.

"They've scanned the rest and are starting to run them, but they put this one first. Inara Morrissey didn't exist until four years ago. The Social Security number matches a two-year-old's who died in the seventies. New York office is sending someone to the last listed place of employment, a restaurant named Evening Star. The address on the ID is a condemned building, but we called the restaurant and got the apartment address. The agent I talked to whistled when he gave it to me; apparently it's a rough neighborhood."

"She told us that," Victor says absently.

"Yes, she's so trustworthy and forthcoming."

He doesn't answer right away, absorbed in studying the ID. He believes his partner that it's a fake, but damn, what a fake. Under ordinary circumstances, he has to admit he'd be fooled by it. "When did she stop showing up for work?"

"Two years ago, according to her boss. Taxes support it."

"Two years . . ." He hands the larger bag back and folds the plastic bag around the single ID until he can tuck it into his back pocket. "Have them run these as quickly as possible; borrow techs from other teams if they can get away with it. Identifying the girls in the hospital has to be a priority. Then get us a couple of earbuds so the techs can pass along updates from the New York office."

"Got it." He scowls at the closed door. "Was she actually talking?"

"Talking hasn't exactly been her problem." He chuckles. "Get married, Eddison, or better yet have teenage daughters. She's better than most, but the patterns are there. You just have to parse through the information for what's significant. Listen to what isn't being said."

"There's a reason I prefer to talk to suspects rather than victims." He stalks into the tech room without waiting for a response.

As long as he's out of the room, he might as well make use of the break. Victor walks briskly down the hall and out into the team's main room, weaving through desks and partial cubes to the corner that serves as a kitchen or break room. He pulls the coffeepot from the machine and gives it a judicious sniff. It's not hot, but it doesn't smell completely stale either. He pours it into two mugs that look clean and pops them in the microwave. While they nuke, he digs through the fridge for anything that might be open season.

Birthday cake isn't quite what he's looking for, but it'll serve, and soon he has paper plates loaded with two thick slices and several packets of sugar and creamer. He hooks his fingers through the handles of the mugs and returns to the tech room.

Eddison scowls but holds the plates for him so he can insert the earbud. Victor doesn't try to hide the wire; the girl's too smart for that. When he's got it settled comfortably, he takes the plates back and enters the room.

He startles her with the cake, and he carefully hides a smile as he slides one of the plates and a mug across the stainless steel surface. "I thought you might be hungry. I don't know how you like your coffee."

"I don't, but thank you." She sips the coffee black, makes a face, but swallows and takes another mouthful.

He waits until her mouth is full of a red frosting rose. "Tell me about the Evening Star, Inara."

She doesn't choke, doesn't flinch, but there's the slightest pause, a moment of absolute stillness that's gone so fast he wouldn't have seen it if he weren't looking for it. She swallows and licks the frosting from her lips, leaving streaks of brilliant red across them. "It's a restaurant, but then you know that."

He pulls the ID from his pocket and places it and the bag on the table. She taps a fingernail against the ID, intermittently obscuring her face. "He kept them?" she asks incredulously. "That seems . . ."

"Foolish?"

"Sure." Her face pulls into a thoughtful frown, and her fingers flatten to hide the plastic card from view. "All of them?"

"As far as we can tell."

She swirls the coffee in the mug, staring at the tiny maelstrom.

"But Inara is as much a construction as Maya, isn't it?" he asks gently. "Your name, your age, none of it's real."

"It's real enough," she corrects softly. "Real for what it needs to be."

"Real enough to get a job and a place to live. But what came before?"

One of the nice things about New York was that no one ever asked questions. It's just one of those places people go to, you know? It's a dream, it's a goal, it's a place you can disappear amidst millions of other people doing the same thing. No one cares where you came from or why you left because they're too focused on themselves and what they want and where they're going. New York has so much history, but everyone in it just wants to know about the future. Even when you're *from* New York City, you can still go to ground somewhere else and they may never find you.

I took the bus to New York with everything I owned in a duffel bag and a suitcase. I found a soup kitchen that didn't care if I slept in the clinic upstairs as long as I helped serve food, and one of the other volunteers told me about a guy who had just made him papers for his wife, who was an illegal from Venezuela. I called the number he gave me and the next day I was at the library, sitting under a statue of a lion and waiting for a complete stranger to approach me.

He didn't inspire much confidence when he finally appeared, an hour and a half after we'd agreed. He was average height and skinny, his clothes stiff with salt and other stains I didn't want to identify. His lank hair was in the process of matting into dreads and he sniffled constantly, his eyes darting around each time before he lifted a sleeve to rub at his cherry red nose. Maybe he was a genius at forgery, but it wasn't hard to guess where the money went.

He didn't ask me my name, or rather, he only asked the name I wanted. Birth date, address, license or ID, did I want to be an organ donor? As we talked, we walked into the library to give us an excuse to be quiet, and when he reached a banner with a swath of clean white, he stood me up against it and took my picture. I'd taken extra care before coming to the library to meet him, even bought some makeup, so I knew I could pull off nineteen. It's about the eyes, really. If you've seen enough, you just look older, no matter what the rest of your face looks like.

He told me to meet him at a particular hot dog cart that evening and he'd have what I needed. When we reconvened—he was late again—he held up an envelope. Such a little thing, really, but it's enough to change a life. He told me it would be a grand, but he'd knock it down to five hundred if I slept with him.

I paid him the grand.

He walked away in one direction and I in another, and when I got back to the hostel where I planned to spend the night—a good ways from the soup kitchen and anyone who might remember a girl being told about illegal papers—I opened the envelope and got my first good look at Inara Morrissey.

"Why didn't you want to be found?" he asks, using a pen to stir the creamer into his coffee.

"I wasn't worried about being found; to be found, someone has to be looking for you."

"Why wouldn't anyone be looking for you?"

"I miss New York. No one asked these kinds of questions there."

Static crackles in his ear as one of the techs opens a line. "New York says she got her GED three years ago. Passed with flying colors but never registered for the SAT or asked for the scores to be passed on to a college or employer."

"Did you drop out of high school?" he asks. "Or did you get your GED so you wouldn't have to produce a diploma?"

"Now that you have a name, it's much easier to dig into my life, isn't it?" She finishes off the cake and sets the plastic fork at a neat angle across the plate, the tines down. Paper crinkles as she tears open one of the sugar packets and empties it into a pile on the plate. Licking the only fingertip not covered in gauze and tape, she presses it against the sugar and sticks it into her mouth. "That only tells you about New York, though."

"I know, so I need you to tell me about what came before."

"I liked being Inara."

"But that isn't who you are," he says gently, and anger flashes through her eyes. Gone just as fast as her almost-smiles or her surprise, but there just the same.

"So a rose by any other name isn't still a rose?"

"That's language, not identity. Who you are isn't a name but it is a history, and I need to know yours."

"Why? My history doesn't tell you about the Gardener, and isn't that what it's really about? The Gardener and his Garden? All his Butterflies?"

"And if he survives to come to trial, we need

50

to provide the jury with credible witnesses. A young woman who won't even tell the truth about her name doesn't cut it."

"It's just a name."

"Not if it's yours."

That not-quite-smile twists her lips briefly. "Bliss said that."

"Bliss?"

Lyonette stood outside the tattoo room as ever, her eyes politely averted from me until I could put on the slinky black dress that had become my only piece of clothing. "Close your eyes," she told me. "Let's take this in stages."

I'd kept my eyes closed so long in that room that the thought of being voluntarily blind again made my skin crawl. But Lyonette had done well by me so far, and she'd clearly done this before for other girls. I made the choice to trust her a bit further. Once I closed my eyes, she took my hand and led me down the hall in the opposite direction than we usually went. It was a long hallway, and we turned left at the end of it. I kept my right hand but against the glass walls, my arm flopping free whenever we passed one of the open doorways.

Then she directed me through one of the doorways and positioned me where she wanted with gentle hands on my upper arms. I felt her step back. "Open your eyes."

51

She stood in front of me, off-center in a room nearly identical to mine. This one had small personal touches: origami creatures on a shelf above the bed, sheets and blankets and pillows, pumpkin-colored curtains hiding the toilet, sink, and shower from sight. The edge of a book stuck out from under the largest pillow and drawers lined the space under the bed.

"What name did he give you?"

"Maya." I staved off the shudder that came from saying it aloud for the first time, from the memory of him saying it over and over while he—

"Maya," she repeated, and gave me another sound to hold on to. "Take a look at yourself now, Maya." She held up a mirror, positioning it so I could use it to look into another mirror behind me.

Large portions of my back were still pink and raw and swollen around the fresh ink, which I knew was darker than it would become once the scabs flaked off. Fingerprints were visible on my sides where the fabric gapped, but there was nothing to obscure the design. It was ugly, and terrible.

And lovely.

The upper wings were golden-brown, tawny like Lyonette's hair and eyes, flecked through with bits of black, white, and deep bronze. The lower wings were shades of rose and purple, also marked through with patterns of black and white. The detail was astonishing, slight color variations giving the impressions of individual scales. The colors were rich, almost saturated, and they filled almost my entire back, from the very tips of my shoulders to a little below the curve of my hips. The wings were tall and narrow, the outer edges just barely curving onto my sides.

The artistry couldn't be denied. Whatever else he was, the Gardener was talented.

I hated it, but it *was* lovely.

A head popped through the doorway, quickly followed by the rest of a tiny girl. She couldn't have topped five feet with her shoulders back, but no one could see those curves and think her a child. She had flawless, frosty-white skin and huge blue-violet eyes, framed by a haphazardly pinned profusion of tight black curls. She was all striking contrasts, with a button nose that leaned toward cute rather than beautiful, but like all the girls I'd glimpsed in the Garden, she was nothing less than stunning.

Beauty loses its meaning when you're surrounded by too much of it.

"So, this is the new girl." She flopped down on the bed, hugging a small pillow to her chest. "What'd the bastard name you?"

"He might hear you," Lyonette chided, but the girl on the bed just shrugged.

"Let him. He's never asked us to love him. So what's he call you?"

"Maya," I said in time with Lyonette, and the

word got a little less hard to hear. I wondered if it would continue to be that way, if in time the word wouldn't hurt at all, or if it was a tiny shard that always would, like the piece of a splinter you can't reach with tweezers.

"Huh, that's not too bad then. Fucker named me Bliss." She rolled her eyes and snorted. "Bliss! Do I look like a blissful person? Ooh, let's see." Her fingers made a twirling motion, and in that moment, she reminded me a little of Hope. With that in mind, I slowly spun to show her my back. "Not too bad. The colors flatter you, anyway. We'll have to look up what kind that is."

"It's a Western Pine Elfin," Lyonette sighed. She shrugged at my sideways look. "It's something to do. Maybe it makes it a little less awful. I'm a Lustrous Copper."

"I'm a Mexican Bluewing," added Bliss. "It's pretty enough. Awful, of course, but it's not like I have to look at it. Anyway, the name thing? He could call us A, B, or Three and it wouldn't matter. Answer to it but don't pretend it's somehow yours. Less confusing that way."

"*Less* confusing?"

"Well sure! Remember who you are and then it's just playing a part. If you start to think of it as you, that's when the identity crisis hits. Identity crisis usually leads to a breakdown, and a breakdown around here leads to—"

"Bliss."

"What? She seems like she can handle it. She isn't crying yet, and we all know what he does when the ink is finished."

Like Hope, but much smarter.

"So what does a breakdown lead to?"

"Check the hallways, just don't do it after you eat."

"You'd just walked through the hallways," Victor reminds her.

"With my eyes closed."

"Then what was in the hallway?"

She swirls the remainder of the coffee in her mug rather than answer, giving him a look that suggests he should already know.

Static crackles in his ear again. "Ramirez just called from the hospital," Eddison says. "She's sending pictures of those the doctors expect to make it. Missing Persons has had some luck. Between them and the ones fresh in the morgue, they've got about half the girls identified. And we have a problem."

"What kind of problem?"

The girl looks at him sharply.

"One of the girls they identified has some important family. She's still calling herself Ravenna, but her fingerprints matched to Patrice Kingsley."

"As in Senator Kingsley's missing daughter?"

Inara settles back in her chair, her expression

clearly amused. Victor isn't sure what she finds funny about what promises to be a hell of a complication.

"Has the senator been informed yet?" he asks.

"Not yet," answers Eddison. "Ramirez wanted to give us a heads-up first. Senator Kingsley has been desperate to find her daughter, Vic; there isn't a chance in hell she won't push into the investigation."

And when that happens, any privacy they may be able to offer these girls will be out the window. Their faces will be plastered on every news network from here to the West Coast. And Inara . . . Victor rubs wearily at his eyes. If the senator learns they have any suspicions about this overly contained young woman, she won't rest until charges are filed.

"Tell Ramirez to hold off as long as she can," he says finally. "We need time."

"Roger."

"Remind me how long she's been missing?"

"Four and a half years."

"Four and a half *years?*"

"Ravenna," Inara murmurs, and Victor stares at her. "No one ever forgets how long they've been there."

"Why not?"

"It changes things, doesn't it? Having a senator involved."

"It changes things for you, as well."

"Of course it does. How could it not?"

She knows, he realizes uneasily. Maybe she doesn't know specifics, but she knows they suspect her of some kind of involvement. He measures the amusement in her eyes, the cynical twist to her mouth. She's a little too comfortable with this new information.

Time to change the subject, then, before he loses the power in the room. "You said the girls in the apartment were your first friends."

She shifts slightly in her seat. "That's right," she answers warily.

"Why is that?"

"Because I hadn't had any before."

"Inara."

She responds to that tone of voice the same way his daughters do—instinctively, grudgingly when she realizes it a moment too late, and just a bit sulky. "You're good at that. You have kids?"

"Three girls."

"And yet you make a career in broken children."

"In trying to rescue broken children," he corrects. "In trying to get justice for broken children."

"You really think broken children care about justice?"

"Wouldn't you?"

"Never really did, no. Justice is a faulty thing at the best of times, and it doesn't actually fix anything."

"Would you say that if you'd gotten justice as a child?"

That not-quite-smile, bitter and gone too fast. "And what would I have needed justice for?"

"My life's work, and you think I won't recognize a broken child when she sits in front of me?"

She inclines her head to concede the point, then bites her lip and winces. "Not entirely accurate. Let's call me a shadow child, over-looked rather than broken. I'm the teddy bear gathering dust bunnies under the bed, not the one-legged soldier."

He smiles slightly and sips his rapidly cooling coffee. She's back to dancing. However disconcerting Eddison might find it, Victor's on familiar ground. "In what way?"

Sometimes you can look at a wedding and realize with a certain sense of resignation that any children produced in that marriage will inevitably be fucked up and fucked over. It's a fact, not a sense of foreboding so much as a grim acceptance that these two people should not— but definitely will—reproduce.

Like my parents.

My mother was twenty-two when she married my father; he was her third marriage. The first was when she was seventeen and married the brother of her mother's then-current husband. He died in

58

less than a year from a heart attack during sex. He left her pretty well off, so a few months later, she married a man only fifteen years older than her, and when they divorced a year later, she came off even a little better. Then came my dad, and if he hadn't knocked her up, I doubt the wedding would have happened. He was good-looking, but he wasn't wealthy and he didn't have prospects and he was only two years older, which to my mother was an insurmountable series of obstacles.

For that we can thank *her* mother, who had nine husbands before early menopause made her decide she was too dried up to remarry. And every single one of them died, each faster than the one before. No foul play about it, either. Just . . . died. Most of them were ancient, of course, and all of them left her with a tidy sum of money, but my mother was raised with certain expectations and her third husband met none of them.

I will say this for them, though: they gave it a try. For the first couple of years we lived near his family and there were cousins and aunts and uncles and I can almost remember playing with other children. Then we moved, and the ties were cut from one end or the other, and it was just me and my parents and their various affairs. They were always either visiting their latest lovers or holing up in their bedrooms, so I became a pretty self-sufficient kid. I learned how to use the microwave, I memorized the bus schedule so I could get to the grocery store, I staked out the days of the week when either of my parents were likely to have cash in their wallets so I could actually buy things at the market.

And you'd think that would look strange, right? But whenever anyone at the store asked—a concerned woman, a cashier—I'd say my mom was out in the car with the baby, keeping the air running. Even in winter they believed that, and they'd smile and tell me what a wonderful daughter and sister I was.

So not only was I self-sufficient, I came to have a pretty low opinion of most people's intelligence.

I was six when they decided to give marriage counseling a go. Not a try, a go. Someone at my dad's office told him insurance would cover counseling, and counseling looked better with a judge and helped speed up a divorce. One of the things the counselor told them to do was take a family trip, just the three of us, somewhere fun and special. A theme park maybe.

We got to the park around ten, and for the first couple of hours things went okay. Then the carousel. I fucking hate carousels. My dad stood at the exit to wait for me to come off, my mom stood at the entrance to help me get on, and they just stood there on opposite sides of the thing and watched me go round and round in circles. I was too small to reach for the iron rings and the horse I was on was so wide it made my hips hurt, but round and round and round I went, and I watched my father walk away with a petite Latina. Another time around and I saw my mother leave with a tall, laughing ginger in a Utilikilt.

A nice older kid helped me down off the horse after he lifted his little sister down, and held my hand as we walked to the exit. I wanted to stay with that family, to be the little sister of someone who went on rides with you and held your hand while walking, someone who smiled down and asked if you had fun. But we got outside the carousel and I thanked him, waving at a woman paying attention to nothing but her cell phone so the boy thought I'd found my mom, and I watched him and his sister walk back to parents who were delighted to see them.

I spent the rest of the day wandering around the park, trying not to get noticed by security, but sunset came and the park closed and I still hadn't found either of my parents. Security noticed and hauled me off to the Hall of Shame. Well, they called it the Lost Parents Place. They cycled a list of calls over the PA system, asking parents missing their children to come claim them. There were others there, too, other kids who'd been forgotten or just wandered away or had been hiding.

Then I heard one of the adults mention child services. Specifically she mentioned calling child services for anyone who wasn't claimed before ten o'clock. My next-door neighbors were a foster home and the thought of living with people like them was horrific. Fortunately, one of the younger kids pissed himself and sent up such a squall that all the adults started fussing over him, trying to calm him, and I managed to sneak out the door and back into the park.

It took some searching, but I finally found the main gate and got out without being seen, attaching myself to the rear of a school group that had gotten stuck for a while on one of the rides, and out into the parking lot. From there it took over an hour for me to walk through all the parking lots to a gas station that was still brightly lit for all the folks heading home. I still had most of the snack money my dad had shoved in my pocket before the carousel so I called their cell phones, and then I called the house phone, and then because I couldn't think of anything else to do, I called my next-door neighbor.

It was almost ten o'clock at night, but he hopped in the car and drove two hours to come pick me up, and another two hours home, and there were no lights on at all in my house.

"Was this the neighbor who was a foster father?" Victor asks when she pauses to lick her chapped lips. He reaches for the empty bottle of water and holds it up toward the one-way mirror, not putting it down until one of the techs says Eddison is on his way.

"Yes."

"But he got you safely home, so why was the thought of living with him so horrific?"

"When we pulled up in front of his house, he told me I needed to thank him for the ride by licking his lollipop."

The plastic bottle shrieks a protest as it crumples in his fist. "Christ."

"When he pulled my head toward his lap, I stuck a finger down my throat, and made myself throw up all over him. Made sure to hit the horn, too, so his wife would come out." She opens another sugar packet and tips half of it into her mouth. "He got arrested for molestation a month or so later, and she moved away."

The door slams open and Eddison tosses a new bottle of water at the girl. Protocol says they're supposed to remove the cap for them—choking hazard—but his other hand is occupied with a sheaf of photo papers that he drops onto the table, along with the bag of IDs in the crook of his elbow. "By not telling us the truth," he snarls, "you're protecting the man who did this."

Inara was right; it is different seeing it than just reading about it. Victor lets out a slow breath, using it to push down the instinctive revulsion. He shifts the first picture off the pile, then the second, the third, the fourth, all depicting portions of the hallways in the ruined garden complex.

She stops him at the seventh one, easing the

paper away so she can look at it more closely. When she sets it back down on top, her finger pets a tawny curve near the center of the image. "That's Lyonette."

"Your friend?"

Her bandaged finger gently moves along the line of glass in the picture. "Yeah," she whispers. "She was."

Birthdays, like names, were best forgotten in the Garden. As I got to know the other girls, I knew they were all fairly young, but ages weren't something you asked about. It just didn't seem necessary. At some point we'd die, and the hallways provided daily reminders of what that would mean, so why compound the tragedy?

Until Lyonette.

I'd been in the Garden for six months, and while I'd become friendly with most of the other girls, I was closest to Lyonette and Bliss. They were the most like me, the ones who really didn't feel up to the high drama of weeping or bemoaning our inevitably tragic fates. We didn't cower before the Gardener, we didn't suck up to him like becoming favorites would somehow change our fortunes. We were the ones who put up with what we had to and otherwise did our own thing.

The Gardener adored us.

Except for meals, which were served at specific times, there was never a place we had to be, so most of the girls room-hopped for comfort. If the Gardener wanted you, he'd simply check the cameras and come find you. When Lyonette asked Bliss and me to spend the night in her room, I didn't think anything of it. It was something we did all the time. I should have recognized the desperation in her voice, the edge to her words, but that was something else the Garden numbed you to. Like beauty, desperation and fear were as common as breathing.

We were provided with clothing for the daytime—always in black, always things that left our backs bare so the wings could be seen—but were given nothing for sleeping. Most of us just slept in our underwear and wished for bras. The hostel and the apartment had been good practice for me; I had far less modesty than most of the other girls had had coming into the Garden, one less humiliation that might break me.

The three of us curled together atop the mattress, waiting for the lights to go out, and gradually we became aware that Lyonette was shaking. Not like a seizure or anything, just a tremor that ran under her skin and electrified every part of her with movement. I sat up, reaching for her hand to lace our fingers together. "What's wrong?"

Tears gleamed in her gold-flecked eyes, making me suddenly nauseated. I'd never seen Lyonette cry before; she hated tears in anyone, especially

65

herself. "Tomorrow's my twenty-first birthday," she whispered.

Bliss squeaked and threw her arms around our friend, burying her face in Lyonette's shoulder. "Fuck, Lyon, I'm so sorry!"

"We have an expiration date then?" I asked quietly. "Twenty-one?"

Lyonette clutched Bliss and me with desperate strength. "I . . . I can't decide if I should fight or not. I'm going to die anyway, and I kind of want to make him earn it, but what if fighting makes it more painful? Shit, I feel like such a coward, but if I have to die, I don't want it to hurt!"

She started sobbing and I wished this was one of the times the solid walls came down around the glass, so we could be trapped in this little space and her weeping wouldn't be heard by everyone down the hall. Lyonette had a reputation for strength among the girls, and I didn't want them to think her weak once she was gone. But for the most part, the walls only came down two mornings a week—what we'd taken to calling the weekend, whether it was or not—so the actual gardeners could do maintenance around our beautiful prison. The hired help never saw us, and the multiple sets of closed doors between us and them guaranteed they never heard us either.

No, wait. The walls came down when a new girl was brought in too. Or when one died.

We didn't like it when the walls came down.

Wishing they would was kind of extraordinary.

We stayed with Lyonette the entire night, long after she'd wept herself into an exhausted sleep and had woken only to weep again. Around four, she roused enough to stumble into the shower, and we helped her wash her hair, brushed it out and arranged it in a regal braided crown. There was a new dress in her closet, an amber silk fancy with glimmering gold threads that was bright as a flame against all the black. The color made her wings glow against her light brown skin, brilliant pumpkin-orange flecked with gold and yellow closest to the black spots and the white fringed bands of black on the very tips. The open wings of a Lustrous Copper.

The Gardener came for her just before daylight.

He was an elegant figure of a man, maybe a little above average height, well built. The type of man who always looked at least ten to fifteen years younger than he really was. Dark blond hair, always perfectly in place and well-trimmed, pale green eyes like the sea. He was handsome, that couldn't be argued, even if my stomach still turned at the sight of him. I'd never seen him dressed all in black before. He stood in the doorway, thumbs hooked in his pockets, and just looked at us.

Taking a deep breath, Lyonette hugged Bliss tightly, whispered something in her ear, before kissing her goodbye. Then she turned to me, her arms painfully tight around my ribs. "My name is Cassidy Lawrence," she whispered, so quietly I could barely hear it. "Please don't forget me. Don't let him be the only one to remember me." She kissed me, closed her eyes, and allowed the Gardener to lead her away.

Bliss and I spent the rest of the morning in Lyonette's room going through the small personal items she'd managed to accumulate over the past five years. Five *years* she'd been there. We took down the privacy curtains, folded them together with the bedding into a neat stack on the edge of the naked mattress. The book she kept under her pillows turned out to be the Bible, with five years of rage and despair and hope scrawled around the verses. There were enough origami animals for all the girls in the Garden and then some, so we spent the afternoon giving them away, along with the black clothing. When we sat down to dinner, there was nothing left of Lyonette in the room.

That night, the walls came down. Bliss and I curled together in my bed, which actually had more bedding than a sewn-on sheet now. Personal touches were things we earned by not being troublesome, by not trying to kill ourselves, so I had sheets and blankets now, the same rich rose and purple as the lower wings on my back. Bliss cried and swore when the walls came down and trapped us in the room. They rose after a few hours, and before they'd come higher than a foot off the floor, she grabbed my hand and squeezed us through so we could search the hallways.

But we only had to go a few feet.

The Gardener stood there, leaning back against the garden-side wall as he studied the girl in the glass. Her head was bowed nearly against her chest, small stirrups under her armpits keeping her upright. Clear resin filled the rest of the space, the gown caught in the liquid like she was underwater. We could see almost every detail of the bright wings on her back, nearly pressed against the glass. Everything that was Lyonette—her fierce smile, her eyes—was hidden away, so the wings were the only focus.

He turned to us and ran a hand through my sleep-tangled hair, gently tugging through the knots he encountered. "You forgot to put your hair up, Maya. I can't see your wings."

I started to gather it to twist into a rough knot but he caught my wrist and pulled me after him.

Into my room.

Bliss swore and ran down the hall, but not before I saw her tears.

The Gardener sat on my bed and brushed my hair until it gleamed like silk, running his fingers through it again and again. Then his hands moved elsewhere, and his mouth, and I closed my eyes and silently recited "The Valley of Unrest."

"Wait, what?" Eddison interrupts, a sickened expression on his face.

She looks away from the picture, giving him a bemused look. " 'The Valley of Unrest,' " she repeats. "It's a poem by Edgar Allan Poe. *They had gone unto the wars, trusting to the mild-eyed stars, nightly, from their azure towers, to keep watch above the flowers'* . . . I like Poe. There's something refreshing about a man who's so unabashedly morose."

"But what—"

"It's what I did whenever the Gardener came to my room," she says baldly. "I wasn't going to fight him, because I didn't want to die, but I wasn't going to participate either. So I let him do his thing, and to keep my mind occupied, I recited Poe's poems."

"The day he finished your tattoo, was that the first time, uh . . . the first time—"

"I recited Poe?" she finishes for him, one eyebrow arched mockingly. Victor flushes but nods. "No, thank God. I'd gotten curious about sex a few months before, so Hope loaned me one of her boys. Sort of."

Eddison makes a choking sound and Victor can't help but be grateful that his wife has these kinds of discussions with their daughters.

In any other setting, we probably would have called Hope a whore, except that Sophia—who actually had been a prostitute until her daughters were taken away by the cops—was a little

70

sensitive about words like that. Plus, Hope was in it for the fun, not the money. She could have made a fortune, though. Male, female, pairs, trios, or groups, Hope was up for anything.

And there really wasn't any such thing as privacy in the apartment. Except for the bathroom, it was all one room, after all, and the curtains between the beds weren't thick enough to conceal much. No canopies, anyway. They certainly didn't make anything soundproof. Hope and Jessica weren't the only girls to bring people home, but they did it with the most frequency, sometimes more than once in a day.

Early exposure—no pun intended—to pedophiles had left me mostly uninterested in sex. That, plus my parents. It seemed a horrific business, not one I wanted any part of, but living with the girls gradually changed that. When they weren't doing it, they were frequently talking about it, and even when they laughed at me, they answered silly questions about it—or in Hope's case, decided to demonstrate how to masturbate—so eventually curiosity won out over the distaste and I decided to give it a try. Well, I decided to think about giving it a try. I backed away from a lot of opportunities at first because I still wasn't sure.

Then one afternoon when I didn't have to go into work in the evening, Hope came home trailing two boys. Jason we worked with, one of

71

the few males on the overwhelmingly female waitstaff, and his friend Topher was a pretty standard fixture in the apartment. They frequently dropped by whether Hope was there or not; we thought they were fun to hang out with. Sometimes they brought food. The three were barely in the door before Hope was busy pulling off Jason's clothing, and the two of them were completely naked by the time they tumbled laughing through the curtains onto her bed.

Topher at least had the grace to blush and kick the trail of clothing closer to the bed.

I was on one of the couches with a book. One of the first things I did once I had a real address was to get a library card, and I made a couple trips a week. Reading had been an escape when I was younger, and even though I didn't have anything I particularly needed to escape from anymore, it was still something I loved. When the clothing was more or less contained, Topher poured two glasses of orange juice—social services had swung by a couple of days ago, so the fridge was actually stocked—and handed one of them to me as he flopped next to me on the couch.

"What, not joining them?" I teased, and his blush deepened.

"It's no mystery that being with Hope is a little like having a time-share, but I don't share at the same time," he mumbled, and I snickered. Hope was *exactly* like a time-share, and proud of it.

Topher was a model, maybe nineteen, who sometimes helped Guilian with the deliveries to make a few extra bucks. He was good-looking in that bland model way—you know, the kind of good-looking that seems really ordinary because it's shoved in your face all the time? He was a decent guy, though. We talked about the matinee a whole slew of us had gone to see the week before, about a gig he had for a few days as a living dummy for a temporary museum exhibit, about one of our mutual acquaintances getting married, and whether or not it would last, all while Hope and Jason went at it screaming and giggling.

So, pretty much a normal afternoon.

Eventually, though, their fun had to end. "It's almost four o'clock!" I yelled over the groaning. "You two need to get to work!"

"Okay, I'll finish him off!"

True to her word, she had Jason grunting in less than thirty seconds, and ten minutes later, they'd both had a quick rinse in the shower and were off to work. Most of the girls were working that night, except for Noémie and Amber, who both had a night class on Wednesdays and wouldn't be back until almost ten. Topher left for a little while but came back with takeout from Taki's on the corner.

I knew Hope's usual invitation to sex was to kiss someone and shove her hand down his or her pants, but I wasn't Hope.

"Hey, Topher?"

"Yeah?"

"Do you want to teach me about sex?"

I was a different kind of straightforward.

Anyone else probably would have blanched, but Topher was a friend of Hope's. Plus, he'd been there for some of the conversations. All he did was smile, and I was reassured by the fact that it wasn't a smirk. "Sure, if you think you're ready for it."

"I think so. I mean, we can always stop."

"Yes, we can. Just tell me if you get uncomfortable, okay?"

"Okay."

He took the remains of our dinner and shoved them into the overflowing trash can by the door; Hope was supposed to take it out when she left for work. When he came back to the couches, he dropped down onto the cushion and gently pulled me to lean against him. "We'll start slow," he said. And he kissed me.

We didn't actually have sex that night; he called it Everything But. It was comfortable, though, and fun, and we laughed as much as anything, which in itself would have been strange just a year before when I'd first moved in. We kept the clothes on after Noémie and Amber came home from class, but he stayed with me that night in my narrow bed and we played more under the sheets until Noémie—in the next bed over—laughed and said if we didn't shut up she was going to join us. It was a few days later that we had the privacy to go all the way, and the first time, I didn't really understand what the big deal was.

Then we did it again, and that time I did.

We spent the next few weeks fooling around, until he met a girl at church he wanted to be serious with, but as easily as we'd become friends with benefits we went back to being friends, without any awkwardness or hurt feelings at all. Neither of us had fallen for the other, neither of us was putting more into it than the other. I loved when he came by the apartment, but not because I expected sex after he started dating his church girl. Topher was just a good guy, someone we all adored.

It did not, however, make me understand my parents' fascination with sex to the exclusion of all else.

She unscrews the cap and takes a long drink of water, rubbing at her sore throat as she swallows. Victor is grateful for the silence and thinks Eddison must be as well, both men staring at the table. Trauma being what it is, Victor can't recall a victim interview where sex was such a frank topic.

He clears his throat, turning the photos over so he doesn't have to see the hallways lined with dead girls in glass and resin. "Your next-door neighbor when you were a child was a pedophile, you said, but when did you see the others?"

"Gran's lawn guy." She stops, blinks, and glowers at the bottle of water, and Victor can't help but think she didn't mean to say it. Perhaps the exhaustion is setting in with a stronger grip. He files that thought away for now, but he'll watch for other opportunities.

"You saw your Gran often?"

She sighs and picks at a scab on one of her fingers. "I lived with her," she answers reluctantly.

"When was this?"

My parents finally got divorced when I was eight. All the questions about money, about the house and cars and all the *things* were taken care of in one meeting. The next eight months were spent with each arguing that the other should be stuck with me.

Isn't that fantastic? Every kid should be forced to sit through eight months of listening to their parents actively not want them.

Eventually it was decided that I'd be sent to live with Gran, my mother's mother, and both my parents would pay her child support. When the day came for me to leave, I sat on my front step with three suitcases, two boxes, and a teddy bear, the grand total of everything I owned. Neither of my parents was home.

A year before, we'd gotten new neighbors across the street, a youngish couple who'd just had their first child. I used to love going over to see the baby, a beautiful little boy who wasn't broken or fucked up yet. With parents like his, maybe he never would be. She'd always give me a plate of cookies and a glass of milk, and he taught me how to play poker and blackjack. They were the ones who took me to the bus station, who helped me buy my ticket with the money my parents had left on my nightstand the day before, the ones who helped me load everything under the bus and introduce me to the driver and help me find a seat. She even gave me a lunch for the trip, complete with oatmeal raisin cookies still warm from the oven. They were another family I wished I could be a part of, but I wasn't theirs. Still, I waved goodbye to them as the bus pulled away, and they stood together on the curb, their baby held between them, and waved until we couldn't see each other anymore.

When I got to the city where Gran lived, I had to take a taxi from the bus station to the house. The driver swore all the way there about people who had no business having kids, and when I asked him what some of the words meant, he even taught me how to use them in sentences. My Gran lived in a big, dilapidated house in a neighborhood that was moneyed sixty years ago but quickly went to shit, and when the driver had helped me unload everything onto her tiny front porch, I paid him and told him to have a great fucking day.

He laughed and tugged my braid, told me to take care of myself.

Menopause did strange things to Gran. She was a serial bride—and widow—when she was younger, but That Time convinced her she was dried up and halfway into the grave, so she holed up in her house and started filling all the rooms and halls with dead things.

No, seriously, *with dead things.* Even the taxidermists thought she was creepy, and you have to be really fucking bad to win that award. She had things she'd purchased premade, like wild game or exotics, things like bears and mountain lions that weren't something you saw in a city. She had birds and armadillos, and my personal most hated, the collection of neighborhood cats and dogs that had been killed in various ways over the years that she'd taken in to be stuffed. They were everywhere, even in the bathrooms and kitchen, and they filled every single room.

When I walked in, dragging my things behind me into the entryway, she was nowhere to be seen. I heard her, though. "If you're a rapist, I'm all dried up, don't waste your time! If you're a thief, I have nothing worth stealing, and if you're a murderer, shame on you!"

I followed the sound of her voice and finally found her in a small family room with narrow walkways between all the stacks of stuffed animals. She was in an easy chair wearing a full-body tiger-print unitard and a dark brown fur coat, chain-smoking as she watched *The Price Is Right* on a seven-inch television whose picture wavered and frequently fell to discoloration.

She didn't even look at me until the commercials. "Oh, you're here. Upstairs, third door on the right. Be a good girl and bring me the bottle of whiskey on the counter before you go."

I got it for her—why not—and watched in amazement as she poured the entire bottle into small dishes and bowls in front of the dead cats and dogs lined up on a couch that would have been hideous under the best of circumstances.

"Drink up, my beauties, being dead is no treat, you've earned it."

Whiskey fumes quickly filled the room, joining with the musty scent of fur and stale cigarettes.

Upstairs, third door on the right led into a room full of so many dead animals they tumbled out when I opened the door. I spent the rest of that day and all that night hauling them out and finding places to stick them so I could bring up my things. I slept curled up on top of the biggest suitcase because the sheets were so gross. I spent the next day cleaning the room top to bottom, beating the dust and mouse droppings—and mouse corpses—out of the mattress, and putting my own sheets from home on the bed. When I had everything arranged as close to home as I could manage, I went back downstairs.

The only indication Gran had moved was her unitard, now a bright, shiny purple.

I waited until the commercials and then cleared my throat. "I've cleaned out the room," I told her. "If you put any more dead things in there while I'm living here, I'll burn the house down."

She laughed and slapped me. "Good girl. I like your gumption."

And that was moving in with my Gran.

The setting changed, but life didn't. She had her groceries delivered once a week by a nervous-looking boy who got a tip almost as big as the grocery bill purely because that was the only way he'd come to our neighborhood. It was pretty simple to call the grocery store and have new things added to the staples. I was enrolled in a school that taught absolutely nothing, where the teachers wouldn't even take attendance because they didn't want truancy to stick them with these kids for another year. There were supposed to be some really good teachers in the school, but they were few and far between and I never got any of them. The rest were burned out and just didn't care anymore as long as they got a paycheck.

The students certainly encouraged that. Drug deals went down right there in the classrooms, even in the elementary school, on behalf of older siblings. When I went up into the middle school, there were metal detectors on every outer door but no one gave a shit or investigated when they went off, which was frequently. No one noticed if you weren't in class, no one called home to check up on students who'd been gone for several days in a row.

I tested that once, stayed home for a full week. I didn't even get makeup work when I went back. I only returned because I was bored. Sad, really. I left everyone else alone so they left me alone too. I didn't leave the house after dark, and every night I fell asleep to a lullaby of gunshots and sirens. And when Gran's lawn guy came twice a month, I hid under my bed in case he came into the house.

He was probably in his late twenties, maybe a little older, and always wore jeans that were too tight and too low, trying to make the best of a package that even at that age I didn't think was very impressive. He liked to call me *pretty girlie,* and if he was there when I came home from school, he'd try to touch me and ask me to bring him things. I kicked him once, right in the balls, and he cursed and chased me into the house, but he tripped over the stag in the entryway and Gran ripped him a new one for making too much noise during her soaps.

After that, I hung out at the gas station a few blocks over until I saw his truck drive past.

"And your parents never questioned your well-being?" He knows it's a stupid question, but it's already out of his mouth, and he nods even as her mouth twists.

"My parents never came to see me, never called, never sent cards or gifts or anything. Mom sent checks for the first three months, Dad for the first five, but then those stopped too. I never saw my parents or heard from them again after I went to Gran's. I honestly don't even know if they're still alive."

They've been at this all day, the birthday cake the first thing he'd had since last night's dinner. He can feel his stomach complaining, knows she must be at least as hungry. It's been almost twenty-four hours since the FBI arrived at the Garden. They've both been awake longer than that.

"Inara, I'm willing to let you tell things in your own way, but I need you to give me a straightforward answer to one question: should we have child services in here?"

"No," she says immediately. "And that's the truth."

"How close is that truth to a lie?"

It's actually a smile this time, crooked and wry, but even so small a smile as that softens her entire face. "I turned eighteen yesterday. Happy birthday to me."

"You were *fourteen* when you got to New York?" Eddison demands.

"Yep."

"What the hell?"

"Gran died." She shrugs, reaching for the water bottle. "I came home from school and she was dead in the chair with burns on her fingers where the cigarette burned all the way down. I'm kind of amazed the whole damn place wasn't on fire from the whiskey fumes. I think her heart gave out or something."

"Did you report it?"

"No. The lawn guy or the grocery boy would find her when they went to get paid, and I didn't want anyone arguing about what to do with me. Maybe they would have tracked down one of my parents and I'd be forced to go with them, or they'd just dump me into the system. Or maybe they would have tracked down one of those uncles or aunts on my dad's side and shoved me off onto yet another relative who didn't want me. I didn't like those options."

"So what did you do?"

"I packed a suitcase and a duffel, then raided Gran's stash."

Victor's not sure if he's going to regret the answer, but he has to ask. "Stash?"

"Of cash. Gran only sort of trusted banks, so any time she got a check, she cashed it and hid half of it up the German shepherd's ass. The tail was on a hinge, so you could reach under and pull out the money." She takes a sip, then purses her lips and presses them against the mouth of the bottle, letting the water soak against the chapped cracks. "There was almost ten grand in there," she continues when she pulls the bottle away. "I hid it away in my suitcase and duffel, spent the night at the house, and in the morning I woke up and walked down to the bus station rather than school, and bought a ticket to New York."

"You spent the night in the house with your dead grandmother."

"She wasn't stuffed yet, but otherwise what was the difference than any other night?"

He's grateful for the static in his ear. "We ordered food for the three of you," Yvonne reports from the observation room. "Couple more minutes on it. And Ramirez called. A few of the girls have started talking. Not much yet; they seem more concerned with the dead ones than themselves. Senator Kingsley is on her way from Massachusetts."

Well, it started out as good news. It's probably too much to hope that the senator will be forced to make an early landing somewhere due to bad weather.

Victor shakes his head and leans back in his chair. The senator isn't here yet; they'll deal with her once she is. "We're going to take a break soon so we can all eat, but one more question before that."

"Only one?"

"Tell us about how you came to the Garden."

"That isn't a question."

Eddison slaps his thigh impatiently, but it's still Victor who speaks. "How did you come to the Garden?"

"I was kidnapped."

Three teenage daughters and he can practically hear the unspoken "duh" at the end of it. "Inara."

"You're *really* good at that."

"Please."

She sighs and brings her feet up onto the edge of the chair, wrapping her bandaged hands around her ankles.

Evening Star was a pretty nice restaurant. Reservation only, unless it was a slow night, but the prices were high enough that most people wouldn't just walk off the street for a meal. On normal nights, the waiters wore tuxedos and the waitresses black strapless gowns with stand-alone collars and cuffs like the tuxes. We even had black bow ties that were a bitch and a half to get right—we weren't allowed clip-ons.

Guilian knew how to cater to the stupidly rich, though, so you could actually rent out the entire restaurant for special occasions and put the waitstaff in costumes. There were a few basic rules—he drew the line at indecency—but within a fairly broad range of options, you could provide the costumes and we would wear them for the event, and then got to keep them. He always gave us warnings about the costumes so we could trade shifts if we didn't think we could deal with it.

Two weeks before my sixteenth birthday—or as far as the girls knew, my twenty-first—the restaurant got rented out by someone doing a fundraiser for one of the theatres. Their first show was going to be a production of *Madame Butterfly*, so we were dressed accordingly. Only girls were allowed to work this one, by request of the client, and we were all given black dresses that came high around a pair of huge wire and silk wings that stayed on with spirit gum and latex—fuck, what a process that was—and we all had to wear our hair completely up.

We all agreed it was better than the shepherdess fetish costumes or the Civil War–themed wedding rehearsal dinner that stuck us all with hoopskirts that we'd finally converted to Christmas light chandeliers when we got sick of them taking up an entire corner of the apartment. Even if it meant getting to work hours early so we could put the damn wings on, the rest of it wasn't that bad, and we could all use the dresses again. Trying to wait tables with large wings behind you was a clusterfuck, though, and by the time the main course had been served, and we could retreat to the kitchen during the fundraising presentation, most of us didn't know whether to swear or laugh. A number of us were doing both.

Rebekah, our lead hostess, sighed and sank

down on a stool, propping her feet up on a sideways crate. Her pregnancy had finally made high heels impossible, and had also spared her from having to bear the indignity of wings. "This thing needs to come out of me now," she groaned.

I squeezed behind the stool as best I could with the wings and started massaging her tight shoulders and back.

Hope peeked out through a gap in the swinging doorway. "Anyone else think the guy in charge is totally fuckable for an old man?"

"He's not that old, and watch your mouth," Whitney retorted. There were certain words Guilian preferred we didn't use at work, even in the kitchens, and *fuck* was one of them.

"Well, his son looks older than me, so he is an old man."

"Then ogle the son."

"No, thanks. He's hot, but there's something wrong with him."

"He isn't looking at you?"

"He's looking a lot, at a bunch of us. He's just wrong. I'd rather eye-fuck the old man."

We stayed in the kitchen, chatting and making up gossip about the guests, until the presentation's intermission, when we circulated with refills and bottles of wine and dessert trays. At the host's table, I got a good look at Hope's old man and his son. Right away I knew what she meant about the son. He *was* handsome, well-muscled and good-featured, with dark brown eyes and his father's dark blond hair, which looked good against his tanned skin.

Even if the tan looked a little fake.

It was something deeper than that, though, a cruelty that showed through in his otherwise charming smile, the way he watched all of us as we moved through the room. Next to him, his father was simply charming, with an easy smile that thanked us all wordlessly for our efforts. He stopped me with two fingers against my wrist, not too familiar, not threatening. "That's a lovely tattoo, my dear."

I glanced down to the slit in my skirt. All of us in the apartment, even Kathryn, had gone out together and gotten matching tattoos a few months before, something we still found absurd and couldn't quite figure out why we'd done it, except that most of us had been a bit tipsy and Hope nagged us until we gave in. It was on the outside of my right ankle, just above the bone, and it was an elegant thing of sweeping black lines. Hope had picked it out. Sophia, the other sober one, argued against the butterfly, because it was overdone and so damn typical, but Hope didn't budge. She was a freaking honey badger when she wanted to be; she called it a tribal butterfly. Normally we had to keep tattoos covered up with clothing or make-up for work, but because of the event theme, Guilian had said we could leave them uncovered.

"Thank you." I poured the sparkling wine into his glass.

"Are you fond of butterflies?"

Not particularly, but that didn't seem a bright thing to mention given the theme of his party. "They're beautiful."

"Yes, but like most beautiful creatures, very short-lived." His pale green eyes traveled from the tattoo on my ankle up my body until he could smile into my eyes. "It is not just your tattoo that's lovely."

I made a note to tell Hope that the old man was as creepy as his son. "Thank you, sir."

"You seem young to be working in a restaurant like this."

One thing no one had ever said to me was that I seemed too young for something. I stared at him a moment too long, saw some kind of satisfaction flicker in his pale eyes. "Some of us are older than our years," I said finally, and promptly cursed myself. The last thing I needed was a wealthy customer convincing Guilian I was lying about my age.

He didn't say anything when I moved on to the next glass, but I felt his eyes on me all the way back to the kitchen.

During the second half of the presentation, I snuck back to the locker room to dig a tampon out of my purse, but when I turned to leave for the bathroom, the son was standing in the doorway.

He was maybe in his mid-twenties, but alone in a small room with him, he definitely gave off a more experienced vibe of menace. I didn't generally credit Hope with being too perceptive, but she was right, there was something really wrong with this guy.

"I'm sorry, but this is a staff-only area."

He ignored me, still blocking the doorway as one hand reached out to flick the edge of one of the wings. "My father has exquisite taste, don't you think?"

"Sir, you need to leave. This is not a customer area."

"I know you're supposed to say that."

"And I say it too." Kegs, one of the busboys, shouldered him roughly out of the way. "I know the owner would be sorry to make you leave the restaurant, but he'll do it without regret if you don't rejoin your party."

The stranger looked him over, but Kegs was tall and burly and perfectly capable of slinging people around like beer kegs, hence the name. With a scowl, the stranger nodded and stalked away.

Kegs watched him until he turned the corner into the main dining room. "You okay, lovely?"

"I am, thanks."

We called him "our" busboy, mainly because Guilian always assigned him to our sections and he considered us his girls. Whether he was working that night or not, Kegs always walked the closing girls to the subway and saw us safely onto the train. He was the one person who inexplicably ignored Guilian's rules about tattoos and piercings. True, he was a busboy, not a waiter, so he wasn't interacting with the customers, but he was still visible. Guilian never commented on the gauged ears, the pierced eyebrow, lip, and tongue, or the heavy black tribal tattoos that marched all the way down both arms and nearly glowed through his white dress shirt. They peeked out from the cuffs onto the backs of his hands and up on the back of his neck when it wasn't obscured by his long hair. Sometimes he knotted the hair up and you could see the tattoos climb onto the shaved lower half of his skull.

He kissed my cheek and walked me to the bathroom, standing outside while I took care of things, and then walked me back to the kitchen. "Be careful around the host's son," he announced to all the girls.

"I told you," giggled Hope.

That night Kegs escorted us all the way to the apartment. The next day, Guilian listened to what had happened with a concerned frown, then told us not to worry too much about it, because the clients had returned to Maryland. Or so we thought.

A couple of weeks later, when Noémie and I left the library one afternoon and bumped into two of her classmates, I waved her on with them and told her I could get the rest of the way home by myself.

I managed three blocks before something stabbed me, and before I could even cry out, my legs fell out from under me, and the world turned black.

"In the afternoon on the streets of New York?" Eddison asks skeptically.

"Like I said, most people in New York don't ask too many questions, and both father and son can be very charming when they want to be. I'm sure they said something that made sense to the people around us."

"And you woke up in the Garden?"

"Yes."

The door opens to show the female tech analyst with her hip still on the handle, her hands full of drinks and food sacks. She nearly drops them on the table, thanking Victor as he helps her steady the cardboard drink caddy.

"There are hot dogs, hamburgers, and fries," Yvonne announces. "I wasn't sure what your tastes are, so I had them put some condiments in on the side."

It takes the girl a moment to realize that she's the one being addressed, and then all she says is thank you.

"Anything new from Ramirez?" Eddison asks.

She shrugs. "Nothing big. They've got another

girl identified, and a couple of them have given their names and addresses, or partial addresses. One girl's family relocated to Paris, poor thing."

As he portions out food, Victor watches Inara study the tech. There are questions in her expression, but he can't make them out. After a moment, she shakes her head and reaches for a packet of ketchup.

"The senator?" asks Eddison.

"Still in the air; they had to detour around a storm front."

Well, Victor almost got his wish. "Thanks, Yvonne."

The analyst taps her ear. "Anything interesting, I'll keep you updated." She nods to Inara and leaves the room. A few seconds later, the mirror rattles slightly as the door to the observation room closes.

Victor eyes Inara as he squeezes mustard and relish onto his hot dog. He isn't sure if he should ask the question. He's never felt uncertain about the power dynamic in a room, not with a victim, but then, she's not exactly a typical victim, is she? That's at least half the problem. He frowns at his meal, unwilling to let the girl think the scowl is aimed at her.

Eddison has that covered.

He has to know, though. "You weren't surprised to hear about Senator Kingsley."

"Should I have been?"

"So you all know each other's real names."

"No." She squeezes ketchup over the patty and fries, then pops a fry in her mouth.

"Then how—"

"Some can't stop talking about their families. Afraid they'll forget, I guess. No names, though. Ravenna said her mother was a senator. That was all we knew."

"Her real name is Patrice," Eddison says.

Inara just shrugs. "What do you call a Butterfly halfway between the Garden and Outside?"

"Well? What do you call them?"

"I suppose it depends on whether or not her mother is a senator. How much damage will it cause if she's forced to become Patrice before she's ready to let go of Ravenna?" She takes a large bite of hamburger and chews slowly, closing her eyes. A soft sound like a groan escapes and her face softens with pleasure.

"Been a while since you had junk food?" Eddison asks with an unwilling smile.

She nods. "Lorraine had strict instructions to make healthy food."

"Lorraine?" Eddison grabs for his notebook and flips through several pages. "The paramedics took in a woman named Lorraine. She said she was an employee. You mean she knew about the Garden?"

"She lives there."

Victor stares at her, vaguely aware of the relish

dripping off his hot dog onto the foil. Inara takes her time with the food and doesn't continue until the last fry is gone.

"I believe I mentioned that some girls tried to suck up?"

Lorraine was one of those once upon a time, someone so desperate to please the Gardener that she was perfectly willing to help him do whatever he wanted to other people if he would just love her. She may have been broken before he took her. Normally the girls like her were given another mark, another set of wings but this time on their faces, to show everyone that they loved being one of his Butterflies. But the Gardener came up with another plan for Lorraine and actually let her out of the Garden.

He sent her to nursing school and to cooking classes on the side, and she was so broken by submission to his interests, so absolutely in love with him, that she never tried to run away, never tried to tell anyone about the Garden or the dead Butterflies or the living ones who still could have had *some* hope. She went to her classes, and when she came back into the Garden she studied and practiced, and on her twenty-first birthday, he took away all those backless, pretty black dresses and gave her a plain grey uniform that covered her entirely, and she became the cook and nurse for the Garden.

He never touched her again, never spoke to her except about her duties, and that's when she finally started to hate him.

Not enough, I guess, because she still didn't tell.

On kinder days—of which there weren't many—I could almost feel sorry for her. She's what, forty-something now? She was one of the first Butterflies; she's known the Garden twice as long as she's known anything else. At some point, maybe you *have* to break. Her way kept her out of the glass, at least, however much she came to regret that.

Our cook-nurse, and we loathed her. Even the suck-ups despised her, because even the suck-ups would have escaped if they could, would have tried to call the police for the sake of the rest of us. Or at least that's what they told themselves. If the opportunity had presented itself, though . . . I don't know. There were stories about a girl who escaped.

"Someone escaped?" demands Eddison.

She smiles crookedly. "There were rumors, but no one knew for sure. Not in our generation, or in Lyonette's. It seemed more apocryphal than anything, something most of us believed simply because we needed to believe escape was possible, not because we thought it was real. It was hard to believe in escape when you had Lorraine choosing to stay, despite everything."

"Would you have tried?" asks Victor. "To escape?"

She gives him a thoughtful look.

Maybe we were a different breed of girl than thirty years ago. Bliss especially enjoyed tormenting Lorraine, mainly because she couldn't do anything in return. The Gardener got pissed if she screwed with our food or medical needs. She was incapable of insulting us, because the words have to have meaning to hurt.

We didn't think the maintenance guys knew about the Butterflies. We were always hidden when they were in the greenhouse, never allowed to be out where we could be seen or heard. The walls came down, opaque and soundproof. We couldn't hear them, just as they couldn't hear us. Lorraine was the only one we *knew* who knew about us, but it was useless trying to ask her to do anything or send a message to anyone. Not only would she not do it, but she'd take it straight to the Gardener.

And then another girl would end up in glass and resin in the hallway.

Sometimes Lorraine looked at those girls on display with such naked envy it was painful to see. Pathetic, of course, and infuriating, because for fuck's sake, she's jealous of murdered girls, but the Gardener *loved* those girls in glass. He greeted them when he passed, he visited just to look at them, he remembered their names, he called them his. Sometimes I think Lorraine looked forward to joining them someday. She missed when the Gardener loved her the way he did the rest of us.

I don't think she realized it would never happen. The girls in the glass were all preserved at the peak of their beauty, the wings on their backs brilliant and bright against young, flawless skin. The Gardener would never bother preserving a woman in her forties—or however old she would be when she died—whose beauty faded decades ago.

Beautiful things are short-lived, he told me the first time we met.

He made sure of that, and then he strove to give his Butterflies a strange breed of immortality.

Neither Victor nor Eddison has a response.

No one asks to be assigned to crimes against children because they're bored. There's always a reason. Victor has always made sure to know the reasons of those who work for him. Eddison stares at his clenched fists on the table, and Victor knows he's thinking of the little sister that went missing when she was eight years old and was never found. Cold cases always hit him hard, anything where families have to wait for answers that may never come.

Victor thinks of his girls. Not because anything's ever happened, but because he knows he'd lose it if anything ever did.

But because it's personal, because they're passionate, agents in crimes against children are often the first to break and burn out. After three decades with the bureau, Victor's seen it happen to a lot of agents, good and bad alike. It nearly happened to him after a particularly bad case, after one too many funerals with too-small caskets for the children they'd been unable to save. His daughters convinced him to stay. They called him their superhero.

This girl has never had a superhero. He wonders if she ever even wanted one.

She watches them both, her face revealing nothing of her thoughts, and he has the uneasy feeling she understands them a lot better than they understand her.

"When the Gardener came to you, did he ever bring his son?" he asks, trying to regain some control of the room.

"*Bring* his son? No. But Avery came and went mostly as he wanted to."

"Did he ever . . . with you?"

"I recited Poe a few times under his attentions," she answers with a shrug. "Avery didn't like me, though. I couldn't give him what he wanted."

"Which was?"

"Fear."

The Gardener only ever killed girls for three reasons.

First, they were too old. The shelf date counted down to twenty-one, and after that, well, beauty is ephemeral and fleeting, and he had to capture it while he could.

Second reason was connected to health. If they were too sick, or too injured, or too pregnant. Well, pregnant, I guess. Being *too* pregnant is a bit like being *too* dead; it's not really a flexible state. He was always a little disgruntled about the pregnancies; Lorraine gave us shots four times a year that were supposed to prevent that sort of inconvenience, but no birth control is completely foolproof.

Third reason was if a girl was completely incapable of settling into the Garden. If after the first few weeks she couldn't stop crying, if she tried to starve herself or kill herself past a certain "allowable" number of times. The girls who fought too hard, the girls who broke.

Avery killed girls for fun, and sometimes by accident. Whenever that happened, his father would ban him from the Garden for a time, but then he'd be back.

I'd been there almost two months before he came looking for me. Lyonette was with a new girl who hadn't been named yet, and Bliss was putting up with the Gardener, so I was on the little cliff above the waterfall with Poe, trying to memorize "Fairy-land." Most of the other girls couldn't go up on the cliff without wanting to throw themselves off, so I usually had it to myself. It was peaceful up there. Quiet, but then, the Garden was always quiet. Even when some of the better-adjusted girls would play tag or hide-and-seek, they were never loud. Everything was subdued, and none of us knew if that was how the Gardener preferred it or if it was just instinct. As a group, all our behaviors were learned from other Butterflies, who had learned it from other Butterflies, because the Gardener had been taking girls for over thirty fucking years.

He didn't kidnap under the age of sixteen, erring on the side of older if he wasn't sure, so the maximum lifespan of a Butterfly was five years. Not counting the overlaps, that was still more than six *generations* of Butterflies.

When I met Avery at the restaurant, he was in a tuxedo like his father. Sitting with my back against a rock, the book across my knees as I basked in the warmth of sunlight through the glass roof, I looked up when his shadow fell over me and found him in jeans and an open button-down dress shirt. There were scratches on his chest and what looked like a bite mark on his neck.

"My father wants to keep you all to himself," he said. "He hasn't talked about you at all, not even your name. He doesn't want me to remember you."

I turned the page and looked back at the book.

His hand grabbed my hair to pull my face up

and his other hand cracked painfully across my face. "There's no busboy here to save you this time. This time you'll get what you're asking for."

I kept hold of the book and didn't say anything.

He hit me again and blood splashed onto my tongue from a split lip, colored lights dancing in front of my eyes. He yanked the book from my hand and threw it into the stream; I watched it disappear over the edge of the waterfall so I wouldn't have to look at him.

"You're coming with me."

He led me by my hair, which Bliss had put up into an elegant French twist that soon came unraveled in his grip. Whenever I didn't move quickly enough for him, he turned and cracked me again. Other girls looked away as we passed them, and one even started crying, though the girls nearest her quickly shushed her in case Avery decided a weeper would be more entertaining.

He hurled me into a room I hadn't been in before, one near the tattoo room at the very front of the Garden. This was a room that was closed and locked unless he was playing. There was a girl in there already, her wrists bound to the wall with heavy rings. Blood thickly coated her thighs and parts of her face, trailed down from a nasty bite on one breast, and her head lolled forward at an awkward angle. She didn't look up even though I landed on the floor with a loud smack.

She wasn't breathing.

Avery stroked the girl's flaming hair, curling his fingers into it to pull her head back. Handprints wrapped around her throat and bone protruded against the skin on one side. "She wasn't as strong as you are."

He dove at me, clearly expecting me to fight, but I didn't. I didn't do anything.

No, not entirely true.

I recited Poe, and when I ran out of lines I knew, I thought them again and again and again until he threw me against the wall with a disgusted snarl and stalked from the room with his jeans undone. I guess you could say I won.

At the moment it didn't feel like much of a victory.

When the room finally stopped spinning, I stood up and looked for a key or a latch, whatever would let the poor girl out of those wide cuffs. Nothing. I found a locked cabinet that, when I pulled the door as far as the lock would allow, showed whips and flails; I found bars and clamps and things my mind shuddered away from; I found any number of things, in fact, except a way to give her any shred of dignity.

So I *found* the remnants of my dress and *found* a way to drape it around her until the most important bits were covered, and I kissed her cheek and apologized with everything in me, as I'd never apologized to anyone before.

"He can't hurt you again, Giselle," I whispered against her bloody skin.

And I walked naked into the hallway.

Everything hurt, and each girl I passed hissed in sympathy. None of them offered to help. We were supposed to go to Lorraine for that, so she could catalogue every injury and report it to the Gardener, but I didn't feel like looking at her stony face or feeling her press harder than she had to against forming bruises. Retrieving the ruins of the poetry book from where it had fetched up in the pond, I returned to my room and sat in my narrow shower stall. The water wouldn't come on until evening—we each had an assigned time, unless we'd just been with the Gardener. The girls who'd been there longer could turn their water on themselves, another earned privilege, but that wasn't me yet. Not for another few months.

I wanted so badly to cry. I'd seen most of the other girls do it time and again, and some of them always seemed to feel better afterward. I hadn't cried since that fucking carousel when I was six years old, when I sat trapped on that beautifully painted horse and went round and round as both of my parents walked away and forgot all about me. And, as it turned out, sitting in the shower stall waiting for water that wouldn't come for hours wasn't going to flip that switch back on.

Bliss found me, water still trickling down her skin from her own shower, her hair wrapped in a brilliant blue towel, the color of the wings inked on her back. "Maya, what—" She stopped short, staring at me. "Fucking hell, what happened?"

It even hurt to talk, my lip swollen and my jaw aching from so many slaps, among other things. "Avery."

"Wait here."

Because there were so many places I was likely to go.

But when she came back, it was with the Gardener, who was unwontedly disheveled. She didn't say a word, just led him into the room, dropped his hand, and walked away.

His hands were shaking.

He stepped slowly across the room, the horror on his face growing as he catalogued each visible injury, each bite mark or scratch, each deepening bruise or handprint. Because the sickest thing was—and there were so many to choose from—he genuinely did care about us, or at least what he thought of as us. He knelt down in front of me and inspected me with concerned eyes and gentle fingers.

"Maya, I am . . . I am so sorry. Truly I am."

"Giselle is dead," I whispered. "I couldn't get her down."

He closed his eyes with a look of genuine pain. "She can wait. Let's get you taken care of."

Until then, I hadn't realized he actually kept a suite in the Garden. As we passed through the tattoo room, he bellowed out Lorraine's name. I could hear her scrambling from the infirmary in the next room, her grey and brown hair fluffing around her face as it escaped her updo.

"Get me bandages, antiseptic. Something to help with the swelling."

"What hap—"

"Just get it," he snapped. He glared at her until she disappeared, returning moments later with a small mesh bag bulging with haphazardly packed supplies.

He punched a code into the pad on the wall and a section slid back and away, revealing a room done in burgundy and deep gold and mahogany. There was a comfortable-looking couch, a recliner positioned under a tall reading lamp, a television mounted on the wall, and that was all I got a chance to see before he led me through another doorway into a bathroom with a floor-set whirlpool tub bigger than my bed. He helped me sit down on the edge and started running the water, then wet a cloth to wipe away the worst of the blood.

"I won't let him do this to you again," he whispered. "My son is . . . my son lacks control."

Among other things.

And just as I let him do other things, I let him fuss over me, and take care of me, and tuck me into his bed while he went to get a tray from Lorraine. I wouldn't have thought I could sleep, but I did, all night with his breath against the back of my neck as he stroked my hair and sides.

The next afternoon, as I relaxed in my own bed with Bliss keeping me company, Lorraine threw a package at me. While Bliss muttered something about foul-tempered bitches who needed to stick their heads in an oven, I unwrapped the plain brown paper and started to laugh.

It was a book of Poe.

"So the Gardener didn't approve of what his son did?"

"The Gardener cherished us, and genuinely regretted killing us. Avery was just . . ." She shakes her head, folding her legs beneath her on the chair. She winces and presses a hand against her stomach. "I'm sorry, but I *really* need to use the bathroom."

The tech analyst opens the door a minute later. Inara gets up and joins her there, then glances back at Victor as if asking for permission. At his nod, they leave and close the door behind them.

Victor shuffles through the photos of the hallways, trying to count the individual sets of wings.

"Do you think that's all the girls he took?" Eddison asks.

"No," Victor sighs. "I wish I could say yes, but what if a girl was injured in such a way that it damaged her wings or back? I doubt he displayed them then, because these are all in perfect condition."

"They're dead."

"But perfectly preserved." He lifts one of the close-ups. "She said glass and resin; have the scene techs confirmed that?"

"I'll find out." He shoves back from the table and pulls his cell phone from his pocket. As long as they've been partners, Victor's never seen him able to stand still while he's on the phone, and as soon as the number's dialed, he starts pacing back and forth across the narrow room like a caged tiger.

Finding the pen attached to Eddison's note-book, Victor scrawls his initials across the bag with the collection of IDs and slits it open, letting the plastic cards spill out over the table. It gets a curious look from Eddison that he largely ignores as he sifts through them until he finds the name he's looking for. Cassidy Lawrence.

Lyonette.

Her driver's license was only three days old when she was taken, and the pretty girl in the picture beams with excitement. It's a face meant for smiles, for joy, and he tries to age that into the fierce-eyed girl who welcomed Inara into the Garden. He can't quite manage it. Even when he places the ID against the picture of those pumpkin wings caught in glass, he can't make himself accept the connection.

"Which one do you suppose is Giselle?" Eddison asks, shoving the phone back in his pocket.

"Too many redheads to guess, unless Inara can tell us which butterfly she had."

"How can he have been doing this for thirty years without us ever noticing?"

"If the police hadn't gotten that call and noticed our flags on some of those names, how much longer do you think he would have gone unnoticed?"

"That's a fucking terrible question."

"What did the techs say?"

"They're closing up the scene for today, giving a tour to the guards for tonight. They said they'd try to open the cases tomorrow."

"Closing up?" He twists his wrist to check his watch. Almost ten o'clock. "Christ."

"Vic . . . we can't release her. She could just disappear again. I'm not convinced she's not part of this."

"I know that."

"Then why aren't you pushing harder?"

"Because she is more than smart enough to turn it back on us, and"—he laughs sharply—"more than enough of a smart-ass to enjoy doing it. Let her tell it in her own way; all it costs us is time, and this is one of the few cases where we *have* the time." He leans forward, clasping his hands against the table. "The suspects are not in good condition; they may or may not survive the night. She's our best chance of learning the larger picture of the Garden."

"If she's telling the truth."

"She hasn't actually lied to us."

"That we know of. People with fake IDs aren't usually innocent, Vic."

"She may be telling the truth about why she has it."

"It's still illegal, and I still don't trust her."

"Give her time. That will also give *us* time for the other girls to recover enough to talk to us. The longer we keep her here, the better our chances of getting the other girls talking."

Eddison scowls but nods. "She's irritating."

"Some people stay broken. Some pick up the pieces and put them back together with all the sharp edges showing."

Rolling his eyes, Eddison scoops the IDs back into the evidence bag. He stacks each photo neatly into a pile and lines the edges with the corner of the table. "We've been up more than thirty-six hours. We need to sleep."

"Yes . . ."

"So what do we do about her? We can't let her disappear. If we take her back to the hospital and the senator hears about her . . ."

"She'll stay here. We'll get some blankets, see if we can find a cot, and in the morning we'll resume."

"You really think that's a good idea?"

"A better idea than letting her go. If we keep her here, rather than moving her to a holding cell, it's still an active interrogation session. Even Senator Kingsley isn't going to butt in during an active interrogation."

"Are we holding our breath on that?" He gathers the trash from dinner, stuffing everything into one of the bags until the paper splits and bursts around the strain, and heads to the door. "I'll hunt down a cot." He yanks open the door, scowls at the returning Inara and Yvonne, and stalks away. Yvonne nods to Victor and returns to the observation room.

"What a pleasant man," Inara notes dryly, and slides into her seat on the far side of the table. The soot streaks and dirt are gone from her face, her hair neatened into a heavy twisted bun.

"He has his uses."

"Please tell me talking to damaged children isn't one of them."

"He's better with suspects," he allows, and wins a hint of a smile. He looks for something to occupy his hands, but Eddison's compulsiveness straightened everything on the table. "Tell us about being in the Garden."

"Meaning?"

"Day to day, when nothing out of the ordinary was happening. What was it like?"

"Boring as all fuck," she answers succinctly.

Victor pinches the bridge of his nose.

• • •

No, but seriously, it was boring.

There were usually twenty to twenty-five of us in the Garden at any given point, not counting Lorraine, because really, why would she have counted for anything? Unless he was out of town, the Gardener "visited" at least one of us a day, sometimes two or three if he didn't have to work or spend time with his family or friends, which meant he still didn't spend time with all of us within a single week. After what Avery did to me and Giselle, he was only allowed in the Garden once a week, and only under his father's supervision, though he defied that as often as he thought he could get away with it. It didn't last long, anyway.

Breakfast was served in the kitchen at seven-thirty, and we had until eight o'clock to eat so Lorraine could get everything cleaned up. You couldn't get away with skipping meals—she watched us eat and reported it to the Gardener—but one meal in a day you were allowed to be "not as hungry." If you did it twice, she'd show up in your room to do a checkup.

After breakfast—except those two mornings of maintenance, when we were stuck behind walls—we were free until twelve, when lunch was served in another half-hour window. Half the girls went back to bed, like they thought sleeping through the days would make them go faster. I usually followed Lyonette's example, even after she was in the glass, and made my mornings available for any girls who needed to talk. The cave under the waterfall became an office of sorts. There were cameras everywhere, and mics, but the crash of even such a small waterfall made it too difficult for conversation to come across clearly.

"And he allowed this?" Victor asks incredulously.

"Once I explained it to him, sure."

"Explained it to him?"

"Yes. He sat me down to dinner one evening in his suite to ask about it, I suppose to make sure we weren't fomenting rebellion or something."

"And how did you explain it?"

"That girls needed some semblance of privacy for mental well-being, and as long as those conversations kept the Butterflies healthy and whole, why the fuck did it matter? Well, I expressed it a little more eloquently than that. The Gardener liked elegance."

"Those conversations with the girls—what were they like?"

With some of them it was just venting. They were restless and scared and pissed off and needed someone to talk all that feeling from them. They'd pace and rage and pound the walls, but at the end, if their hands and hearts were sore, they were at least a little further from breaking. These were the girls like Bliss, only they lacked her courage.

Bliss said whatever she wanted, wherever and whenever she wanted. Like she said the first time I met her, the Gardener never asked us to love him. He wanted us to, I think, but he never asked us to. I think he valued her honesty, just as he came to value my straightforwardness.

Some of the girls needed comfort, something I was not especially good at. I could have patience with the occasional tears, or the tears that came of that first month in the Garden, but when it went on and on and on, for weeks and months and even years . . . well, that was generally when I lost patience and told them to get over it.

Or, if I was feeling magnanimous that day, I sent them on to Evita.

Evita was an American Lady, her back inked in faded oranges and dull yellows before the wing-tips spread to intricate black patterns. Evita was sweet, but not quite bright. I don't say that to be mean, but because it's true. She had the understanding of a six-year-old, so the Garden was a daily source of wonder for her. The Gardener only came to her once or twice a month because she always got so confused and scared by what he wanted from her, and Avery wasn't allowed to go near her at all. Every time the Gardener came, we all worried that she'd end up in glass, but that simple sweetness was something he seemed to treasure.

That simple sweetness meant you could go to her, bawling your eyes out, and she'd hug and stroke and make silly sounds until you stopped crying; and she'd listen to you pour your heart out, without saying a word. For those girls, being around Evita's sunny smile always made them feel better.

For my part, being around Evita just made me sad, but when the Gardener came to her, she came to me, and she was the one person whose tears I could always forgive.

"Do we need to get a special needs advocate to the hospital?"

The girl shakes her head. "She died about six months ago. An accident."

Around eleven-fifteen, the "office" closed and a group of us ran laps through the hallways. Lorraine would glare at us if she was present but never said anything against it, because it was really the only exercise we got. The Gardener wouldn't give us weights or treadmills or anything because he was worried we'd use them to injure ourselves. Then, after lunch, the afternoon was ours until dinner at eight o'clock.

That was when the boredom set in.

The cliff top became my place even more than the waterfall cave, because I was one of the few who enjoyed climbing up and sprawling close to the glass that marked the edge of our prison. Most of the girls did better pretending the sky wasn't so close, pretending that our world was bigger than it was and that nothing waited Outside. If it helped them, I wasn't going to argue with them. But I loved it up there. Some days I'd even climb the trees and stretch out and press my hand against the glass. I liked reminding myself that there was a world beyond my cage, even if I'd never see it again.

Early on, sometimes Lyonette, Bliss, and I would sprawl in the afternoon sun and talk, or read. Lyonette would fold her origami creations, Bliss would play with the polymer clay the Gardener bought for her, and I'd read aloud from plays and novels and poetry.

But sometimes we'd go down to the main level, where the stream bisected the almost jungle-like growth, and we'd spend time with the other girls. Sometimes we'd just read together, or talk of less sensitive things, but there were games too, when we got bored enough.

Those were the days that seemed to make the Gardener happiest. We knew there were cameras everywhere because at night you could see the winking red eyes, but on days when we played, he'd come into the Garden and watch us from the rocks by the waterfall, a soft smile on his face like this was everything he could have dreamed of.

I think it's a tribute to just how bored we got

that we didn't all scatter to our rooms and solitary activities the minute we saw him.

Six months ago, about ten of us were playing hide-and-seek, and Danelle was It. She had to count off to a hundred while standing near the Gardener, because it was the one place none of us were likely to hide, and so the only place she wouldn't easily hear us hiding. I'm not sure if he was aware of the logic or not, but he seemed charmed to be part of the game, even peripherally.

I nearly always climbed the tree during these games, mainly because practicing for two years on the fire escape of the apartment meant I could climb higher and faster than anyone else. They might find me pretty easily, but they couldn't actually reach me to tag.

Evita was scared of heights, just like she was scared of enclosed spaces. Someone always stayed with her at night in case the walls came down so she wouldn't be alone and terrified. Evita *never* climbed. Except that day. I don't know why she wanted to, especially not when we could see how scared she was once she got about six feet off the ground, but even when we called across that it was okay, she could still hide somewhere else, she was determined. "I can be brave," she said. "I can be brave like Maya."

From beside Danelle, the Gardener watched us with worried eyes, like he did whenever one of us went against our habits.

117

Danelle reached ninety-nine and just stopped, giving Evita more time to hide. We all did that sometimes, if we could hear her. Danelle kept her back turned and her hands over her tattooed face, waiting for silence.

It took Evita almost ten minutes, but she pulled herself up the tree inch by inch until she was fifteen feet up and sitting on one of the branches. Tears tracked down her face, but she looked at me in a nearby tree and gave me a wavering smile. "I can be brave," she said.

"You're very brave, Evita," I told her. "Braver than all the rest of us."

She nodded and looked down between her feet at the ground that seemed so far away. "I don't like it up here."

"Do you want me to help you down?"

She nodded again.

I stood carefully on my branch and turned so I could start down my tree, only to hear Ravenna cry out behind me. "Evita, no! Wait for Maya!"

I looked back over my shoulder in time to see Evita windmilling wildly and teetering down the branch until it was too narrow to support her weight. The branch snapped and Evita shrieked as she dropped. Everyone rushed from their hiding places to try to help, but then her head struck a lower branch with a sickening crack and her screams abruptly stopped.

She fell into the pond with a great splash, and was still.

I shimmied down the tree as quickly as I could, scraping my legs and arms on the bark, but no one else moved, not even the Gardener. They all stared at the girl in the pond, at the blood floating away from her pale blonde hair. Wading into the stream, I grabbed her ankle and pulled her closer to me.

Finally the Gardener came running, and heedless of his fine clothing, he helped me get her out of the water onto dry land. Evita's lovely blue eyes were frozen open, but there wasn't any sense in trying to make her breathe.

Part of that crack had been her neck breaking.

Death was a strange thing in the Garden, an omnipresent threat but not something we actually *saw*. Girls were simply taken away and a pair of wings in a display case in the halls took their place. For most of the girls, this was their first time seeing death firsthand.

The Gardener's hands shook as he smoothed Evita's wet hair back from her face and cradled the wet mess on the back of her skull where she'd hit the branch. Then we were all staring at him rather than Evita because he was *weeping*. His entire body moved with the strength of his sobs, his eyes screwing shut against this unexpected pain, and he rocked back and forth with Evita's body clasped to his chest, blood staining his sleeve and water soaking through his shirt and trousers.

It was like he'd taken even our tears from us, then. Alerted by the screams, the other girls had come running from their rooms or elsewhere in the Garden, and together all twenty-two of us stood in dry-eyed silence as our captor wept for the death of the one girl he *hadn't* killed.

She takes the stack of hallway photos and flicks through them until she finds the one she wants. "He arranged her hair so the damage wouldn't show," she tells Victor, laying it out for him to see. "He spent the rest of that day and night doing something, off where we couldn't see him, and the walls came down, and the next day she was up in the glass and he was asleep in front of her, his eyes red and swollen. He stayed there the rest of the day, right in front of her. Right up until a couple of days ago, he touched the glass every time he passed it, until he didn't even seem to realize he was doing it. Even when the glass was covered, he touched the wall."

"She wasn't the only accidental death though, was she?"

She shakes her head. "No, not by a long shot. But Evita was . . . well, she was sweet. Utterly innocent, incapable of comprehending the bad things. When they happened to her, they touched her lightly and then let her go. In a way, I think she was the happiest of us, purely because she didn't know any other way to be."

Eddison bursts in with a groan of cheap metal, dragging a cot behind him with the other arm full of blankets and thin pillows. He drops them in the far corner and, panting, turns to his partner. "Just got a call from Ramirez; the son is dead."

"Which one?"

The words are said so softly, so full of air and some indefinable emotion, Victor isn't entirely sure he even heard it. He looks at the girl, but her eyes are fixed on Eddison, one fingernail digging under the gauze until scarlet blooms along her finger.

Eddison is equally taken aback. He glances at Victor, who shrugs. "Avery," Eddison answers, nonplussed.

She folds in on herself, hiding her face in her arms. Victor wonders if she's crying, but when she lifts her head a minute or so later, she's dry-eyed. Haunted, in some new and inexplicable way, but dry-eyed.

Eddison gives Victor a significant look, but Victor can't begin to guess what's running through this girl's head. Shouldn't she be happy her tormentor is dead? Or, at the least, relieved? And maybe that is there, buried in her complexity, but she seems more resigned than anything else.

"Inara?"

Her pale brown eyes flick over to the cot, her fingers digging under the gauze on both hands now. "Does this mean I can sleep?" she asks dully.

Victor stands and motions for Eddison to give him the room. He does so without comment, taking the pictures and evidence bags, and in less than a minute, Victor is alone with the broken child he may never understand. Without speaking, he unfolds the squeaking legs of the cot and stands it up in the farthest corner from the door, where the table can be between the girl and anyone entering, and wraps one of the blankets around it like a sheet. The other he drapes at the foot, with the pillows piled near the head.

When he's done, he takes a knee next to her chair and gently lays a hand against her back. "Inara, I know you're tired, so we'll let you sleep now. We'll be back in the morning with breakfast and more questions, and hopefully an update for you on the other girls. But. Before I go—"

"Does it have to be tonight?"

"Did the younger son already know about the Garden?"

She bites her lip until blood dribbles down her chin.

With a deep sigh, he hands her a tissue from his pocket and walks to the door.

"Des."

He looks back at her, still with one hand on the door, but her eyes are closed and her face is written over with a pain he can't begin to name. "I'm sorry?"

"His name is Des. Desmond. And yes, he knew about the Garden. About us."

Her voice breaks and even though he knows a good agent should take advantage of this crack, this vulnerability, he sees his daughters sitting there with that pain and he just can't do it. "There'll be someone watching from the tech room," he says softly. "If you need anything, they'll help you. Sleep well."

That fractured sound might be a laugh, but it's not one he wants to hear again.

He pulls the door closed with a quiet click behind him.

II

The girl—strange to call her Inara, when he knows it isn't her real name—is still asleep, her face buried in the collar of his jacket, when Victor arrives and checks in with the yawning night-shift tech analysts. One of the techs hands him a stack of messages: reports from the hospital throughout the night, from the agents out at the property, background on as many of the players as possible. He sorts through them as he drinks his cafeteria coffee—marginally better than the questionable swill left standing in the pot in the team kitchen—trying to match the pictures to the names in the girl's stories.

It's barely six o'clock when Yvonne enters, her eyes puffy from lack of sleep. "Good morning, Agent Hanoverian."

"Your shift doesn't start till eight; why aren't you sleeping?"

The tech analyst just shakes her head. "Couldn't sleep. I sat up all night in my daughter's room, rocking in the chair and staring at her. If some-one ever . . ." She shakes her head again, more sharply this time, as if sloughing off the bad thoughts. "I left as soon as my mother-in-law was awake enough to deal with the baby."

He considers telling her to find an office and take a nap, but then, he doubts anyone on the team slept well last night. He certainly didn't, plagued by the hallway photos and the distant memories of his daughters running around the yard wearing costume butterfly wings. It's easier for the horrors to catch up once you have nothing to do.

Victor hefts the canvas bag at his feet. "I have a fresh-made cinnamon roll for you if you do me a favor," he says, and watches her stand straight with sudden energy. "Holly gave me clothes for Inara; think you could walk her down to the lockers and let her shower?"

"Your daughter is an angel." She glances through the glass at the sleeping girl. "I hate to wake her up, though."

"Better you than Eddison."

She walks out of the tech room without another word, and a moment later the door to the inter-view room opens with the slightest squeak.

It's enough; the girl sits up in a tangle of hair and blanket, her back against the wall until she identifies Yvonne, standing in the doorway with her hands out and open. They stare at each other until Yvonne tries a small smile. "Good reflexes."

"He used to stand in the doorways some-times; he always seemed disappointed if you didn't realize he was there." She yawns and stretches, joints popping and cracking from the uncomfortable cot.

"We thought you might appreciate a shower," says Yvonne, holding out the canvas bag. "We've got some clothing that should fit well enough, and some soaps."

"I could kiss you if I were into that sort of thing." On her way to the door, she taps against the glass. "Thank you, FBI Special Agent in Charge Victor Hanoverian."

He laughs but doesn't try to answer.

While she's gone, he moves into the interview room to continue parsing through the new information. Another of the girls has died in the night, but the rest are expected to live. Counting Inara, that makes for a total of thirteen. Thirteen survivors. Perhaps fourteen, depending on what she can tell them of the boy. If he's the Gardener's son, is he part of what his father and brother did?

She's still in the locker room when Eddison comes in, cleanly shaven and wearing a suit this time. He drops a box of Danishes on the table. "Where is she?"

"Yvonne has her down at the showers."

"Think she'll tell us anything today?"

"In her own way."

A snort tells him what his partner thinks of that idea.

"Yes, well." He hands him the stack of papers he's already gone through, and for a time the only sounds are the shuffling of pages and the occasional slurp of coffee.

"Ramirez says Senator Kingsley has set up camp in the hospital lobby," Eddison says a few minutes later.

"Saw that."

"She says the daughter didn't want to see the senator; claimed she wasn't ready."

"Saw that too." Victor drops his papers to the table and rubs his eyes. "Can you blame her? She grew up on camera, with everything she did reflecting on her mother. She knows—probably better than any of the others—the media blitz waiting for them. Seeing her mother is the start of that."

"Ever wonder if we're really the good guys?"

"Don't let her get to you." He grins at his partner's startled look. "Do we have a perfect job? No. Do we *do* a perfect job? No. It isn't possible. But we do our job, and at the end of the day, we do a hell of a lot more good than harm. Inara's good at deflecting; you can't let her get under your skin."

Eddison reads another report before saying anything. "Patrice Kingsley—Ravenna—told Ramirez she wants to talk to Maya before making a decision about her mother."

"Wanting advice? Or someone to make the decision for her?"

"Didn't say. Vic . . ."

Victor waits him out.

"How do we know she isn't like Lorraine? She took care of these girls. How do we know it wasn't to please the Gardener?"

"We don't," admits Vic. "Yet. One way or the other, we'll find out."

"Before we die of old age?"

The senior agent rolls his eyes and turns back to his papers.

It's a different girl who finally reenters with Yvonne, her hair combed in a straight fall to her hips. The jeans don't quite fit, tight across her hips with the buttons undone to give a little more space, but the layered edges of the tank tops mostly cover that, and the mossy green sweater hugs soft curves. Thin flip-flops slap quietly against the floor as she walks. The bandages are off and Victor winces at the purple-red burns that wrap around her hands, marked through with gashes from glass and debris from their escape.

She follows his gaze to her hands and holds them up for further inspection as she drops into her seat at the far side of the table. "They feel worse than they look, but the doctors said as long as I'm not stupid, I shouldn't see any loss of function."

"How is the rest of you?"

"There are some lovely bruises and the stitches are a little pink and tender around the edges, but not really swollen. A doctor should probably give them a look-see at some point. But, you know, I'm alive, which is more than I can say about a lot of people I know."

She's expecting him to start out with the boy. He can see it in her face, in the tension in her shoulders, in the way her fingertips press over the scabs on the opposite hand. She's prepared for that. So instead, he pushes across the remaining cup—hot chocolate rather than coffee, given her distaste for it yesterday—and opens the tinfoil wrapping on the rolls. He hands one to Yvonne, who murmurs a thank-you and retreats to the observation room.

Inara's brows pull together at the sight, her head tilting like a bird's as she studies the contents. "What kind of bakery wraps things in aluminum?"

"The bakery known as my mother."

"Your *mother* made your breakfast?" Her mouth moves in something that might be a smile with less shock. "Did she make your lunch in a little brown sack, too?"

"Even wrote a note, telling me to make good choices today," he lies with a straight face, and she rolls her lips in to stop the smile from growing. "But you never had that, did you?" he continues more softly.

"Once," she corrects, and there's no trace of the humor now. "The couple across the street took me to the bus station, right? She made me a lunch, and inside there was this note, saying how glad they were to know me, how much they'd miss me. Their phone number was there, and they asked me to call them when I got to Gran's to let them know that I was safe. To call them whenever I wanted, just to talk. They'd signed it with hugs, both of them, and even the baby had a crayon scribble on the bottom."

"You didn't call, did you?"

"Once," she says again, almost a whisper. Her fingertips trace the lines of each cut and gash. "When I got to the station near Gran's, I called them to tell them I'd gotten there. They asked to speak to Gran, but I said she was arranging for the taxi. They told me to call back as often as I wanted. I stood at the curb of the station, waiting for a taxi, and kept staring at that silly piece of paper. Then I threw it away."

"Why?"

"Because keeping it felt too much like hurting myself." She sits up in the chair, crossing her legs at the knee, and leans her elbows against the table. "You seem to have this strange image of me as a lost child, like I've just been thrown on the side of the road like garbage, or roadkill, but kids like me? We're not lost. We may be the only ones who never are. We always know exactly where we are and where we can go. And where we can't."

Victor shakes his head, unwilling to argue the point but equally incapable of agreeing with it.

"Why didn't the girls in New York report you missing?"

She rolls her eyes. "We didn't have that kind of relationship."

"But you were friends."

"Yes. Friends who were all running from other things. Before I moved in, the bed was vacant because the last girl suddenly picked up and left. Hard on her heels was a pissed-off uncle who wanted to know what she'd done with the baby he'd raped into her three years before. No matter how carefully you hide, there's always *someone* who can find you."

"Only if they're looking."

"Or if you're really just that unlucky."

"What do you mean?" asks Eddison.

"What, you think I wanted the Gardener to kidnap me? The whole city to disappear in, but he found me."

"That doesn't explain—"

"It does," she says simply. "If you're a certain kind of person."

Victor sips his coffee, trying to decide if he should push the conversation in a necessary direction or let it go in what may or may not prove to be a useful one. "What kind of person, Inara?" he prompts eventually.

"If you expect to be overlooked or forgotten, you're always at least a little surprised when someone remembers you. You're always outside understanding those strange creatures who actually expect people to remember and come back."

She takes her time then, eating her cinnamon roll, but Victor can tell she isn't finished with the thought yet. Maybe it isn't fully formed yet—his youngest daughter will do that sometimes, just trail off until she knows the rest of the words. He isn't sure if that's Inara's reason, but it's still a pattern he knows, so he kicks Eddison under the table to keep him silent when his partner's mouth opens.

Eddison glares at him and scoots his chair several inches away, but says nothing.

"Sophia's girls expect her to come back," she continues softly. She licks the icing off her injured fingers and winces. "They've been with their foster family for . . . well, they'd been there nearly four years when I was taken. Anyone could have understood if they'd given up hope. They didn't, though. No matter what happened, no matter how bad things got, they knew she was fighting for them. They know she will always, *always* come back for them. I don't get it. I don't think I ever will. But then, I never had a Sophia."

"But you have Sophia."

"Had," she corrects. "And it's not the same. I'm not her daughter."

"Her family, though. Yes?"

"Friends. It's not the same."

He's not sure he believes that. He's not sure she

does either. Maybe it's easier for her to pretend she does.

"Your girls always believe you'll come home, don't they, Agent Hanoverian?" She smooths a hand along the soft sleeve of the sweater. "They're afraid that one day you might die in the line of duty, but they don't believe anything could keep you away if you were still alive."

"Keep your mouth off his girls," snaps Eddison, and she smirks.

"You can see his girls in his eyes every time he looks at me or one of those pictures. They're why he does what he does."

"Yes, they are," Victor says, finishing his coffee. "And one of them sent along something else for you." He reaches into his pocket and pulls out a tube of deep berry lip gloss. "This is from my eldest, who also gave the clothing."

It startles a smile from her, a real one that makes her whole face shine for a few seconds, her amber-flecked eyes crinkling at the corners. "Lip gloss."

"She said it's a girl thing."

"I'd hope so; this would be a very unflattering shade on you." Gingerly unscrewing the cap, she squeezes the tube until a bead of shimmering color oozes from the end. She rolls it along her lower lip, managing the upper with no mess or missed places despite her eyes never going to the one-way mirror. "We used to do our makeup on the train on the way to work. Most of us could put our whole face on without ever looking in a mirror."

"I have to admit, it's not something I've ever tried," he says dryly.

Eddison straightens the stack of papers, lining their edges precisely with the edge of the table. Victor watches him, used to his partner's compulsions but still amused by them. Eddison sees him watching and frowns.

"Inara," Victor says finally, and she reluctantly opens her eyes. "We need to start."

"Des," she sighs.

He nods. "Tell me about Desmond."

I was the only one who liked to find the high places in the Garden, so I was the one to find the *other* garden. Up on the little cliff, there was this small stand of trees—and by stand, I mean five— that grew right up against the glass. At least a couple times a week, I climbed one of the trees, settled into the highest curve of branches that could support me, and pressed my cheek against the glass. Sometimes if I closed my eyes, I could pretend I was out on our fire escape, against our bank of windows, hearing Sophia talk about her girls, or listening to a boy in another building play violin, as Kathryn sat beside me. To my front and left, I could see almost the entire Garden, except for the hallways that wrapped around us and what was hidden by the edge of the cliff. In the afternoon, I could see the girls playing tag or hide-and-seek along the stream, one or two floating in the small pond, or sitting among the rocks or bushes, with books and crosswords and various things.

But I could also see out of the Garden, just a little. As far as I could tell, the greenhouse we called the Garden was actually one of two, one inside the other like nesting dolls. Ours was the one in the center, impossibly tall, with our hallways wrapped around it in a square. The ceilings in our rooms weren't especially high, but the walls rose all the way up to the trees on the cliff, black and flat-topped, and on the other side, another glass roof, sloping down over another greenhouse. It was more of a border than a proper square on its own, broad path lined—at least on the side I could see—with plant life. It was hard to see, even from the tops of the trees. Just a sliver here or there, where the angle was just right. In *that* greenhouse was the real world, with gardeners no one hid from and doors that led Outside, where the seasons changed and life didn't count down to twenty-one.

The real world had not the Gardener, but the man non-Butterflies knew him to be, a man who was involved with arts and philanthropy, and some kind of business venture—or rather, many kinds of business ventures, from what he sometimes hinted. That man had a house some-where on the property, not visible even from the trees. That man had a wife and family.

Well, he had Avery, and clearly the asshole had to come from somewhere, but still.

There was a wife.

And she and the Gardener walked through that outer greenhouse together almost every afternoon from two to three, her hand tucked through his elbow for support. She was slender almost to the point of sickliness, with dark hair and impec-cable style. From so far away, that was all I could see. They'd walk slowly down the leg of the square, stopping from time to time to inspect a flower or plant more closely, and then slowly walk on until they passed from my limited range of sight. They'd be back once or twice more before their walk was done.

She was the one who determined their pace, and whenever she lagged, he turned to her solicitously. It was the same tenderness he showed to his Butterflies, soft and sincere in a way that sent spiders crawling under my skin.

It was the same tenderness with which he touched the glass of the display cases, with which he wept over Evita. It was in the way his hands trembled when he saw what Avery had done to me.

It was love, as he knew it.

Two or three times a week, Avery accompanied

them, trailing along behind and rarely staying for the full hour. He usually did a single revolution and then walked into the Garden, where he looked for someone who was sweet and innocent and so easily gave him the fear he craved.

And twice a week, on consecutive days that were the same as our maintenance mornings, there was a younger son, with his mother's dark hair and slim build. As with his mother, the detail was lost to distance, but it was clear she doted on him. When he joined them, she moved between her husband and younger son.

For months, I watched them unobserved, until one day, the Gardener looked up.

Right at me.

I kept my cheek pressed against the glass, curled within the leaves high in my tree, and didn't move.

It was another three days before we spoke of it, and even then only over the bed of a stranger, not even a Butterfly.

Victor takes a deep breath, pushing away that bizarre image of normalcy. Most of the sickos he arrests seem normal on the surface. "He'd kidnapped another girl?"

"He took several a year, but never until the previous one was fully marked and more or less settled in."

"Why?"

"Why he took several a year? Or why he waited between them?"

"Yes," Victor tells her, and she smirks.

"For the first—attrition. He never took more than the Garden could support, so generally he only went shopping when one of the Butterflies died. That wasn't always the case, but usually. For the second . . ." She shrugs and presses her palms flat against the table, studying the stippling of burned tissue across the backs. "A new girl was a stressful time in the Garden. Everyone got on edge, remembering their own kidnapping and how it was when they woke up the first time, and then the inevitable tears just made it all worse. Once a new girl settled, things were quiet for a while, until the next death, the next wings on display, the next new girl. The Gardener was always—mostly—exquisitely sensitive to the prevailing mood in the Garden."

"Is that why he allowed Lyonette to act as a guide?"

"Because it helped, yes."

"Then how did you end up doing it?"

"Because someone had to, and Bliss was too angry, the rest too skittish."

It wasn't the girl after me but the next one that I first helped with, because Avery had brought the flu into the Garden and it was cutting a hell of a swath through the girls.

Lyonette was a train wreck. She was pale and sweating, her tawny hair plastered to her neck and face, and the toilet bowl was a much truer friend than I could ever be. Bliss and I told her to stay in bed, to let the Gardener deal with his own mess for once, but as soon as the walls lifted to let us out of our rooms, she pulled on clothes and staggered out into the hallway.

Swearing, I tied on a dress and jogged after her until I could loop one of her arms around my shoulders. She was so dizzy she couldn't walk without keeping a hand to the wall. She didn't flinch away from the display cases like she usually did even after almost five years. "Why does it have to be you?"

"Because it has to be someone," she whispered, and stopped to swallow back her need to vomit. Again. Even though she'd been kneeling in front of the toilet for most of the past eighteen hours.

I didn't agree, not at that point.

Maybe not ever.

The Gardener was very, very good at guessing ages, better than any carnival whack I'd ever heard of. A few girls came in at seventeen, but most were sixteen. He wouldn't kidnap younger—and if he thought there was a chance of fifteen or less, he said he chose someone else—but he tried not to go any older. I guess he wanted the full five years whenever possible.

The things that man felt comfortable talking

about with his captives . . . or maybe just with me.

The new girl was in a room that was every bit as naked as the one I'd woken up in. Mine was slowly starting to accumulate personal touches, but for now she had a plain grey fitted sheet and nothing else. Her skin tone was dark and, combined with the cast of her features, suggested mixed race: Mexican and African, I'd find out later. She wasn't much taller than Bliss, and except for a rather astonishing set of tits that looked like they'd been a *quinceañera* gift, she was reed-slender. Small holes marched all the way up one ear and most of the other. Another hole on the edge of her nostril and yet another around her navel suggested they'd been pierced as well.

"Why'd he take them all out?"

"Maybe he thought they were tacky," groaned Lyonette, sinking to the floor beside the unshielded toilet.

"My ears were double pierced when I came. Still are."

"Maybe he thinks yours are classy."

"Plus the cartilage cuff on the right."

"Maya, don't be a bitch. This is rough enough, all right?"

Surprisingly, that actually was enough to make me stop. It wasn't just that she was clearly pathetic at the moment. It was also the undercurrent. Trying to make sense of why the Gardener did what he did was an exercise in futility, and completely unnecessary besides. We didn't need to know why. We just needed to know what.

"Not that you're actually capable of going anywhere, but wait here."

She flapped her hand and closed her eyes.

There were two refrigerators in the kitchen attached to our dining room. One held our meal ingredients and was always kept locked, Lorraine having the only key. The other held drinks and what snacks we were allowed to have between meals. I grabbed a couple bottles of water for Lyonette and a juice for myself, then pillaged a book from the library to read aloud to her while we waited for the new girl to wake up.

"There was a library?" Eddison asks incredulously.

"Well, yeah. He wanted us to be happy there. That meant keeping us occupied."

"What kinds of books did he give you?"

"Whatever we asked for, really." She shrugs and settles back into her chair, arms crossed loosely over her chest. "It was mostly classics at first, but those of us who genuinely enjoyed reading started a wish list by the doorway, and every now and then he'd add a few dozen or so volumes. And some of us had personal books, direct gifts from him, that stayed in our rooms."

"And you were one of the readers."

She starts to give him a disgusted look, then

reconsiders. "Oh, right, you weren't here for that part."

"What part?"

"The part where I explained that being in the Garden was usually boring as fuck."

"If *that's* boring, you're clearly not doing it right," he mutters, and it startles a laugh out of her.

"It wasn't boring when it was my choice," she admits. "But that was before the Garden."

Victor knows he should drag the conversation back to the original question, but the sight of the two of them in agreement about something is far too entertaining, so he lets it go, even ignores the slight trace of a lie in the girl's face.

"And I suppose your favorite was Poe?"

"Oh, no, Poe had a purpose: to distract. I liked the fairy tales. Not the watered-down Disney shit, or the sanitized Perrault versions. I liked the real ones, where horrible things happened to everyone and you really understood it wasn't intended for children."

"No illusions?" Victor asks, and she nods.

"Exactly."

New Girl took a long time to regain consciousness, long enough that Lyonette even debated sending for Lorraine. I talked her out of it. If the girl was going to die from it, there was little enough our nurse could do to prevent it, and that pinch-faced bitch wasn't the first thing *I* would want to see. Lyonette used that to insist I be the first thing New Girl saw.

Given that Lyonette looked like death warmed over, I didn't even argue . . . much.

It was late in the afternoon before the girl finally stirred, and I closed *Oliver Twist* on a finger to see if she was actually waking up. We got another two hours of reading in before you could call her any sort of coherent. Under Lyonette's instructions, I poured a glass of water to have ready and wet down a few cloths to help against the headache. When I folded one of them under the girl's neck, she batted at my hand and swore at me in Spanish.

Good enough.

Eventually she gathered enough of her wits to pull the washcloths away from her face and try to sit up, her entire body swaying with the force of her nausea.

"Careful there," I said quietly. "Here's some water, it'll help."

"Get away from me, you sick fuck!"

"I'm not the one who kidnapped you, so save it. Either you want the water and aspirin or you can eat shit and die, your choice."

Lyonette groaned. "Maya."

The girl blinked at me, but meekly took the pills and the cup.

"Better. You're being held by a man known as the Gardener. He gives us new names, so don't bother telling us yours. Remember it, but don't say it. I'm called Maya, and the lovely one with the flu over there is Lyonette."

"I'm—"

"No one," I reminded her sharply. "Not until he gives you a name. Don't make it harder than it has to be."

"Maya!"

I glanced over at Lyonette, who was giving me the pathetic, exasperated, incredulous, what-the-fuck-are-you-doing-to-me look she usually reserved for Evita. "You do it, then. You weren't the first face she saw, hooray! Now you can take over if you don't like how I'm doing it."

I'd had Sophia as a maternal example for young children. New Girl wasn't that young, and I wasn't Sophia.

Lyonette closed her eyes and whispered a prayer for patience. Before she could finish, though, she had to fold herself over the toilet bowl again.

The new girl's hands started to shake, so I took them between my own. It was always warm in the Garden, except sometimes in the cave behind the waterfall, but I knew the shivers were from shock more than anything. "Here's the thing, and it's terrifying and bewildering and fuck-all unfair, but it's still the thing: we are here as the unwilling guests of a man who will come to you for company and, as often as not, sex. Sometimes his son will come to you. You belong to them now, and they will do what they want to you, including mark you as theirs. There are quite a few of us here, and we support each other as we can, but the only way you're getting out of here is to die, so you're going to have to decide if this life of ours is better or worse than death."

"Suicide is a mortal sin," she whispered.

"Good, that means you're not too likely to want to off yourself."

"Jesus, Maya, why not just hand her some rope?"

The girl swallowed hard but—God love her for it—squeezed my hands. "How long have you been here?"

"About four months."

She looked over at Lyonette.

"Almost five years," she murmured. If I'd known then . . . but it didn't matter. It never did. Knowing it didn't change anything.

"And you're still alive, and Mama always says, where there's life there's hope. I'll hope."

"Just be careful with the hope," I cautioned her. "A little is fine. Too much is crippling."

"Maya . . ."

"So, New Girl, want to take a tour?"

"I'm naked."

"Not so much a thing here. You'll get used to it."

"Maya!"

"Did you bring a dress?" I asked pointedly, and

Lyonette flushed beneath her sickly pallor. "And I'm not letting her borrow yours; you've probably puked all down the front."

She hadn't, but her black dress went all the way to the floor. No way tiny little New Girl was going to manage in that. I would've loaned her mine if it would be any better.

"Wait here," I sighed. "I'll get something from Bliss."

Our friend wasn't in her room when I got there, so I just grabbed something and returned to the new girl's room, which was, as ever, studiously avoided by the other Butterflies. She made a face at the black fabric—even I had to admit it wasn't a flattering color on her—but you learned to fear colored clothing in the Garden.

When you were given something other than black, it was because that was the gown the Gardener wanted you to die in.

She obeyed when I told her not to look in the hallway—even I wasn't so much of a bitch as to show her that right off. She was at the far end of the Garden from my room, just down the hall from Lyonette's, and bordering one side of the no-man's-land that held the rooms we weren't supposed to go in, the door to Outside that we were supposed to pretend didn't exist. From that position, she was able to see the full breadth of the Garden in one look: all the rich, growing things, the vibrant flowers and white sand paths, the waterfall and stream and pond, the cliff, all the tiny stands of trees, the actual butterflies hovering over plants, and the clear glass roof that seemed so impossibly far away.

She burst into tears.

Lyonette lurched forward but pulled back immediately in a violent shivering fit. The flu probably wasn't the best way to welcome someone to our verdant cage. I . . . well, I just wasn't that maternal. As amply evidenced. I watched the new girl as she crumpled to the ground, curled into a tiny ball, as she clutched her arms across her stomach like this was a physical blow she could ward off.

Eventually, when the heaving, soul-shattering sobs had trailed off into whimpers and gasps for breath, I sank down onto my knees beside her, one hand on her yet-unmarked back. "This isn't the worst pain," I told her as gently as I could. "But I think it's the worst shock. From here on out, you can expect it a little."

At first I wasn't sure if she'd heard me, because the whimpers continued unabated. Then she threw herself to the side, wrapping her arms around my waist and burying her face in my lap as her shock and grief deepened into full-throated sobs once more. I didn't pet or stroke her, didn't move my hand—she'd learn to hate that gesture from the Gardener—but I kept my hand against her warm skin so she knew I was there.

". . ."

"Do you still have the hallway pictures in here?" she asks abruptly, and the agents shake themselves from the spell of her words. It's Eddison who hands her the stack, his fists clenched against his thighs as he watches her riffle through them. She pulls out a photo, stares at it for a moment, then places it face-up on the table where the men can see. "A Chiricahua White." She traces a finger over the sharp delineation of white and black on the wings. "He named her Johanna."

Victor blinks. "Johanna?"

"I don't know that there was a system to how he named us. I think he just looked through names until he found one he liked. I mean, she sure as hell didn't *look* like a Johanna, but whatever."

Victor forces himself to examine the wings in the glass. She's right, the girl was tiny, though her exact height is difficult to gauge from her position. "What happened to her?"

"She was . . . mercurial. For the most part she seemed to settle in okay, but then suddenly she'd get these mood swings that sent a storm through the whole Garden. And then Lyonette died, and then the Gardener brought in a new new girl."

He clears his throat when she doesn't go on. "What happened to her?" he asks again, and Inara sighs.

"The walls came down so the Gardener could get the new girl for a tattoo session, but Johanna managed to stay out in the Garden. When the walls went up, we found her in the pond." In one fluid motion, she grabs the photo and slams it face-down on the metal. "So much for mortal sin."

Sliding another stack of photos and papers before him, Victor silently sifts through them until he finds the one he's looking for. It's a young man, probably a little older than he looks, with artistically disheveled hair so dark brown it's nearly black. Pale green eyes stand out sharply in a slender, pale face. He's a good-looking boy, even in this over-pixelated likeness, someone who—at least by appearance—he wouldn't mind Holly bringing home for him to meet. He should bring the conversation back to this boy.

Not yet. Just a little longer.

He isn't sure if it's for her benefit or his own.

"When the Gardener noticed you in the trees."

"What of it?"

"You said he came to talk to you over a stranger's bed; was this the girl after Johanna?"

It's not a smile, more like a grimace to acknowledge his statement. "No. The one after that."

A little longer. "What did her name end up being?"

She closes her eyes. "She never got one."

"Why wouldn't—"

"Timing. Sometimes that's all it came down to."

She had skin like ebony, almost blue-black against the dove-grey fitted sheet, with a smoothly shaven head and features that wouldn't have been out of place on the walls of an Egyptian tomb. In the days following Lyonette's death, I desperately needed something—anything—to do, but unlike Bliss and Lyonette, I had neither talent nor interest in creating things. I read, and read a lot, but I didn't make anything of my own. Bliss buried herself in polymer clay, filling the oven with figurines, half of which she later destroyed in fits of temper, but I didn't have that outlet, either the making or the destroying.

Three days later, though, the Gardener brought in the new girl, and there was no more Lyonette to give her a graceful introduction. None of the other girls wanted to go near her until she was settled and I wondered just how long Lyonette had been doing her job that no one else even seemed to think about it.

In the days following Johanna's death, I'd wondered how much—if at all—I was to blame for her choice. If I'd given her a more graceful introduction to her situation, if I'd been more sympathetic or more comforting, maybe she would have been able to cling to that hope her mama told her to have. Or maybe not. Maybe that first view of the Garden, that first moment where it was *real,* was what made the difference.

It wasn't like I could ask her.

So I stuck with the new girl, as patient with her as I could be, and tucked the more acerbic comments away. Considering how frequently she burst into tears, it took more patience than I knew I had. Bliss rescued me sometimes.

Not by coming herself—that would have been a very bad idea—but by sending Evita to be sweet and sincere and in many ways such a better person than I could ever hope to be.

The day after the third of her tattoo sessions, I stayed with her through the evening until her drugged dinner took effect. Normally that's when I left, but I'd seen something I wanted to investigate without alarming her, which meant she needed to be fully asleep. Even after her deep, steady breathing, and the way all the tension left her body told me she was asleep, I let the drug work even further.

Maybe an hour after she fell asleep, I set aside my book and rolled her over onto her stomach. She usually slept on her back, but the process of the tattoo made her sleep on her side to keep pressure off the tender areas. The butterfly book in the library—with Lyonette's handwriting scrawled in the margins, listing names and locations in the halls—told me the Gardener had chosen a Falcate Orangetip for her, mostly white with a splash of orange on the edge of each upper wing. He liked to choose white and the palest yellows for the darker-skinned girls, for some reason. I guess he was afraid the darker colors wouldn't show with the same clarity. For this one, he'd finished the orange and moved into the white sections, and something about them just looked wrong.

Now that I could actually bend close to see it without giving her alarm, I could see the added puffiness, the scale-like swellings under the ink, the way the white bubbled grotesquely in huge blisters. The orange wingtips were nearly as bad. Tracing in closer to her spine, even the black outlines and veins pearled. I pulled out one of my earrings—the Gardener never had taken them—and used the post to carefully pierce one of the smaller blisters. Mostly clear fluid leaked out from the tiny puncture, but when I pressed down gently, a milky white spilled out as well.

I washed the earring off in the sink and replaced it in my ear as I tried to think of a solution. I couldn't be sure if she was reacting to the inks or to the needles, but there was definitely an allergic reaction of some sort. Not immediately life-threatening like a peanut allergy can be, but it wasn't letting the ink heal. Infection could kill just as much as a histamine response, or so Lorraine had told us on one of her rare friendly days.

Of course, she'd been causing Bliss all sorts of pain by digging around in her feet for splinters, so that probably contributed to the good mood.

For lack of a better idea, I returned to the girl's

side and tried to measure how bad the reaction was in each area. I'd gotten through the orange and half the white when I felt the change.

The Gardener was there.

He leaned against the doorway, thumbs hooked through the pockets of his pressed khakis. Lights were going out all over the Garden as girls went to bed, waiting to see if this would be the night they'd be required to entertain their captor. He'd never called for Lyonette when she was settling a new girl, but then, I wasn't Lyonette.

"You look worried," he said instead of a greeting.

I gestured to the girl's back. "She's not going to heal."

As he stepped into the room, he unbuttoned his cuffs and rolled the sleeves of his dark green shirt up to his elbows. The color made his pale eyes glow against his face. He pressed against her back with gentle hands, finding the same things I did, and gradually the concern changed to a look of deep sorrow. "Everyone reacts differently to tattoos."

I should have felt sorrow, or rage, or confusion.

All I felt was numb.

"What do you do with the girls who never get their full wings?" I asked quietly.

He gave me a swift, thoughtful look, and I wondered if I was the first girl to ever ask that. "I see them properly buried on the estate."

· · ·

Eddison growls and reaches for his notebook. "Did he say where on the estate?"

"No, but I think it overlooked a river. Sometimes he'd come to the Garden with mud on his shoes and this wistful look on his face, and on those days, he'd give Bliss river stones to use as a base for some of her figures. Nothing I could see from the trees."

He balls up the aluminum foil and tosses it at the one-way mirror. "Get a team out to the riverbank, look for graves."

"You could say please."

"I'm giving them an assignment, not asking for a favor," he retorts through gritted teeth.

She shrugs. "Guilian always said please. Rebekah, too, even when she was just assigning sections. But then, I guess that's why I loved working for Guilian. He made it a very pleasant and respectful place."

She might as well have slapped him in the face. Victor sees the angry flush climb up from his partner's collar and looks away so he won't smile. Or at least so Eddison won't see it. "Was it just the girls who died before the wings were finished?" he asks quickly.

"No. If they died in such a way that it ruined the wings, he didn't display them. Avery put several girls into the ground instead of the glass, when he whipped them hard enough to scar across the ink." She lightly touches her neck. "Giselle."

"That wasn't where the conversation ended, was it?"

"No, but you already know that."

"Yes, but I'd like to hear the rest," he replies, just as he would to his daughters.

She quirks an eyebrow at him.

Like Lyonette had, I usually borrowed a stool from the infirmary to keep beside the girl's bed. Sitting *on* the bed probably would have been fine, but this gave her a little space. Gave her a territory that was hers. The Gardener didn't really recognize territory in that way. He sat with his back against the headboard, placing the girl's head in his lap so he could run his hand over her shaven skull. So far as I knew, he never visited the girls in their rooms until after they were fully marked, until after he'd raped them for the first time.

After all, that was what made them *his*.

But then, he wasn't there to see the new girl. He was there to talk to me.

And he didn't seem in any big hurry to do it.

I pulled my ankles up onto the seat, sitting cross-legged on the narrow stool, and spread my book across my lap, reading to fill the empty space until he reached over and gently closed it. Then I gave him my attention.

"How long have you been watching my family?"

"Nearly since my wings were done."

"But you haven't said anything."

"Not to you or anyone." Not even to Lyonette or Bliss, though I'd been tempted. I wasn't sure why. Maybe it was easier to think of him as just our captor. Putting a family in there made it . . . well, more wrong somehow. Just the fact that it could *be* more wrong was disturbing enough.

"And what do you think when you see us?"

"I think your wife is sick." I rarely lied to the Gardener; the truth was the one thing that could always be mine. "I think she's scared of Avery and doesn't want to show it, and I think she dotes on your younger boy. I think she treasures those walks with you as the only time she has your undivided attention."

"All that from a stand of trees?" Thank God, he looked more amused than anything. He settled his back more comfortably against the headboard, one arm bent behind him to act as a cushion for his head.

"Am I wrong?"

"No." He looked down at the girl in his lap, then back at me. "She's been struggling for years against a heart condition. It isn't severe enough that she qualifies for a transplant, but it causes a significant drop in quality of life."

So his wife was a kind of butterfly too. "That's one."

"And she does dote on our younger son. She's

quite proud of him. He keeps perfect grades, is always polite, and is a treat to hear on the piano and violin."

"That's two."

"Between the Garden and my business, and her own charitable functions and planning, our schedules are often in conflict. We both make time for our afternoon walks unless we're out of town. It's good for her heart."

"That's three."

And all that was left was the hard one, the one no parent wants to admit.

So he didn't. He left it unsaid, and in the silence there was truth.

"You pay a great deal of attention to things, don't you, Maya? To people, to patterns, to events. You find more meaning than others."

"I pay attention," I agreed. "I don't know that I find more meaning."

"You observed a walk in a greenhouse and made it mean all that."

"I didn't *make* it mean anything. I just noticed body language."

Body language was one of the things that told me my next-door neighbor was a pedophile long before the first time he exposed himself, long before the first time he touched me or asked me to touch him. It was in the way he watched me and the other kids in the neighborhood, in the bruised looks of the foster kids who lived with him. I was prepared for his advances because I knew they'd be coming. Body language warned me about Gran's lawn guy, about the kids in school who would try to beat you up just because they could. Body language was better than a flashing light for warnings.

And body language told me that as much as he wanted to seem perfectly relaxed right now, he couldn't.

"I don't intend to tell anyone, you know."

There it was. Not all of the tension left his body, but most of it. Except when his lust got the better of him, he was a remarkably self-contained man.

"We don't know about them . . . and they don't know about us, do they?"

"No," he whispered. "Some things . . ." He never did finish that thought, not out loud at least. "I would never willingly hurt Eleanor."

I didn't know his name, but now I knew his wife's.

"And your son?"

"Desmond?" He actually seemed surprised for a moment, then shook his head. "Desmond is very different from Avery."

Even then, all I could think was *Thank God.*

He lifted the girl's head from his lap and eased off the bed, extending his hand to me. "I'd like to ask you something, if I may."

I wasn't sure why asking me something would involve moving, but I obediently stood and took his hand, leaving the book on the stool. The girl wouldn't be awake until morning, so I wasn't strictly needed at her bedside. He walked us through the hallways, absently touching each occupied display case as he passed. If I'd had a mind to, I could have asked him to name them, and he could have. Every single name, every single Butterfly, he knew and remembered them all.

I never wanted to know.

I thought he was taking me to my room, but he turned aside at the last moment and led us into the cave behind the waterfall. Except for the moonlight that filtered through the glass roof of the greenhouse and fractured through the falling water, the cave was completely dark.

Oh, and the blinking red eye of the camera.

We stood in silence in the darkness, listening to the waterfall hit the stream and the decorative rocks. Pia, who'd been there about a year longer than I had, had a theory that there were pipes in the bottom of the pond that kept the water at a certain level by draining it and funneling it through another pipe way up to the tiny pond atop the cliff that fed into the waterfall. She was probably right. Given that I couldn't swim, I never tried to go down to the bottom of the pond to see for sure. Pia liked to poke at things and figure out how they worked. When the walls came up to reveal Johanna in glass, Pia went to the pond, and said there were sensors along the edge now.

"I've wondered about what draws you to this place," he said after a time. "The cliff top I can almost understand. It's open, it's free, the height gives you a sense of safety. But this place . . . what can this cave offer you?"

The ability to say whatever the fuck I want to without worrying about reprisals, because the roaring of the waterfall was strong enough to obscure whatever the mics might pick up.

But he was looking for something more personal than that, something with the meaning he thought I gave everything. It took me a minute or two to come up with that answer for him, something close enough to truth. "There's no illusion in here," I said finally. "It's not lush and green and growing and waiting for death and the possibility of decay. It's just rock and water."

Here the girls and I sat face-to-face and knee to knee, and it was usually easy to pretend there were no Butterflies. The suck-ups had the wings marked around their eyes like Carnevale masks, but even then, in the misty dimness of the cave, it was easy to think it a trick of the shadows. We'd take our hair down, put our backs against the rocks, and there were no fucking Butterflies. Just for a few moments.

So perhaps there was illusion in here after all, but it was *our* illusion, not one he'd manufactured for us.

He dropped my hand and then he was pulling out all the pins that kept my hair up in its braided crown, until it fell in a crimped mass to my hips. Hiding the wings. It was the one thing he never did, unless he was brushing it out. But he just left it down around me, tucking the pins into the breast pocket of his shirt.

"You are quite unlike any of the others," he said eventually.

Not entirely true. I had a temper like Bliss, only I didn't let it go. I had impatience like Lyonette, which I did my best to spread out. I read like Zara, ran like Glenys, danced like Ravenna, and braided hair like Hailee. I had bits and pieces of most of the others in me, save for Evita's sweet simplicity.

The only thing that made me truly different was that I was the only one who never cried.

Who never could.

Fucking carousel.

"You put requests for books on the lists but never overtly ask for anything. You assist the other girls, you listen to them, calm them. You keep their secrets, and apparently mine as well, but you give no one else secrets to keep for you."

"My secrets are old friends; I would feel like a poor friend if I abandoned them now."

His low chuckle echoed around the chamber before the waterfall swallowed the sound. "I'm not asking you to share them, Maya; your life before is your own."

162

She gives Eddison a pointed look, and Victor can't help but laugh. "I'm not going to apologize," Eddison tells her bluntly. "This is my job, and we have to know the truth to put together a strong case against him. The doctors are fairly confident he'll survive to stand trial."

"Pity."

"A trial means justice," he snaps.

"In a sense, sure."

"In a sense? It—"

"Does 'justice' change any of what he did? Any of what we went through? Does it bring the girls in glass back to life?"

"Well, no, but it keeps him from doing it again."

"So would his death, and without the sensationalism and tax money."

"Back to the waterfall," Victor announces over the beginning of Eddison's protest.

"Spoilsport," mutters the girl.

"Ask me for one thing, Maya."

There was a challenge in his eyes, layered through his voice. He expected me to ask for something impossible, like freedom. Or maybe he expected me to be like Lorraine, to ask for something that could have gotten me out of the Garden but wasn't freedom at all.

I knew better than that. Like throwing away

well-intentioned phone numbers, I knew better than to ask for things I clearly couldn't have.

"Can this one camera be disabled without another one going up in its place?" I asked promptly, and watched shock pass across his shadowed face. "No cameras, no mics?"

"That's it?"

"It would be nice to have one place that's genuinely private," I explained with a shrug. It almost felt strange to have my hair shifting across my back and shoulders with the gesture. "You can see us everywhere else we go, even watch us on the toilet if you had a wish to. Having just a single place devoid of cameras would be beneficial. A mental-health exercise, in a way."

He watched me for a long time before answering. "Something that benefits all of you."

"Yes."

"I tell you to ask for anything, and you ask for something that benefits all of you."

"It benefits me too."

He laughed again and reached for me, pulling me against his chest so he could kiss me. His hands moved over the fastenings of my dress, and as he lowered me to the mist-damp stone, I closed my eyes and let my thoughts drift off to Annabel Lee and her grave in the kingdom by the sea.

I didn't think angels would ever be jealous of me.

● ● ●

It's astonishing how much of a question she can answer without ever actually answering the question. There's a small, inappropriate part of Victor that would love to put her on the stand right now and watch both sets of lawyers tear their hair out in frustration. Even when she seems forthcoming, her answers almost always veer sideways, providing something like substance without giving away the heart. Ask about the boy and she starts there, or seems to, and somehow it ends in a completely different conversation, and the boy is barely glimpsed. Yes, the lawyers will hate her come trial. He shoves the impulse aside and takes the picture of the boy from its stack, setting it on the table so she can see it right-side up.

She looks away at first, eyes flicking to the mirror, to the floor, to her burned and cut-up hands, before a sigh shudders through her body and she turns her face to the photo. She lifts it gently by the edges, studying the unenhanced blowup from his driver's license. The glossy paper trembles in her grasp, but no one mentions that.

"You get used to things in the Garden," she says pensively. "Even the new girls coming in are something you just get used to, something you expect when another one dies. And then, suddenly, everything changes."

"When?"

"Just shy of six months ago. A few days after Evita died."

Maybe it was that Evita was one of those people you couldn't help but love. Maybe it was that her death was an accident, nothing we could have prepared for. Maybe it was the Gardener's reaction, the openness of it.

Whatever it was, the Garden stank of despair in the days following Evita's accident. Most of the girls kept to their rooms, and Lorraine had to put all the meals on trays and bring them to us, and God, didn't that piss her off to no end. Of course, she was in a mood same as the rest of us, though for a different reason. We mourned Evita. She mourned another filled display case that didn't include her.

Sick fuck.

I left my room at night, unable to bear the four walls and silence. We weren't coming into a weekend, so I didn't have to worry about maintenance or the solid walls coming down. There wasn't a reason in the world I couldn't spend the night wandering around. Sometimes the illusion of freedom, of choice, was more painful than captivity.

It's not like the Gardener couldn't find me if he wanted me, though he was with someone else.

At night the Garden was mostly silent. There

was the waterfall, of course, and the babble of the stream, the hum of machinery and moving air, and the muffled sound of girls crying from scattered points on the perimeter, but compared to the day, it was close enough to silent. I took my book and book light up the cliff to sit on one of the large rocks. I called it the sunbathing rock.

Bliss called it Pride Rock, and laughed when I dared her to find a lion to dangle off the edge.

She made one from polymer clay, and when I'd managed to start breathing again from laughing so hard, she gave him to me. He lived on the shelf above my bed, along with the other things most precious to me. I guess he's there still, or was, until . . .

Bliss joined me up on the cliff around midnight, tossing me a figurine. I held it under the book light to discover a dragon curled around itself. It was dark blue, his head hunched into his shoulders, and somehow the shape of the brow ridge over huge black eyes gave him the most pathetic look a clay figure could possibly have. "Why is he so sad?"

She glared at me.

Right.

The dragon's home was next to Simba, and where the lion was just a joke, the dragon actually came to mean something.

But that day he was new and sad, and Bliss was angry and sad, so I rested him on my knee and went back to reading *Antigone* until she felt up to saying something.

"If my room is intact, do you think there's a chance of my getting the figures back? And the origami menagerie? And the . . . well, all of it, really."

"We can ask," Victor hedges, and she sighs.

"Why *Antigone*?" Eddison asks.

"I always thought she was pretty cool. She's strong and brave and resourceful, not above a certain level of emotional manipulation, and she dies, but on her own terms. She's sentenced to live out the rest of her days in a tomb and she says fuck that, I'm going to hang myself. And then there's her betrothed, who loves her so much that he flips his shit at her death and tries to kill his own father. And then, of course, he dies too, because come on, it's a Greek tragedy, and the Greeks and Shakespeare really love killing people off. It's a great lesson, really. Everyone dies." She lays the photo down and covers the boy's face with her hands. Victor can't be sure she even realizes she's done it. "But I might have picked something else if I'd known Bliss was going to join me."

"Oh?"

"It seemed to inspire her."

• • •

She paced around me as I read, snatching leaves off plants and shredding them as she walked until you could follow her progress by the slaughter of green bits on the rock. She snarled and swore with every step, so I didn't bother to look up until she fell silent.

She stood on the very edge of the false cliff, her toes curled over the rock, with her arms spread wide beside her. Her pale skin glowed in the moonlight where it showed through the gaps in her knee-length black dress. "I could jump," she whispered.

"But you won't."

"I could," she insisted, and I shook my head.

"But you won't."

"I will!"

"No, you won't."

"And why the fuck not?" she demanded, spinning to face me with her fists planted on her hips.

"Because you can't guarantee that you would die, and if you were injured, it might not be badly enough for him to kill you. It's not that high a fall."

"Evita fell from lower."

"Evita broke her neck on a tree branch. You have luck like mine; if you tried, you'd fuck it up and be fine except for a few bruises."

"Godfuckingdammit!" She flopped beside me on the stone, her face buried in her arms as she wept. Bliss had been there three months longer than I had. Twenty-one months, for her. "Why isn't there a better option?"

"Johanna drowned herself. Think that's less painful than an uncertain fall?"

"Pia says it won't work. He added sensors in the bank; if the water rises, it sends him an alarm and he can check the cameras. She said you can see the nearest cameras move to focus on whoever's swimming."

"If you waited till he was out of the house, or even out of town, it would probably give you enough time to drown if you really wanted to."

"I don't want to drown," she sighed, sitting up to mop at her tears with her dress. "I don't want to die."

"Everyone dies."

"Then I don't want to die now," she snarled.

"Then why jump?"

"You have absolutely no sense of sympathy."

Not entirely true, and she knew it, but true enough.

I closed the book and turned off the book light, setting them both on the ground with the sad little dragon on top of them so I could twist onto my stomach to lie alongside her.

"I get so sick of this place," she whispered, and even though we weren't in the cave—the one place we were truly private—I thought she'd probably said it softly enough to avoid getting picked up. None of us knew if he went back through the recordings, never knew if it was safe to talk even when we knew for a fact he wasn't sitting at a monitor.

"We all do."

"Then why can't I make the best of it, like you do?"

"You had a happy home, right?"

"Right."

"That's why you can't make the best of it."

I'd been happy in the apartment, which had eventually become home, but I'd lived through bad things before getting there, so I'd lived through bad things before coming here. Bliss never had, or at least, not nearly to the same extent. She had too much good to compare this to.

"Tell me something from before."

"You know I won't."

"Not something personal. Just . . . something."

"One of my neighbors had a weed garden on the roof," I said after a moment. "When I moved there it was just a corner, but as time went by and no one reported it, it expanded until it covered half the roof. Some of the children from the lower floors used to play hide-and-seek in it. Eventually, though, someone tipped off the police, and he saw them coming, panicked, and set the whole damn crop on fire. We were all a little bit high for a week, and we had to wash everything we owned multiple times to get the smell out."

Bliss shook her head. "I can't even imagine."

"That's not a bad thing."

"I'm forgetting things from home," she confessed. "I was trying to remember my street address earlier and I couldn't remember if it was a road or an avenue or a street or what. I still can't. One-oh-nine-two-nine Northwest Fifty-Eighth . . . something."

Which was really what all the fuss came down to. I shifted to lay one of my hands over hers, because there was nothing I could say.

"Every morning when I wake up and every night before I fall asleep, I tell myself my name, my family's names. I remind myself what they looked like."

I'd seen Bliss's family, a collection of clay figures. She made so many figures that there was no reason to give this set any special significance, unless you noticed the glossy parts where her fingers had worn the clay smooth, or that they were positioned in such a way that they were the first and last things she saw in a day.

Maybe the Gardener was right, and I do give everything a meaning.

"What happens when that isn't enough?"

"Keep reminding yourself," I told her. "Just keep doing it, and it'll have to be enough."

"Does it work for you?"

I never memorized my address in New York. When I had to put it down on a form, I asked one of the other girls, and they laughed at me every time but never actually made me learn it. I never changed my license from the fake one because I didn't know how well it would stand up to real scrutiny, or if the DMV would do more than a cursory check of the information.

But I remembered Sophia, the faded plumpness she grew into after she kicked the addictions, and Whitney's red-gold hair, and Hope's laugh, and Jessica's nervous giggle. I remembered Noémie's gorgeous bone structure, from a Blackfoot father and a Cherokee mother, remembered the way Kathryn's smile could light up a room on the rare occasions she gave it. I remembered Amber's bright, flashy clothing, the patterns never working together and yet always working, because she loved them so much. I didn't remind myself of them, didn't strain to keep them in my memory, because they were indelibly written there.

Just like I could have gladly forgotten my mother's and father's faces, my Gran's stretchy unitards, almost all the people from before New York. But I remembered them too, and in a misty way I even remembered aunts and uncles and cousins, and running around in convoluted games I never understood, and posing for pictures I never saw. I just remembered things, remembered people.

Even when I would rather not.

We sat up at the same time, propping ourselves

on our elbows, as a door opened and a flashlight beam swept into the far end of the Garden.

"The fuck?" Bliss whispered, and I nodded in silent agreement.

The Gardener was in Danelle's room, seeking comfort and ostensibly giving her comfort as well for being the one to count in Evita's final game of hide-and-seek. Even if he was leaving, he never needed a flashlight. Neither did Avery, who was banned from the Garden for another two weeks for breaking Pia's arm, or Lorraine, who was either asleep or crying herself to sleep at this time of night. There was a button in the infirmary that buzzed in her room and the kitchen if she was needed in her capacity as nurse.

The figure was dressed all in black, which might have seemed like a good idea until he stepped onto one of those white sand paths. He moved cautiously, the cone of light sweeping before every step, but we could tell from his posture that he was gawking at everything.

I never questioned that I immediately labeled the intruder as male. Something about the way he walked, maybe. Or the idiocy of bringing a flashlight if you're trying to sneak around.

"Which do you think would get us in more trouble?" Bliss breathed against my ear. "Finding out who he is, or ignoring him?"

I realized I had a pretty good idea of who the intruder was, but I'd told the Gardener I wouldn't tell anyone. Not that a promise to a serial killer holds a great deal of weight, but still. I pretty much never made promises, simply because then I felt bound to keep them.

But what the fuck was the Gardener's younger son doing breaking into the inner greenhouse complex? And what did it—could it—mean for us?

The first question answered itself almost as soon as it crossed my mind, because it was the same reason I climbed those trees almost every afternoon to catch those glimpses of a real world Outside the glass. Curiosity, among other things, for me. Probably just curiosity for him.

The second question . . .

There were girls who could die if we chose the wrong thing to do. If he was just in the Garden itself that would be fine—it was a private garden space, who cared?—but if he explored the hallways at all . . .

Maybe he'd see the dead girls and call the police.

But maybe he wouldn't, and then Bliss and I would be left explaining why we saw an intruder and did nothing.

Swearing under my breath, I slipped off the rock, crouching low to the ground. "Stay here, and keep an eye on him."

"And do what if he does something?"

"Scream?"

"And you are—"

"Giving this to the Gardener to deal with."

She shook her head but didn't try to stop me. In her eyes, I could see the same awareness of being stuck. We couldn't risk everyone's lives on hoping this boy would be better than the rest of his family. And it wasn't like seeing the Gardener with someone would be a first for me. He usually went for the privacy of a room, but every now and then . . . well. Like I said, he was a remarkably self-contained man, until he wasn't.

I nearly crawled down the path on the far side of the cliff, where there was actually a slope rather than a mostly sheer face. The sand muffled my steps when I reached the ground, and by moving slowly I was able to step into the stream without a splash. I ducked behind the waterfall and moved quickly down the back hall to Danelle's room.

The Gardener had pulled his trousers on but not his shirt or shoes, and he sat on the edge of the bed working a brush through Danelle's auburn curls until they fluffed into a mane all around her. More than any of the rest of us, Danelle loathed his fascination with our hair because it always made hers unmanageable.

They both looked up when I slipped into the room, Danelle's confusion echoed but edged in anger in the Gardener's face. "I'm sorry," I whispered, "but it's important."

Danelle cocked an eyebrow at me. When she'd first come to the Garden four years ago, she'd thought sucking up to the Gardener would get her home and had the inked wings on her face to show for it, a mask of red and purple. She'd mellowed through the years, though, and graduated to the "let him do whatever, just don't participate" way of thinking. I knew what she was asking, but I only shrugged. Whether or not I told her would largely depend on what actually happened.

Stuffing his feet into his shoes and grabbing his shirt, the Gardener followed me out into the hall. "That—"

"There's someone in the Garden," I interrupted as quietly as I could. "I think it's your younger son."

His eyes widened. "Where is he?"

"Near the pond when I came to get you."

He shrugged into his shirt and gestured for me to button it while he ran his hands through his hair to get rid of the dishevelment. He was kind of screwed on the funky smell, though. When he set off down the hallway, I followed. After all, he didn't tell me not to. Well, at least not until we got to one of the doorways and he could see the boy for himself, still waving around the silly flashlight. The man watched his son for a long time in silence, and I couldn't read the expression on his face. With a hand on my shoulder, he pointed down, which could have meant either sit or stay.

I was the wrong kind of bitch for sit, so I chose stay, and he didn't argue with me.

From the hallway, I watched him walk out into the Garden, openly and without apparent hesitation. His voice broke the near silence like a gunshot. "Desmond!"

The boy's head whipped around and he dropped the flashlight. It bounced off a rock with the sound of cracking plastic, and when it fell to the sand the light flickered and died. "Father!"

The Gardener's hand went into his pocket, and a moment later the walls came down around me, locking the other girls into their rooms and hiding the display cases. And left Bliss and me somewhat stranded, her up on the rock and me in the hall. And I hadn't exactly told the Gardener she was up there. Shit.

I leaned against the wall and waited.

"What the hell are you doing here? I told you the inner greenhouse was off limits."

"I . . . I heard Avery talking about it, and I just . . . I just wanted to see it. I'm sorry I disobeyed you, Father."

It was hard to put an age to his voice. It was a light tenor, which had the effect of making him sound young. He was uncomfortable and embarrassed, clearly, but he didn't actually seem scared.

"How did you even get in here?"

And could a Butterfly use it to get out?

The boy—Desmond, I supposed—hesitated. "A

few weeks ago, I saw Avery pull aside a panel by one of the maintenance doors," he said finally. "He closed it again when he saw I was there, but not before I saw a punch pad."

"Which has a security code, so how did you get in?"

"Avery uses the same three passwords for everything. I just tried those."

I had the feeling Avery was going to have to create a fourth password pretty soon. We weren't supposed to loiter near the main entrance. That stretch, a little to either side of that locked door, had Lorraine's room, Avery's playroom before it had been dismantled, the infirmary and kitchen/dining room, the tattoo room that led into the Gardener's suite, and a couple of rooms we didn't know the purpose of, but could guess. Whatever he did in those rooms, that was where we died. All things we weren't supposed to pay excessive attention to, minus the kitchen, and neither the Gardener nor Avery left while there was a Butterfly who could see them do it.

"Just what did you think you were going to find?" asked the Gardener.

"A . . . a garden . . ." the boy answered slowly. "I just wanted to see why it was so special."

"Because it was private," his father sighed, and I wondered if that was the reason he'd actually removed the camera and mic from the cave behind the waterfall. Because he valued his privacy enough to let us pretend we had ours. "If you truly wish to become a psychologist, Desmond, you will have to respect people's privacy."

"Except when that privacy forms a block to their mental well-being, in which case I'd be professionally obligated to urge them to talk through those secrets."

Funny, Whitney had never mentioned that kind of ethical jiggering when she talked about her psych seminars.

"You will then be professionally obligated to keep those secrets to yourself," the Gardener reminded him. "Now, let's go."

"Do you sleep here?"

"Occasionally. Let's go, Desmond."

"Why?"

I bit my lip against a laugh. It was a rare treat to hear the Gardener truly flummoxed.

"Because I find it peaceful," he eventually answered. "Pick up your flashlight. I'll walk you back to the house."

"But—"

"But what?" he snapped.

"Why do you keep this place such a secret? It's just a garden."

The Gardener didn't answer right away, and I knew he had to be thinking through his options. Tell his son the truth, and hope he buys into it, keeps it secret? Lie to him and risk the truth being found out anyway, because a son disobedient once might prove disobedient again? Or was he thinking something worse, that somehow a son could be just as disposable as a Butterfly?

"*If* I tell you, you must keep it an absolute secret," he said finally. "You cannot breathe a word about it outside these walls. Don't even speak about it to your brother. Not a word, do you understand me?"

"Y-yes, sir." It still wasn't fear, but there was something there, something a little hard-edged and desperate.

He wanted to make his father proud.

A year ago, the Gardener had told me that his *wife* was proud of their younger son, not necessarily that he was. He hadn't sounded disappointed, but maybe against his mother's easy-shown pride, his father's was harder to detect. Or perhaps his father simply withheld praise until he felt it had been earned. There were any number of possible explanations, but this boy wanted to make his father proud, wanted to feel a part of something greater.

Stupid, stupid boy.

There were footsteps then, growing softer, moving away. I stayed where I was, stuck until the walls lifted. A minute or two later, the Gardener stepped into the far end of the hall and beckoned to me. I obeyed, like I always did, and he absently ran a hand over my hair, now back in a messy knot. He was seeking comfort, I guess.

"Come with me, please."

He actually waited for me to nod before putting his hand on my back and giving me a gentle shove down the hall. The tattoo room was open, the machines shrouded in plastic dustcovers until there was a new girl again; once inside, he pulled a small black remote from his pocket, hit a button, and the door came down behind us. Through the room, the door to his private suite was also open. The punch pad beeped when the door closed. His son stood in front of the bookshelves, turning at the sound of the lock engaging.

He stared at me in openmouthed shock.

Up close, it was easy to see that he'd inherited his father's eyes, but most of him belonged to his mother. He had a slender build and long, elegant fingers. Musician's hands, I thought, when I recalled what his father had said of him. It was still hard to guess his age. He could have been my age, maybe a little older. I wasn't as good at that game as the Gardener.

His father pointed to the armchair under the lamp. "Sit down, please." For himself, he chose a seat on the couch and tugged me down next to him, all while keeping my back from sight. I curled my legs beside me and leaned back against the well-padded cushions, my hands folded in my lap. His son was still on his feet, still staring at me. "Desmond, sit down."

His legs fell out from under him and he collapsed into the recliner.

If I spilled horror stories to this shocked boy, could he get the police here faster than his father could kill me? Or would his father simply kill him to silence him? The trouble with sociopaths, really, is that you never know where they draw their boundaries.

I couldn't quite decide if it was worth the risk, and in the end, what stopped me was the thought of all the other girls. All the air for the Garden came from a centralized system. All the Gardener had to do to take out the entire flock was put a pesticide or something into the air. After all, he had to keep all sorts of chemicals stocked for the care of the greenhouses.

"Maya, this is Desmond. He's a junior this year at Washington College."

Which would explain why he only walked with his parents on weekends.

"Desmond, this is Maya. She lives here in the inner garden."

"Lives . . . lives here?"

"Lives here," he affirmed. "As do others." The Gardener sat forward on the edge of the couch, his hands clasped loosely between his knees. "Your brother and I rescue them from the streets and bring them back here for a better life. We feed them, clothe them, and take care of them."

Very few of us were from the streets, and in no

sense were we rescued from anything, but the rest of it could be true from a certain skewed perspective. The Gardener never seemed to think of himself as villainous, anyway.

"Your mother does not know about this, nor can she. The strain of caring for so many people would put too much work on her heart." He sounded so earnest, so sincere. And I could actually *see* his son believing him. Relief worked over his face, chasing away the momentary flash of horror that his father had been keeping a harem for his own pleasure.

Stupid, *stupid* boy.

He'd learn better. The first time he heard a girl crying, the first time he saw someone's wings, the first time the walls came up and showed all those girls in resin and glass, he'd know better. For now, he swallowed it all. By the time he learned better, would he be in too deep to do the right thing?

We sat together in that room for almost an hour as the Gardener explained his version of things, occasionally looking to me to nod and smile along. I did so, my stomach churning, but much like Bliss, I didn't want to die yet. I didn't quite have the hope that Johanna's mother had espoused, but if I had a few years left, I wanted them, even like this. I'd had too many opportunities to give up, give in, and I'd kept going. If I hadn't fallen to suicide, I wasn't going to go meekly to my death.

Finally the Gardener checked his watch. "It's

almost two o'clock in the morning," he sighed, "and you have class at nine. Come, I'll walk you back to the house. And remember, not a word, not even to Avery unless you're here. We'll put in a code for you when I'm sure you can be trusted with it."

I would have stood as well, but when I swung my feet to the floor, he made a subtle gesture that had me sinking back into the couch.

I guess I was the right kind of bitch after all.

He called us Butterflies, but really we were well-trained dogs.

I stayed on the couch exactly as he left me, not even getting up to wander around the rest of the suite. There wasn't a window or another door, so there wasn't a point. I'd seen it all already, of course, but this time there wasn't the blur of pain and shock. This was something private for him, something even more so than the Garden. Even Butterflies didn't belong here.

So why the fuck was I here? Especially without him being present?

He returned maybe half an hour later. "Turn around," he ordered hoarsely, tugging at his clothing and dropping it into careless piles on the carpet. I obeyed before he could see my face, twisting to sit back on my ankles with open air behind me. He dropped to his knees, tracing every line on my back with trembling fingers and lips, and somehow I knew this was him coming apart from the stress of telling his son, the excitement that perhaps this younger son might share his interests in a gentler way than the elder. He fumbled with the hooks on my dress and when he couldn't get them on the first or second try, he simply tore the fabric away from the fastenings, leaving me in shreds of black silk.

Yet if hope has flown away in a night, or in a day, or in none, is it therefore the less gone? All that we see or seem is but a dream within a dream.

But then, by that point I'd been in the Garden for a year and a half, and even Poe was more a habit than a true distraction. I was more aware than I would have liked of what he was doing, of the sweat that splashed from his chest onto my spine, of his groans every time he pulled me back even closer against him. Too aware of all the ways he worked to pull responses from me, and all the ways my body betrayed me by obeying, because there was never enough fear from me or brutality from him to shut things off completely.

Even when it seemed like he was finished, he stayed where he was, and he blew little puffs of air against the outlines of the wings, and after a full circuit he did it again with kisses, soft as prayers, and then he did the whole thing over again, and I thought how fucking unfair it was that he made us butterflies, of all things.

Real butterflies could fly away, out of reach.

The Gardener's Butterflies could only ever fall, and that but rarely.

She pulls the lip gloss from her pocket and reapplies it with shaking hands. Watching her, seeing the tattered shreds of dignity the gesture helps her wrap around herself, Victor makes a note to thank his daughter for her thoughtfulness. Such a simple thing, but more than he could have guessed.

"And that was meeting Desmond," she says after a minute.

Eddison scowls at the stacks of photos and other papers. "How could he—"

"Those who want to believe something badly enough generally do," she says simply. "He wanted his father to have a good, reasonable explanation, and when he was provided with one, he wanted to believe, so he did. For a while, he did."

"You said you'd been there a year and a half at that point," murmurs Victor. "You kept track?"

"Not at first. Then I got an unexpected present on my anniversary."

"From Bliss?"

"From Avery."

After that first time, when his father raked him over the coals for what he'd done to me and Giselle, Avery had only touched me twice, and only with his father's specific consent and the threat that anything untoward that happened to me would also be happening to Avery. He didn't slap me or choke me, didn't bind me past tying my wrists together at the small of my back, but Avery knew other ways to make things painful.

After each of those two times with Avery, I spent most of the following week dehydrated, because if it was going to hurt to piss anyway, at least I was going to make sure it didn't happen more often.

He still watched me all the time, though, much as Desmond probably looked at those hints of the inner garden until he found a way in. I was something that wasn't supposed to be touched, therefore I was fascinating and desirable.

The fourth time I had to put up with him started out like the recent ones, with the Gardener coming to me and explaining that Avery had asked permission for some time with me, but that he had his limits, just like the last two times. It was the Gardener's way of being comforting. We still couldn't say no, because that displeased him, but he thought it was reassuring to know that Avery couldn't hurt us without repercussion.

The fact that the repercussions could only happen after we'd been maimed or killed was less than reassuring, but he never seemed to connect those dots. Or maybe he did and just dismissed the concern out of hand. After all, this was the man who genuinely seemed to believe that he was giving us a better life than what we'd had Outside, that he was taking care of us.

So, not particularly comforted, I obediently followed Avery to his playroom and watched him close the door, took off my clothes when he ordered me to, and let him lock me into the restraints on the wall, let him tie a blindfold too tightly around my head. I'd moved on to Poe's prose by that point, because it was more challenging to memorize when it didn't rhyme, and I dusted off as much as I could recall of "The Tell-Tale Heart" and prepared to silently recite it.

Unlike the Gardener, Avery didn't believe in preparation or foreplay, didn't care about making us ready or at the very least lubing us up, because he enjoyed causing us pain. It didn't surprise me that he went right to it.

A quarter of the way through the story, it did surprise me when he pulled out without finishing. I could hear him at the far end of the room, where he stored most of his toys, but even as time passed he didn't come back to me. Gradually, though, I became aware of a light smell. I couldn't identify it, something like stale coffee or a pot on the burner after all the water's boiled away. Finally I could hear his heavy footsteps against the cold metal floor as he came back, then oh fucking God the pain as he pressed something into my hip that burned and tore. It was unlike anything I'd ever felt before, the agony so tight it pulled everything in me to a single point and tried to shatter it.

I screamed, my throat clenching around the sound that tore through it.

Avery laughed. "Happy anniversary, you arrogant bitch."

The door slammed open and he spun away, but even after the tool was drawn away the agony remained, stealing all the breath from me as my scream finally choked and died. There were sounds in the room, but I couldn't make sense of them. I gasped and tried to suck in air, but it felt like my lungs had forgotten how to work.

Then hands fumbled at the cuffs at my wrists and ankles, and I flinched.

"It's me, Maya, just me." I recognized the Gardener's voice, felt familiar hands tearing away my blindfold so I could see him. On the floor behind him, Avery sprawled inelegantly, a hypodermic quivering in his neck. "I'm so very sorry, I never thought . . . he'd been so . . . I'm sorry. He will never, ever touch you again."

The tool was on the floor next to Avery. When I saw it, I bit my tongue to keep the nausea from overwhelming me. The Gardener got the last of the bonds unfastened and I nearly screamed again when I tried to take a step.

He swept my feet out from under me and hefted me into a cradle carry, staggering out of Avery's playroom and partway down the hall to the infirmary. He nearly dropped me on the narrow cot so he could punch Lorraine's call button. Then he knelt beside me, clasping my hand in both of his and telling me over and over again how sorry he was, even after Lorraine came rushing and panting into the room and set to work.

On the plus side, I didn't have to deal with Avery for a long time after that, and his playroom was completely dismantled. But. His father couldn't deny him completely—the Garden was nearly the only leash he had on Avery—so he still had his other ways to hurt the other girls. Silver lining and all that bullshit.

He doesn't want to know. He really, truly doesn't want to know, and he can see that same wish mirrored in Eddison.

But they have to know.

"The hospital didn't say anything."

"You all dragged me here before the hospital could do the rape kit they'd intended."

He takes a deep, shaky breath and lets it out on almost a whistle. "Inara."

Without a word, she stands and folds the sweater and tank tops halfway up her stomach, exposing other burns, cuts, and the bottom edge of a line of stitches on her side. The button on her jeans is already undone, so she tugs down the zipper, then reaches to her left side and hooks a thumb through the denim and her green striped cotton

191

underwear, pulling them down just enough for the agents to see.

The scar tissue is bright pink and thickly ridged along her hip bone. Only the edges of the wings are faded to pale pink and white. She gives them a crooked almost-smile. "They say everything comes in threes."

Three butterflies for a broken girl: one for personality, one for possession, and one for pettiness.

She fixes her clothing and sits down, pulling a cheese Danish from the box that got forgotten in favor of the homemade cinnamon rolls. "Any chance I could get some water, please?"

There's a tap from the other side of the glass in answer.

Victor thinks it's probably Yvonne. Because it's easier when you have something to do.

The door opens, but it's a male analyst who sticks his head in, tossing three bottles of water to Eddison before closing the door again. Eddison hands one to Victor, then unscrews the cap on another and puts it in front of Inara. She looks at her damaged hands, at the ridges on the plastic cap, and nods, taking a long drink.

Victor reaches for the picture of the boy and lays it prominently on the table. "Tell us about Desmond and the Garden, Inara."

She presses the heels of her hands against her eyes. For a moment, the spread of pinks, reds, and purples across her face looks like a mask.

Almost like a butterfly.

Victor shudders, but he reaches across the table to gently pull her arms down. He keeps his hands over hers, careful not to put too much pressure on the burns, and waits for her to find the words. After several minutes of silence, she turns her hands under his until she can lightly clasp his wrists, and he returns the grip.

"Desmond didn't know the true nature of the Garden for a while," she tells his hands. "Maybe a long while, by the way of things. His father made sure of that."

The Gardener didn't give an access code to his younger son right away. For the first couple of weeks, he escorted Desmond through the Garden, controlling what he saw and who he spoke to. Bliss, for example, was one of the later introductions, after the Gardener had a chance for several long conversations with her about what was and was not appropriate to show or tell his son.

Desmond wasn't shown the criers or the suck-ups, and those of us he was allowed to interact with received a dress with a back.

Bliss hurt herself laughing when she found hers neatly folded outside her room. Lorraine was the one to deliver them, and for a moment she seemed so satisfied. She didn't know that Desmond had discovered the Garden, didn't know that this was temporary.

She thought we were sharing her punishment, her exile.

The dresses were simple but elegant, like everything else in our wardrobes. He knew all our sizes and had probably sent Lorraine out to get them—regardless of her panic attacks at the thought of leaving the safety of the Garden—but we had them so fast there couldn't have been another way. Still black, of course. Mine was almost a shirt, sleeveless and collared with buttons to the waist where it disappeared under a wide black stretch belt and became a swishy skirt to my knees. I secretly loved it.

Our wings were hidden, but much to the Gardener's delight, I still had some wings showing. The black tribal butterfly I'd gotten with the girls in the apartment was still stark and fresh on my right ankle. As long as our wings were hidden anyway, we were even allowed to wear our hair however we liked. Bliss left hers down in a riot of curls that got tangled in everything, while I wore mine back in a simple braid. It felt remarkably self-indulgent.

The Desmond of the first two weeks was his father's shadow, polite and respectful, mindful of his questions so as not to strain his father's patience. We were all carefully coached in our responses. If he asked anything about our lives before, we were to cast our eyes down and murmur something about painful things being best forgotten. It wasn't until the fifth or sixth time he heard this that something struck him as odd.

That it struck him at all made me revise my initial estimation of his intelligence.

Only a little, though. After all, he was still buying into his father's story.

He came in the evenings for a few hours, not every evening but most of them. After classes were done, and if he didn't have too much homework. During that introduction, Avery was banned from the Garden completely and the Gardener didn't touch any of us while Desmond was there. He touched us later, of course, or before, but not where his son could see. The walls stayed down over the girls in glass, not just from the outside but the sidewalls in the rooms as well. We went *weeks* without seeing any dead girls, and though there was guilt at wanting to forget or ignore them, it was glorious to not have that constant reminder of our impending mortality and immortality.

Desmond's introduction was like the way Lyonette brought girls into the Garden. First you make them feel better. Then you show them, tell them, a piece at a time. You don't bring the markings up right away, you don't bring up the sex right away. You acclimate them to one aspect and then, when they don't balk at that anymore, you introduce another.

One of the many reasons my introductions weren't nearly as graceful as Lyonette's.

I mostly kept to my routine whether Desmond was in the Garden or not. I spent the mornings talking to girls in the cave, ran my laps before lunch, and spent my afternoons either reading up on the cliff or playing games down on the ground. Wherever he and his father started in the afternoon, they usually ended conversing with me up on the cliff. Bliss was sometimes there for that.

More often, she saw them coming up the path and climbed down the face to avoid them.

As much as he liked Bliss's temper and spirit, the Gardener was all right with that. It meant less of a risk that his son would discover the truth before his father had adequately prepared him.

That last evening of direct supervision, the Gardener started the conversation with me and Desmond, then left it in our hands as he made his way down the path and into the hallways. The display cases had been covered, after all, and I think he missed them. But the conversation petered out not long after he left, and when Desmond couldn't find a way to continue it— because it was certainly not my responsibility to do so—I turned back to my book.

"*Antigone*?" Eddison asks.

"*Lysistrata*," she corrects with a small smile. "I needed something a little lighter."

"Can't say I've read that one."

"Doesn't surprise me; it's the kind of thing you appreciate more when you've got a steady woman in your life."

"How—"

"Really? The way you snap and snarl, the graceless way you interact, and you want to try to tell me you have a wife or girlfriend?"

An ugly flush stains his cheeks but—he's learning. He doesn't rise to the bait.

She flashes him a grin. "Spoilsport."

"Some of us have jobs to do," he retorts. "You try dating when your job can call you in at any time."

"Hanoverian is married."

"He got married in college."

"Eddison was too busy getting arrested in college," Victor remarks. A flush mottles the back of his partner's neck.

Inara perks up. "Drunk and disorderly? Lewd and lascivious?"

"Assault."

"Vic—"

But Victor cuts him off. "Campus and local cops bungled the investigation into a series of rapes across campus. Possibly on purpose—the suspect was the police chief's son. No charges were filed. The school imposed no discipline."

"And Eddison went after the boy."

Both men nod.

"A vigilante." She settles back in her chair, a thoughtful expression on her face. "When you don't receive justice, you make it."

"That was a long time ago," mutters Eddison.

"Was it?"

"I uphold the law. It isn't perfect but it's the law, and it's what we have. Without justice, we have no order and no hope."

Victor watches the girl absorb that, turn it over.

"I like your idea of justice," she says finally. "I'm just not sure it really exists."

"This," Eddison says, and taps the table, "this is part of justice too. This is where we start to find truth."

She smiles slightly.

And shrugs.

We sat in silence for long enough that he grew uncomfortable, fidgeting on the rock and tugging off his sweater in the reflected heat from the glass roof. I mostly ignored him, until his cleared throat indicated his desire to finally speak. I closed the book on a finger and gave him my attention.

He shrank back. "You're, uh . . . a very *direct* person, aren't you?"

"Is that a bad thing?"

"No . . ." he said slowly, like he wasn't entirely sure. He took a deep breath, and closed his eyes. "How much of what my father is telling me is complete shit?"

That was worth finding the bookmark. I slid it between the pages and set the book carefully on the rock behind me. "What makes you think any of it is?"

"He's trying too hard. And . . . well, that whole thing with it being private. When I was little, he took me into his office, showed me around, and explained that he worked very hard there and needed me to never come in there to interrupt him. He *showed* me. He never did with this place, so I knew it had to be different."

I turned to face him more fully, cross-legged on the sun-warmed rock as I arranged my skirt to cover everything important. "Different in what way?"

He followed my example, so close that our knees touched. "Is he really rescuing you?"

"Don't you think that's a question you should put to your father?"

"I'd rather put it to someone who might tell me the truth."

"And you think that's me?"

"Why not? You're a very direct sort of person."

I smiled in spite of myself. "Direct doesn't mean honest. It could just mean that I'm very direct and straightforward with my lies."

"So you plan to lie to me?"

"I plan to tell you to ask your father."

"Maya, what is my father really doing here?"

"Desmond, if you thought your father was doing

anything inappropriate, what would you do?" Did he have any idea how important his answer could be?

"I would . . . well, I would . . ." He shakes his head, scratching at his slightly overgrown hair. "I guess it would depend on what that inappropriate thing was."

"Then what do you think he's doing?"

"Besides cheating on my mother?"

Point.

He takes another deep breath. "I think he comes to you all for sex."

"And if he is?"

"He's cheating on my mother."

"Which would be your mother's concern, not yours."

"He's my father."

"Not your spouse."

"Why aren't you giving me a direct answer?"

"Why are you asking me, instead of him?"

"Because I'm not sure I can trust what he says." He blushed, like questioning the word of his father was somehow shameful.

"And you think you can trust me?"

"All the others do." His gesture took in the whole of the Garden, the handful of girls allowed out of their rooms when Desmond was there.

But all the walls were down on the girls who used to suck up in hopes of release, their second sets of wings displayed on their faces. They were down on the weepers and the listless and—except for Bliss—the chronically bitchy. They were down over all those dozens of girls in glass, and the scattering of empty cases that weren't enough to hold the current generations, and no one knew what he was going to do when he ran out.

"You're not one of us," I said flatly. "Because of who you are, what you are, you never will be."

"Because I'm privileged?"

"More than you can ever fathom. They trust me because I've proven to them they can. I have no interest in proving that to you."

"What do you think his reaction would be if I asked him?"

"I don't know, but he's coming up the path, and I'll thank you not to ask him in front of me."

"It isn't easy to ask him for anything," he murmured.

I knew why that was true for us. I thought it cowardice that it was apparently true for him.

His father rejoined us then, standing over us with a smile. "Getting along well enough, Desmond?"

"Yes, sir. Maya's very pleasant to talk with."

"I'm glad to hear it." His hand twitched as if to touch my hair, but at the last second he brought it up to rub at his jaw. "It's time for us to join your mother for dinner. I'll check in on you later, Maya."

"Of course."

Desmond stood and brought my knuckles to his lips. Seriously? "Thank you for your company."

"Of course," I repeated. I watched them make their way back through the Garden. Soon they'd be sitting down in a dining room with Eleanor and Avery, a perfectly normal family conversing over a meal, never mind the lies that hovered over the table like fog.

A few minutes later I heard Bliss come up beside me. "What a tool." She snorted.

"Maybe."

"Will he go to the police?"

"No," I said reluctantly. "I don't think he will."

"Then he's a tool."

Sometimes it was hard to argue with Bliss's logic, such as it was.

But sometimes, tools could be used.

"Why didn't you think he'd go to the police?"

"For the same reason he wasn't going to ask his father those important questions," she answers with a shrug. "Because he was scared. What if he went to the police and his father's explanation was actually true? Or worse, what if it wasn't? Maybe he wanted to do the right thing, but he was barely twenty-one. How many of us know the right thing at that age?"

"You haven't even reached that age yet," Eddison points out, and the girl nods.

"And I don't claim to know the right thing. He

wanted to believe his father. I've never had anyone I wanted to believe that badly. I never felt that kind of need for someone to be proud of me."

She smiles suddenly, soft and sour and slightly sad. "Lotte worried about that, though."

"Lotte?"

"Sophia's younger girl. I remember one time, after we'd worked till three in the morning, Sophia was at the girls' school at eight-thirty in the morning so she could see their class plays. She told us about it after she'd gotten a nap in." The smile spreads, deepens, and for a moment Victor thinks he sees the real Inara Morrissey, the girl who found a home in that strange apartment. "Jillie was fearless, confident, the kind of kid who could throw herself into any-thing, no hesitation. Lotte was . . . not. Girls with older sisters like Jillie probably never are.

"Anyway, there we were around the coffee table, sitting on the floor to eat a crazy assortment of food from Taki's, and Sophia's too tired to bother getting dressed. She just pads over in her underwear, her hair covering most of her ink and not much of her tits, and plops down to eat. Lotte had been fretting about her line for weeks, practicing it over and over again with each of us when we went with her mother to visit, and we all wanted to know if she'd remembered it."

Victor's been to those class plays. "Did she?"

"Half of it. Jillie shouted the rest of it from the

203

audience." The smile shifts, fades. "I've never been an envious person, never really saw a point to it. Those girls, though, what they had with each other and Sophia . . . they were worth envying."

"Inara—"

"You could get anything at Taki's," she interrupts briskly, flicking her burned and sliced fingers as if to dismiss the sentimentality. "It was between the station and our building, never closed, and he'd make anything, even if you bought the stuff at the bodega next door. Working in the restaurant, none of us ever wanted to cook."

The moment he could have pushed is gone as quickly as it came, but he makes a mental note of it. He's not naïve enough to think she trusts them. Still, he doesn't think she means to reveal this much emotion. Whatever she's hiding—and he agrees with Eddison, she's hiding something important—she's so focused on it that other things are starting to slip.

He likes Inara, and he sees his daughters every time he looks at her, but he has a job to do. "And the Garden?" he asks neutrally. "I think you mentioned Lorraine had orders to make only healthy food?"

She makes a face. "Cafeteria style. You stood in line, received your meal, and then sat down at these tables complete with benches to make you feel like you were back in grade school. Unless you wanted to take the tray back to your room, which you could pretty much do whenever you felt like it as long as you brought it back at the next meal."

"What if you didn't like what was being served?"

"You ate what you could off the plate. If there was an actual allergy involved, there was forgiveness, but if you didn't eat enough or if you were too picky, things didn't end well for you."

There was a set of twins there when I first arrived. They looked identical, right down to the wings tattooed on their backs, but they were very, very different people. Magdalene and Magdalena. Maggie, the elder by several minutes, was allergic to life. Seriously, she couldn't even go out into the main Garden because she couldn't breathe out there. If you ever needed help falling asleep, all you had to do was ask her to list her food allergies. Lena, on the other hand, wasn't allergic to anything. In one of his rare lapses into insensitivity, the Gardener kept them in the same room and always visited them at the same time.

Lena liked to run around in the Garden, and as often as not ended up soaked and muddy and covered in plant bits. This created a rather large problem when she tried to go back to the room to shower. Even if Maggie was in the dining room, she'd come back later, find a shred of grass on the floor, and freak the fuck out. Maggie was allergic to the first twenty or so soaps the Gardener provided, and even then she complained about how dry her skin was, how lank her hair was, and always, *always* how she couldn't breathe and why her eyes were so blurry and none of us had any sympathy for her, oh holy fuck.

Maggie was used to her parents falling over themselves to make her comfortable at every step.

I liked Lena, though. Lena never complained—even when Maggie was at her most annoying—and she explored the Garden just as much as I did. Sometimes the Gardener even hid little treasures for her to find, simply because he knew she would. She loved to laugh and seized on any excuse to do so, creating one of those relentlessly cheerful outlooks that would be irritating if you didn't *know* she knew the gravity of the situation. She chose to be happy because she didn't like being sad or pissed off.

She tried to explain it to me, and I sort of got it, but not really, because let's face it: I'm not that person. I don't choose to be sad or pissed off, but I don't exactly choose to be happy, either.

Maggie never ate with the rest of us because she said just being in the same room with things would make her have a severe reaction. Her sister nearly always had to take her a tray of specially prepared food, then swing by to pick it up before the next meal. But then, Lena had the time for that, because you could put any meal before her and she'd suck it down under five minutes. Lena would eat everything without a complaint.

And Lena was one of the very few people in the Garden I genuinely feared for, because most of us understood that if the Gardener kept the twins as a pair in all other things, he would in death as well.

They'd been there for six months when I got there, with Lyonette running careful interference between Maggie and the rest of our little world, and fortunately the Gardener seemed more amused than anything else with Maggie's need for special attention.

At least until he wasn't.

I was there when that change began, and there was no more Lyonette to run interference.

Every so often, the Gardener felt the urge to dine with us en masse, like a king with his court. Or, as Bliss put it, the Sultan with his harem. He had Lorraine inform all of us during breakfast that he'd be there for dinner that night, I suppose so we could take extra effort with our appearances.

That afternoon found me in Danelle's room with a bowl of water in my lap so I could carefully rewet her hair each time I needed to run the brush through it. She sat in front of me on the bed twining ribbons through sections of Evita's hair before she twisted them up into a mass on the back of her blonde head. For Danelle, I braided small sections of hair to drape between two high buns, and others to fall down her back. They were too thin to obscure the wings, but they were her small defiance. Hailee sat behind me doing something with brush and pins, while Simone stood behind her with ribbons and twists and oil.

I'd never gone to a school dance, but it might have looked like we were preparing for something like that, something fun and wonderful, something to look forward to, and at the end of the evening you'd have a whole set of memories to cherish. Not so much here in the Garden. With the presence of the water and the chance for spilling, none of us were wearing more than underwear, and no one was giggling or chattering like girls off to a dance probably would be.

Lena walked in, still dripping from a shower—or a dip in the pond, knowing her—and dropped onto the floor. "She says she's not going."

"She's going," sighed Danelle. I finished the last braid and let it drop against her back.

"She says she's not."

"We'll take care of it." She patted the back of Evita's head and slid off the bed with the brush. "Sit up." She sank to her knees behind Lena, who promptly obeyed.

It should have been the end of it, especially once Danelle got to Maggie's room, but as the rest of us dressed and gathered in the hallway, we could hear them arguing. Something shattered against a wall, and a minute later a pink-cheeked Danelle stalked out. Only parts of the handprint showed through the red and purple wings. "She's getting dressed. Let's go."

The Gardener wasn't yet in the dining room when we arrived, two by two like Madeline and her classmates. Danelle and I hung back to let the others enter, twitching dresses to hang correctly, fixing a pin here or there. When they were all in and seated, I leaned against the wall.

"Is she actually getting dressed?"

She rolled her eyes. "God I hope so."

"I think I'll go make sure of that."

"Maya . . ." She stopped, then shook her head. "Never mind, go ahead. You do you." Danelle had shaken off her post-suck-up apathy in order to help me after Lyonette went into glass. I hadn't figured out how to tell her how grateful I was.

Maggie wasn't getting dressed. As a matter of fact she was quite busy trying to stuff all of her clothing—which she shared with her twin— down the toilet. She flinched when I cleared my throat from the doorway, then panted with exertion as she defiantly met my eye. She had the same dark blonde hair as the Gardener and Avery, currently in a mess about her face. With her hazel eyes and strong nose, she could easily have passed for his daughter.

Which, you know, ew.

"I'm not going."

"Yes, you are, because you are endangering your sister."

"And she doesn't *endanger* me every time she waltzes in with things that could kill me clinging all over her?" she demanded.

"Allergies are not the same as pissing off the Gardener, and you know it."

"I'm not going! I'm not, I'm not, I'm not!"

I slapped her.

It made a ringing sound in the small room, the skin immediately pinking up around the impact. She stared at me, tears filling her eyes as she clutched her cheek with one hand. Avery wasn't allowed to touch her because of the allergies, so I doubt she'd ever been slapped before, however quick she was to do it to others. As long as she was shocked into stillness anyway, I grabbed her hair and pulled it into a knot high on her head, securing it with a few spiral pins.

I got a good grip on her upper arm and hauled her into the hallway. "Come on."

"I'm not going," she sobbed, and scratched at my hand and arm. "I'm not!"

"If you could have been the least bit mature, you could have been dressed and calm and this would have all been over in an hour or so, but no, you had to be a spoiled little princess about it, so now you get to be naked and worked up and *you* get to explain to the Gardener why you would disrespect him in such a way."

"Just tell him I'm sick!"

"He already knows you aren't," I growled.

"Lorraine would have told him, or didn't you think it was strange that she checked in on everyone through the afternoon?"

"That was hours ago!"

"You got all the allergies and Lena got all the brains," I muttered, and blew a stray hair out of my mouth. "Magdalene, please try not to be a *complete* idiot. It's one meal. Your food will still be prepared separately, and we'll still sit you down at the far end of the table away from everyone else's plates."

"Why don't any of you understand?" She tried to kick at me, and when that didn't work, she tried to drop to the ground. I just kept dragging her after me until the friction on her side made her struggle back to her feet. "I could get really sick! I could die!"

That was it.

I turned and slammed her against one of the glass display cases, her head between the open wings of ink. The girl had been there before Lyonette, before the one who welcomed Lyonette, and none of us knew her name, only that she was a Gulf Fritillary, and what a fucked-up thing to know. "If you don't join us for dinner, you *will* die, and so will your sister. Get a fucking clue."

She started crying harder, great big heaving sobs and gobs of snot. Disgusted, I renewed my grip on her arm and got around the corner.

The Gardener stood in the doorway to the dining

room, his arms crossed over his chest and a faint frown on his face.

Fuck.

"Is there a problem, ladies?" he asked.

I glanced at the naked, sobbing Maggie and the bright-pink handprint on her cheek, as well as the beginnings of what would probably be a charming bruise on her arm where I gripped it. "No?"

"I see."

Unfortunately, he did. He watched all through dinner, sitting at the end of a table between me and Danelle, as Maggie picked at her specially prepared plate without eating a single bite. He watched as she refused to enter the conversation, or even answer things put directly to her. He watched her roll her glass of ice water across her cheek—while Danelle simply pretended her own swollen cheek didn't bother her—watched how she curled into herself as far as the table would allow to hide her nakedness.

As we sat a little awkwardly over cheesecake and coffee, he cleared his throat and leaned close to me. "Was the slap really necessary?"

"Yes, to calm her down."

"That was calm?"

I considered the best way to answer. I didn't want to screw Maggie—Lena, really—over, but I didn't want to get screwed myself, either. "Calmer."

All he did was nod, and when I looked at

Danelle and saw the grim resignation in her eyes, my stomach sank.

"How long?" Eddison asks.

"Another two weeks," she murmurs. "You know that saying, what is seen cannot be unseen? After that evening, he always had this frown when he looked at either of the twins. Then one night the walls came down. Two days later, they were placed immediately to the right of the dining room."

Victor hands her the stack of hallway photos. A minute or so later, she hands it back with a different picture on top. "Together?"

"In death as in life," she agrees grimly.

Side by side in the same case, the twins are positioned closely together, their inner hands linked between them. "Swamp Metalmarks," the girl adds as he traces a finger over the mottled orange and copper wings. One has her head resting against the other's shoulder; her sister's head rests against hers. They look . . .

"They never got along that well when they were alive."

She takes the stack of photos from the hall-way, sifting through them with an unreadable expression. After a moment, she starts sorting them into two stacks in front of her. When she's done, the one on the left is far taller. She slides it to the far edge of the table, then lays her hands

213

over the shorter stack, fingers laced together.

"I know these girls," she says quietly. Her face is still impossible to decipher. "Some of them not very well, and some of them were like pieces of my soul, but I knew them. I knew the names he gave them. And after Lyonette introduced us to Cassidy Lawrence, introduced us to the part that could live on after Lyonette went into the glass, others used the hours before death to introduce us to the names they'd had before."

"You know their real names?"

"You don't think that at some point the Butterfly names became real?"

"Their legal names, then."

"Some of them."

"We could have been notifying their families by now," says Eddison. "Why didn't you tell us this earlier?"

"Because I don't like you," she says bluntly, and he yanks the photos out from under her hands.

The girl cocks an eyebrow. "You really believe knowledge brings closure, don't you?" she asks. She might be incredulous, or mocking; Victor isn't sure. Maybe it's something else entirely.

"The families deserve to know what happened."

"Do they?"

"Yes!" Shoving back from the table, Eddison starts pacing before the one-way mirror. "Some of them have been waiting for *decades* to get word of their loved ones. If they can just know—know that they can finally give up . . .”

Her eyes track him back and forth across the small room. “So you never heard.”

“What?”

“Whoever went missing. You never heard.”

Victor curses under his breath at his partner’s stricken face. Oh, the girl is good, he can admit that. Not that it’s hard to irritate Eddison, but to really get under his skin? “Go see about getting some food delivered,” he orders. “Take a few minutes.”

The door slams behind Eddison.

“Who was it?” asks Inara.

“Do you really think it’s any of your business?”

“How much of what you’ve asked me is really any of yours?”

It’s not the same, and they both know it.

“I don’t believe the knowledge helps,” Inara says after a moment. “If my parents are alive, if they’re dead, it doesn’t change what happened way back then. It stopped hurting a long time ago, as soon as I accepted that they weren’t coming back.”

“Your parents chose to leave,” he reminds her. “None of you chose to be kidnapped.”

She looks down at her burned hands. “I guess I don’t see the difference.”

“If one of Sophia’s girls was kidnapped, do you think she’d ever rest until she knew?”

Inara blinks. "But how does it help? To know they've been dead for years; to know they were raped and murdered and then violated further in death?"

"Because then they no longer have to wonder. Don't you think the girls in the apartment worried about you?"

"People leave," she says with a shrug.

"But you would have gone back if you could," he hazards.

She doesn't answer. Has it ever occurred to her to go back? That she could?

He sighs and rubs tiredly at his face. This isn't a debate either of them can win.

The door smacks against the wall as it opens too quickly, and Eddison stalks back in. Victor swears under his breath and starts to rise, but Eddison shakes his head. "Let me go, Vic. I know the line."

Crossing that line in college got the FBI interested in hiring him; crossing it a few times since has gotten him in trouble. Beneath the remnants of red-faced fury, though, Victor can see calm determination. It's enough for Victor to sit back down. Just in case, he stays on the edge of his seat.

Eddison walks around the table so he can lean over Inara. "As you like to say, here's the thing: most people are missed. I'm sorry that you had such a shitty family. I am. No child deserves to grow up that way. I am sorry no one missed you,

216

but you don't get to decide for all those other girls that no one's missing them."

He sets a picture frame on the table; Victor doesn't have to look to know what the frame holds.

"This is my sister, Faith," says Eddison. "She disappeared when she was eight, and no, we never heard. We don't know if she's alive or dead. Twenty *years* my family has searched and waited for word. Even if we'd found her body, at least we'd finally know. I'd stop looking at blondes in their late twenties and wondering if one of them is Faith, if I'm walking right by her and don't know it. My mother could stop updating the website she hopes Faith will stumble across. My father could take the reward for information money he's been saving all these years and fix the house that's falling down around them. We could finally put my sister to rest and let her go.

"Not knowing is crippling. It will take a long time to get those girls out of the resin, even longer to make positive IDs. Too long. You have the chance to give these families peace. You have the chance to let them finally grieve and move on with their lives. You have the chance to give these girls back to their families."

The little girl in the picture is wearing a pink glitter tiara and a Ninja Turtle costume—complete with eye mask and pink tutu—and holding a Wonder Woman pillowcase in one hand. A much younger Eddison holds her other hand, smiling down at her. He's not in a costume, but the girl grinning back at him with two bottom teeth missing doesn't seem to care.

Inara touches the child's glass-covered smile. She touched Lyonette's photo that way. "He took pictures of us," she says eventually. "Front and back, once the tattoos were done. If he took them, he must have kept them. Not in his Garden suite—I looked once—but Lyonette thought he probably put them into some kind of book, to keep him company when he had to be away from the Garden." She studies the photo another moment, then hands the frame back to him. "Lotte was nearly eight."

"I'll call CSU," Eddison tells Victor, "have them check the house again." He carefully tucks the frame under one arm and leaves the room.

The silence that follows is broken by Inara's soft snort. "I still don't like him."

"You're allowed," Victor says with a laugh. "Did Desmond ever see this book?"

She shrugs. "If he did, he never mentioned it."

"But at some point he discovered the true nature of the Garden."

"At some point."

The first time Desmond used his new codes was after midnight on a Thursday. Well, technically Friday. It was a week or so after his father finally programmed him into the security system, a week of visiting only with his father, of not asking questions even when his father had walked away. Three weeks now he'd known of the Garden, but not the real one.

I'd spent most of the day secluded in Simone's room, helping her with cold cloths and glasses of water as she suffered through constant nausea and vomiting. It was the third day in a row and we'd thus far managed to keep it from Lorraine, but I wasn't sure how long that could last. Between the nausea and some specific points of tenderness, I had the bad feeling Simone was pregnant.

It happened sometimes, because no contraception is completely foolproof, but it always meant another filled display case and a temporarily empty room. I don't think Simone had realized her condition yet. She thought Avery had brought the flu back into the Garden. She was finally asleep, one hand pressed against her stomach, and Danelle had promised to stay with her until the morning.

The smell of sour, stale vomit clung to me, strong enough to make me semi-nauseated as well. I'd long since earned the privilege of turning my shower on whenever I wanted, but the idea of being stuck in another little room was almost physically painful. I stopped by the room just long enough to shove my dress and underwear down the laundry chute—far too narrow for a person to fit through, as Bliss had informed me—and went out into the Garden itself.

At night the Garden was a place of shadows and moonlight, where you could more clearly hear all the illusions that went into making it what it was. During the day there was conversation and movement, sometimes games or songs, and it masked the sound of the pipes feeding water and nutrients through the beds, of the fans that circulated the air. At night, the creature that was the Garden peeled back its synthetic skin to show the skeleton beneath.

I liked the Garden at night for the same reason I loved the original fairy tales. It was what it was, nothing more and nothing less. Unless the Gardener was visiting you, darkness in the Garden was the closest we got to truth.

I stepped through the echoing cave and into the falls, letting the water pour over me and wash away the sourness of sickness and coming death. It was just strong enough to beat at muscles sore and tired from three days of bending over someone, of perching on an uncomfortable stool and expecting every second for Lorraine or the Gardener to come investigate. I let the water pound that away, then used the mist-dampened rocks to haul myself up to the top of the cliff and the sun rock. I wrung most of the water from my hair and then lay back with closed eyes, sprawled inelegantly over the rock with its trace of sun warmth left over from the day. Breath by breath, I could feel my muscles slowly relax.

"Direct, but not very modest."

I sat up so fast something seized in my back, and I spent the next several minutes swearing at people who couldn't give proper warning. Desmond stood on the path five or ten yards away, hands shoved deep in his pockets, craning his neck back to stare at the glass tiles of the greenhouse roof.

"Good evening," I said sourly, rearranging myself more comfortably on the rock. All of my clothing was either in my room or waiting to be laundered, so there wasn't much point in shrieking and trying to find something to cover myself with. "Come to take in the view?"

"Rather more of a view than I expected."

"I thought I was alone."

"Alone?" he repeated, meeting my eyes and very carefully not looking any lower. "In an entire garden full of other girls?"

"Who are all either sleeping or occupying themselves in their rooms," I retorted.

"Ah."

That was the last thing said for some time. It sure as hell wasn't my job to supply conversation, so I turned on the stone and looked out into the Garden, watching the surface of the pond ripple and sway where water emptied from the stream. Eventually I heard his footsteps on the stone and then something dark hovered in front of me.

When I reached out to touch it, it dropped into my lap.

His sweater.

The color was hard to determine in the moonlight, maybe a burgundy of some sort, with a school crest sewn onto one breast. It smelled like soap and aftershave and cedar, something warm and masculine and mostly unfamiliar in the Garden. I twisted my wet hair into a messy knot atop my head and pulled on the sweater, and when everything was covered, he sat next to me on the rock.

"I couldn't sleep," he said quietly.

"So you came out here."

"I just can't make sense of this place."

"Given that it doesn't make sense, that's understandable."

"So you're not here by choice."

I sighed and rolled my eyes. "Stop looking for information you have no intention of actually using."

"How do you know I won't use it?"

"Because you want him to be proud of you," I said sharply. "And you know if you tell anyone about all this, he won't be. Given that, what does it matter whether we're here by choice or not?"

"You . . . you must think I'm a despicable excuse for a human being."

"I think you have the potential to be." I looked at his sad, earnest face and decided to take a risk

222

for pretty much the first time since coming to the Garden. "I also think you have the potential to be better."

He was silent for a long time. Such a tiny step, a minuscule nudge, but already it seemed too big. How could a parent have so much control over a child, that paternal pride meant more than what was right? "Our choices make us who we are," he said eventually.

It wasn't what I'd call a substantive response.

"What choices are you making, Desmond?"

"I don't think I'm making any choices right now."

"Then you're automatically making the wrong ones." He straightened, mouth open to protest, but I held up my hand. "Not making a choice *is* a choice. Neutrality is a concept, not a fact. No one actually gets to live their lives that way."

"Seemed to work for Switzerland."

"As a nation, maybe. How do you think individuals felt, when they learned the truth of what their neutrality allowed to transpire? When they learned of the camps, and the gas chambers, and the experimentation, do you think they were pleased with their neutrality then?"

"Then why don't you just leave?" he demanded. "Rather than judge my father for giving you food and clothing and comfortable shelter, why don't you just go back out there?"

"You don't really think we have codes, do you?"

He deflated, the indignation fading as quickly as it flared. "He keeps you locked in?"

"Collectors don't let butterflies fly free. It defeats the purpose."

"You could ask."

"It isn't easy to ask him for anything," I said, parroting his words from a week or so ago.

He flinched.

He was blind, but he wasn't stupid. That he chose to be ignorant really pissed me off. I shrugged out of the sweater and dropped it in his lap, sliding off the rock. "Thank you for the conversation," I muttered, walking quickly down the path that sloped to the main level from the far end of the cliff. I could hear him tripping and fumbling after me.

"Maya, wait. Wait!" His hand closed around my wrist and tugged back, nearly pulling me off my feet. "I'm sorry."

"You're between me and food. Apologize for that, if you like, and get out of my way."

He let go of my wrist but kept following me across the Garden. He hopped first across the small stream and reached out to steady me from the other side, something I found both bizarre and charming. The main lights in the dining room—and the attached open kitchen—were dark, but a dim light shone from above the stove for anyone seeking a late-night snack. The sight of the larger, locked fridge momentarily distracted him.

I yanked open the door to the smaller one and studied what was inside. I was genuinely hungry, but as being around vomiting people doesn't do much for the appetite, nothing seemed appealing.

"What is that on your back?"

I slammed the door shut, blocking out the light, but it was too late.

He stepped closer behind me, walking us both over to the oven, and in the dim glow of the stove light he studied the wings in all their exquisite, excruciating detail. Under normal circumstances, I could have mostly forgotten what they looked like. He'd give us mirrors if we asked for them; I never had. Bliss, though, made a point of showing everyone their wings on a regular basis.

So we couldn't forget what we were.

Butterflies are short-lived creatures, and that too was part of her reminder.

His fingertips brushed against the darker veins of brown against the fawn-colored upper wings, stretching as the lines splayed outward into the delicate chevrons. I stood perfectly still despite the goose bumps that crawled down my spine at his tentative exploration. He hadn't asked, but then, he was his father's son, I supposed. My eyes closed, my hands curling into fists at my sides, as his fingers moved lower into the bottom wings of roses and purples. He didn't follow the lines down, but in, toward my spine, until he could run a thumb up the entire length of black ink that ran down the center of my back.

"That's gorgeous," he whispered. "Why a butterfly?"

"Ask your father."

Suddenly his hand was trembling against my skin, against the mark of his father's ownership. He didn't move it away, though. "He did this to you?"

I didn't answer.

"How badly did it hurt?"

What hurt most was lying there *letting* him do it, but I didn't say that. I didn't say that it hurt so fucking badly to see those first lines appear on each new girl's back, didn't say that the skin had been so raw I hadn't slept on my back for weeks, didn't say that I still couldn't sleep on my stomach because it made me remember that first rape on the tattoo bench, when he drove himself into me and gave me a new name.

I didn't say anything.

"Does he . . . does he do this to all of you?" he asked shakily.

I nodded.

"Oh, God."

Run, I screamed silently. Run and tell the police, or open the doors and let us tell the police ourselves. Just do something—anything—other than stand there!

But he didn't. He stayed behind me, his hand

against the map of ink and scars, until the silence became a living, gasping thing between us. So I was the one to move away, to open the fridge again and pretend there was anything normal about this moment. I pulled out an orange, swung the door closed with my hip, and leaned against the part of the counter that ran perpendicular to the rest. It wasn't quite an island, but it created a waist-high separation between the kitchen and the dining room.

Desmond tried to join me there but his legs gave out, and he slid to the floor next to my feet, his back against the cabinets. His shoulder brushed against my knee as I methodically peeled the orange. I always tried to get it off in one piece, a perfect spiral. So far I never had. It always broke partway through.

"Why does he do it?"

"Why do you think?"

"Shit." He brought his knees up and hunched over them, his arms crossed against the back of his head.

I freed the first wedge and sucked it dry, setting the seeds on the peel as I found them.

And the silence grew.

When all the juice was gone from the wedge, I popped the whole thing in my mouth and chewed. Hope used to tease me about how I ate oranges, saying I made boys very uncomfortable. I'd stuck my tongue out at her and told her boys didn't have to watch. Desmond certainly wasn't watching, anyway. I moved on to the second wedge, then the third and the fourth.

"Still awake, Maya?" came the Gardener's light voice from the doorway. "Are you feeling well?"

Desmond looked up, his face pale and stricken, but he didn't stand or say anything to announce his presence. Sitting on the floor against the cabinets, he wouldn't be seen unless the Gardener came all the way to the counter and looked straight down. The Gardener never came into the kitchen itself.

"I'm feeling fine," I answered. "I just decided to get a snack after rinsing off in the falls."

"And didn't want to be bothered with clothing?" He laughed and entered the dining room, sitting down in the large, padded chair that was reserved for him. So far as I knew, he'd never seen the rough crown Bliss had scratched into the back. It was vaguely throne-like, I'd given her that, with a deep cushion of dark red velvet and nearly black polished wood rising into ornate scrolls above his head. He pushed it back, one elbow resting on the edge of the table because the chair had no arms.

I shrugged, picking another wedge from the orange. "It seemed a little silly to worry."

He looked strangely casual, sitting in the shadows wearing nothing but a pair of silky pajama pants. His plain gold wedding band gleamed with fractures of light from the stove. I couldn't tell if he'd been sleeping in his suite or if he'd been with one of the other girls, though he didn't generally sleep in our rooms. Unless his wife was out of town, he usually spent at least part of each night in the house I'd never seen, couldn't see, even from the tallest tree in the Garden. "Come sit with me."

At my feet, Desmond pressed his fist against his mouth with a pained look.

Leaving the rest of the orange on the counter with the peel and seeds, I obediently came around the counter and crossed into the shadows to join him at his table. I started to lower myself onto the nearest bench, but he pulled me into his lap. One hand stroked along my back and hip, something he did without thinking, while the other clasped one of my hands against my thigh.

"How are the girls reacting to Desmond being here?"

If he'd had any idea how *here* Desmond was, I doubted we'd be having this conversation.

"They're . . . wary," I answered finally. "I think we're all waiting to see if he's more like you or Avery."

"And hoping for?" I slanted him a sideways look and he actually laughed, pressing a kiss against my collarbone. "They're not afraid of him, surely? Desmond would never hurt anyone."

"I'm sure they'll all adjust to his being here."

"And you, Maya? What do you think of my younger son?"

I almost looked toward the kitchen, but if he didn't want his father to know he was there, I wouldn't give him away. "I think he's confused. He doesn't really know what to make of all this." I took a deep breath, gave myself a moment to convince myself that the next question was for Desmond's sake, to give him another view into the reality of the Garden. "Why the displays?"

"What do you mean?"

"After keeping us, why do you keep us?"

He didn't answer for a time, his fingers tracing nonsense symbols on my skin. "My father collected butterflies," he said eventually. "He went hunting for them, and if he couldn't capture them in good condition he paid others for them, and he pinned them into their display cases while they were still alive. Every one of them had a black velvet background, a little bronze plaque giving its common and proper names, creating a veritable museum of shadowboxes on his office walls. Sometimes he'd hang my mother's embroidery between the cases. Sometimes they were single butterflies, sometimes entire bouquets, picked out in beautiful colors on the cloth."

His hand left my thigh and traveled up my back, tracing the wings. He didn't even have to look at them to know their shapes. "He was happiest in that room, and once he retired he spent almost every day in there. But there was a small electrical fire in that section of the house, and all the butterflies were ruined. Every single one, the collection he'd spent decades acquiring and working on. He was never quite the same after that, and died not long after. I suppose he felt as though his entire life had been burned away in that fire.

"The day after his funeral, Mother and I had to attend an Independence Day fair in town. They were presenting Mother with an award for her charity work and she didn't want to disappoint anyone by not attending. I left her in the company of sympathetic friends and wandered through the small fair, and then I saw her: a girl, wearing a butterfly mask made of feathers and passing out little feather and silk rose petal butterflies to the children who came through the silk maze. She was so vibrant and bright, so very alive, it was hard to believe that butterflies could ever die.

"When I smiled at her and went into the maze, she followed me in. It wasn't hard to get her home from there. I kept her in the basement at first, until I could build the garden to be a proper home. I was in school and I'd just taken over my father's business, and before too long I was married, so I think she was very lonely, even once I moved her into the garden, so I brought in Lorraine for her, and others, to be her friends." He was lost in memory, but for him it wasn't painful.

For him, it only made sense, was only right. Rather than bringing his Eve to a garden, he'd built one around her, and served as the angel with the flaming sword to keep her in. He rearranged me on his lap, tugging me against his chest until he could lay my head between his neck and shoulder. "Her death was heartbreaking, and I couldn't bear to think that brief existence was all she would ever have. I didn't want to forget her. As long as I could remember her, a part of her would still live. I built the cases, researched ways to preserve her against decay."

"The resin," I whispered, and he nodded.

"But first the embalming. My company keeps formaldehyde and formaldehyde resins on hand in the manufacturing division, for clothing if you can believe it. It's easy to order more than they need and bring the rest here. Replacing the blood with the formaldehyde retards decay, enough for the resin to preserve everything else. Even when you're gone, Maya, you will not be forgotten."

The sick thing was, he genuinely meant it to be comforting. Unless an accident happened or I pissed him off, in three and a half years he would run formaldehyde through my veins. I knew just enough to know that he would stay with me the entire time, maybe even brushing my hair and pinning it into its final arrangement, and when all my blood was gone, he'd place me in a glass case and pump it full of clear resin to give me a second life no mere electrical fire could end. He would touch the glass and whisper my name every time he passed, and he would remember me.

And sitting in his lap left no illusions as to how he felt about all of that.

He gently pushed me off his lap, spreading his legs to make me kneel between them, one hand tangling in my hair. "Show me that you won't forget me, Maya." He pulled my head closer, his other hand busy at the drawstring of his pants. "Not even then."

Not even when I was long dead and gone, and the sight of me would still be enough to make him hard.

And I obeyed because I always obeyed, because I still wanted those three and a half years even if it meant this man telling me he loved me. I obeyed when he damn near choked me, and I obeyed when he yanked me back onto his lap, obeyed when he told me to promise I wouldn't ever forget him.

And this time, instead of writing someone else's poems and stories against the inside of my skull, I wondered about the boy on the other side of the kitchen counter, listening to it all.

The thing that convinced me my long-ago next-door neighbor was a pedophile was more than the looks he gave me. It was the looks the foster children gave each other, the bruised, sick knowledge they shared between them. All of them knew what was happening, not just to themselves but to each other. None of them would say a word. I saw those bruised looks and I knew it would only be a matter of time before he put his hand up my dress, before he took my hand and put it in his lap and whispered about a present for me.

The Gardener kissed me when he was done and told me to make sure I got some rest. He was still pulling his pants back in place as he walked out of the dining room. I walked back to the other side of the counter, picked up the rest of my orange, and sat down next to Desmond, whose face was wet and shiny with tears. He stared at me with dull eyes.

Bruised eyes.

I ate the rest of the orange in the time it took him to find something to say, and then he didn't say anything at all, just handed me his sweater. I put it on and when he reached for my hand, I let him take it.

He was never going to go to the police.

We both knew it.

All that the past half hour had changed was that now he hated himself a little for it.

"You haven't asked who survived."

"You're not going to let me go see them until I've told you everything you want to know."

"True."

"So I'll find out when we're done, when I can actually spend time with them. My being there now can't change anything anyway."

"Suddenly I can believe you haven't cried since you were six."

A faint smile flickers across her face. "Fucking carousel," she agrees pleasantly.

Bliss made a carousel, did I mention that?

She could make damn near anything out of polymer clay, baking sheet after sheet in the oven with Lorraine scowling at her the entire time as supervision. She was the only one of us with oven privileges. She was also the only one who'd ever asked.

The night before she died, in those long hours we spent curled together on her bed, Lyonette told us stories about when she was younger. She didn't give us names or locations, but she told them just the same, and the one that made her smile, the one that she loved more than any of the others, was about a carousel.

Her father made the figures for a lot of carousels, and sometimes little Cassidy Lawrence would draw some out and her father would incorporate the designs into the next project, let her choose the colors or the expression on a face. Once her father let her go with him to deliver the horses and sleighs to a traveling carnival. They placed the figures all around the disc and she sat on the rail and watched as they ran the wiring through the golden poles so the horses moved up and down, and when everything was done, she ran around and around the carousel, petting the horses and whispering their names in their ears so they wouldn't forget. She knew every single one, and she loved them all.

The Gardener's traits don't exist in isolation, just in extremes.

But the horses weren't hers, and when it came time to go home, she had to leave them all behind, probably to never see them again. She couldn't cry because she'd promised her father she wouldn't, promised she wouldn't make a scene when they had to go.

That was when she made her first origami horse.

In the cab of the truck on the way home, she made her first two dozen origami horses, using notebook paper and fast-food receipts to practice until she could make them well, and when she got home, she graduated to using computer paper. She made horse after horse after horse and colored them all to match the ones she'd left behind, whispering their names as she did, and when she was done, she carefully painted thin dowels and stuck them through the middles with a little bit of glue.

She drew out and colored the patterns on the floor, all the paintings on the sloped ceiling, even the pictures framed in the elaborate curlicues that ran along the base of the tent top, and her mother helped her put them all together. Her father even helped her make a crank for the base so the whole thing could slowly spin. Her parents were so proud of her.

The morning of the day she was kidnapped, when she left the house for school, the carousel was still sitting in pride of place on the mantel.

After Lyonette died, I had the nameless new girl to keep me occupied.

Bliss had her polymer clay.

She didn't show anyone what she was working on and none of us asked, letting her work through her grief in her own way. She was unusually focused on this project. Honestly, as long as it wasn't a Lustrous Copper figurine, I wasn't too worried. She'd done that for a few of the other dead girls and somehow I found those two-inch-tall butterflies more macabre and disturbing than the girls in the glass.

But then the new girl's infection reached a critical point—her tattoo was never going to heal properly. Even if the infection didn't kill her, the wings would be hopelessly flawed, and that was something the Gardener couldn't accept. Not when beauty was why he chose us.

The doors had come down in the dark hours of earliest morning, like they would have for her normal tattoo session, but when they came up, she wasn't in the tattoo room or her bed. She never

237

appeared in the display cases. There was no goodbye.

There was just . . . nothing.

There was literally nothing left of her, not even a name.

Bliss was in my room when I came back from looking, sitting cross-legged on my bed with a wrap skirt draped over a bundle in her lap. Dark shadows bruised the pale skin under her eyes and I wondered how much she'd slept since Lyonette had said goodbye to us.

I sank down next to her on the bed, one leg curled under my body, and leaned my back against the wall.

"Is she dead?"

"If not, she soon will be," I sighed.

"And then you'll sit through another new girl's arrival and tattoos."

"Probably."

"Why?"

I'd wondered that myself over the past week or so. "Because Lyonette thought it was important."

She pulled the fabric away from her lap, and there was the carousel.

Lyonette had made another origami carousel when she came to the Garden; it had been sitting on the shelf above Bliss's bed since her death. She'd reproduced all the patterns and designs and colors, and so had Bliss in her own medium. The golden poles even had the spiral ridges. I reached out and nudged the red pennant on top and the whole thing spun just a little.

"I had to make it," she whispered, "but I can't keep it."

Bliss broke into furious, heartbroken sobs on my bed. She didn't know about my carousel. She didn't know that I'd sat on a black-and-red painted horse and finally understood that my parents didn't love me, or at least didn't love me nearly enough. The day I finally understood—and accepted—that I wasn't wanted.

I lifted it gently out of her lap and nudged her knee with my toe. "Shower."

She hiccupped and slid off the bed to obey, and while she washed away two weeks of grief and rage, I studied the horses to see if any of them matched the one that I'd splashed with the last of my tears ten years before.

And the answer was almost. This horse had silver chasings instead of gold, and it had red ribbons tied into its black mane, but otherwise they were very, very close. I shifted onto my knees and placed it on the shelf next to Simba, next to the origami menagerie and the other polymer figures, next to the rocks Evita had painted and the poem Danelle had written and all the other things I'd somehow managed to accumulate after six months in the Garden. I wondered if I could have Bliss make a tiny girl with dark hair and golden skin to sit on that black-and-red horse and spin and spin and spin on the carousel and watch all the rest of the world walk away from her.

But if I'd asked, she would have asked why, and that little girl didn't need the sympathy so much as she needed to just finally be forgotten.

Bliss came out of the shower, body and hair wrapped in violet and rose towels, and finally slept curled against me like one of Sophia's girls. I kept one arm behind my head and I stayed against the wall, and every now and then I reached out and gave the carousel a little nudge so I could watch the black-and-red horse glide just a little farther away.

•

He wishes he could let her have that distraction. Let the conversation derail, let her avoid the train wreck he has to put her through.

But Victor sits forward in his chair and clears his throat, and when she turns her miserable eyes on him, he nods slowly.

She sighs and folds her hands in her lap.

For the next week, Desmond stayed out of the Garden completely. He didn't use his codes, didn't come in with his father, he just stayed away. Bliss was the one to ask the Gardener about it, in her usual appallingly blunt fashion, but he laughed and said not to worry, his son was just focusing on his upcoming finals.

I was okay with that.

Whether he was hiding, staying away, or just thinking through things, I didn't mind the absence of another male to entertain. I appreciated the space to think.

Avery was back in the Garden, after all, which meant a constant, subtle interference had to be played to protect the more fragile girls from his interest. Running it all from Simone's bedside just made it more difficult.

She'd noticeably lost weight in the past week and a half, unable to keep anything down longer than a half hour or so. During the days, I stayed with her, and during the nights, when Danelle came to relieve me, I went into the Garden and slept out on the sun rock, where I could pretend the walls weren't closing in and time wasn't running out.

I *liked* Simone. She was funny and wry, never buying into the bullshit but making the best of it anyway. I helped her back into bed from another toilet dive and she clutched my hand. "I'm going to have to take a test, aren't I?"

Bliss said Lorraine had stayed at breakfast, asking questions. "Yes," I answered slowly. "I think you will."

"It'll come up positive, won't it?"

"I think so."

She closed her eyes, one hand pulling away the sweat-damp hair from her forehead. "I should have realized sooner. I saw both my mom and my oldest sister go through pregnancies and they were sick for two months solid."

"Want me to pee on the stick for you?"

"What the hell is wrong with us that *that* is a declaration of love and friendship?" But she shook her head slowly. "I don't want us both dead, which we both know would be the result."

We sat in silence for a while, because some things just don't have an answer.

"Can you do me a favor?" she asked eventually.

"What do you need?"

"If we have the book in the library, can you read it to me?"

When she told me what she wanted, I almost laughed. Almost. Not because it was funny but because I was relieved that this was one thing I could do for her. I retrieved it from the library, settled next to her on the bed with her hand in mine, and opened the book to the proper page so I could start to read.

"Most terribly cold it was; it snowed, and was nearly quite dark, and evening—the last evening of the year. In this cold and darkness there went along the street a poor little girl, bareheaded, and with naked feet."

"What book is that?"

"Part of a book," the girl corrects. "It's 'The Little Match Girl' by Hans Christian Andersen."

Victor can almost remember it, something

from a ballet his daughter Brittany did when she was much younger, but it's lost to memories of *The Nutcracker* and *The Steadfast Tin Soldier*.

"It's the kind of story that makes more sense in the Garden than in the real world."

I went on to other stories when that one was done, but fell silent when Lorraine walked in. She had a tray with two lunches on it and sitting between them was a pregnancy test kit.

"I have to be here when you take it," she said.

"No shit."

Sighing, Simone sat up against the headboard and reached for her glass of water, downing it all in one go. I handed her another glass off the tray, this one of fruit juice, and she drank it down as well. She made a good attempt at lunch, which was just soup and toast, but most of it went untouched. When the water finally got through her system, she grabbed the kit off the tray, stalked to her little toilet, and tugged the curtain to conceal herself.

Lorraine hovered in the doorway like a vulture, her shoulders hunched and her eyes on the fabric screen.

Simone leaned forward to catch my eye, then jerked her head toward the bitch in the doorway. Nodding, I took a deep breath and started reading "The Steadfast Tin Soldier."

At the top of my lungs.

It earned me a ferocious scowl from the cook-nurse, but at least it let Simone piss in peace. We heard the flush and a moment later, she came out from behind the curtain and tossed the dripping stick of plastic at the older woman. "Have fun. Go report. Just get out."

"Don't you want to—"

"No. Get out." Simone threw herself onto the bed, draping her upper half over my lap. "Will you keep reading?"

I laid the book across her back, hiding the dull brown wings of a Mitchell's Satyr, and picked back up where we'd left off. She slept through much of the afternoon, waking up from time to time to hurl herself toward the toilet. Danelle joined us for a bit later on, brushing Simone's dark brown hair into an elegant twist. Bliss brought us dinner, and pinned small polymer larkspur blooms into the twist, and when I'd eaten and Simone had pushed her food around the plate, Bliss took the trays back to the kitchen for Lorraine.

As the deepening evening made the shadows shift in the hallway, the Gardener appeared in the doorway.

With a dress.

It was a multi-layered confection of sheer silks in shades of brown and creams, all meant to echo her wings and flatter her dusky skin tone. Simone looked up at our sudden silence, saw the dress, and quickly turned her face away before he could see her tears.

"Ladies?"

Blinking rapidly, Danelle kissed the curve of Simone's ear, the closest to her face she could reach, and silently left the room. Simone slowly pushed herself up to sitting and wrapped her arms around me, burying her nose in my shoulder. I squeezed back as tightly as I could, feeling the tremors start.

"My name is Rachel," she whispered against my skin. "Rachel Young. Will you remember?"

"I will." I kissed her cheek and reluctantly let her go. With the book of fairy tales in hand, I walked to the doorway, where the Gardener lightly kissed me.

"She won't be in pain," he murmured.

She'll be dead.

This was the part where I was supposed to go back to my room, or Bliss's room, or Danelle's room. This was the part where we were supposed to gather in small groups, pretending we're anything other than what we are, and mourn the loss that hadn't actually happened yet. This was where we were supposed to wait for Simone to die.

And for the first time, I couldn't do it.

I just couldn't do it.

The lights flickered, our warning to get to our rooms before the walls came down over the doorways. I stepped out onto the sand path, aware of movement in the shadows in the far side of the Garden. I wasn't sure if it was Avery, Desmond, or another of the girls, and at the moment I didn't care. The lights went out and the walls hissed behind me, settling into their grooves with heavy thumps that fell flat against the silence.

Walking deeper into the Garden, I stepped along the bank of the stream until I reached the waterfall. I dropped the book on a rock a safe distance from the water and spray and crossed my arms across my stomach, clutching my elbows against a solid weight growing in my chest. My head lolled back on my neck and, leaning against the cliff, I stared up at the panes of glass overhead. Stars were winking into sight against the deepening night, some bright and silver, some pale and blue or yellow and one lone red light that might have been a plane.

A tiny flash of light streaked across the sky, and even though I knew the science—knew that it was just space debris, just rock or metal or scrap from a satellite burning up in the atmosphere—all I could think of was that stupid story. *"Someone is just dead!" said the little girl; for her old grandmother, the only person who had loved her, and who was now no more, had told her, that when a star falls, a soul ascends to God.*

And that stupid little girl stood in the winter and kept lighting matches to catch glimpses of families that weren't—could never be—hers and froze to death in those harsh moments of reality between matches, because even though matches can burn, they're light, not heat.

My breath caught against that solid, expanding weight and couldn't get past it. I couldn't breathe in, couldn't breathe out, just this knot of stale air choking me. Leaves and branches rattled in the distance as I fell to my knees, gasping for breaths that wouldn't come. I curled my hand into a fist and pounded it into my chest but aside from a second, throbbing pain, nothing changed. Why couldn't I breathe?

A hand touched my shoulder and I whirled around, slapping it away as I fell back from the uncoordinated movement.

Desmond.

I rolled onto my hands and knees, scrambled to my feet and through the waterfall into the cave, but he followed me, catching me when I tripped on a dip in the floor and fell again. He lowered me gently to the ground and knelt in front of me. He studied my face as I struggled for air. "I know you don't have any reason to trust me, but do it anyway, just for a minute."

His hand came toward my face and I slapped it away again. Shaking his head, he spun me quickly and pinned my arms to my side with one arm, and his other hand covered my nose and mouth. "Breathe in," he whispered against my ear.

"Doesn't matter if it's a full breath, you'll still get some air. Breathe in."

I tried, and maybe he was right, maybe there was some, but I couldn't feel it. All I could feel was his hand between me and what I needed to live.

"All I'm doing is forcing you to breathe in a high concentration of carbon dioxide," he continued calmly. "Breathe in. The carbon dioxide attaches to your bloodstream in place of oxygen and slows your body's responses. Breathe in. When your body gets to a critical point, when you're on the verge of passing out, your body's natural responses push past the psychological factors. Breathe in."

Each time he gave me the instruction, I tried to obey, I truly did, but there just wasn't any air. I stopped struggling, my limbs leaden and heavy, and sagged against his chest. His hand stayed sealed over my nose and mouth. With all of me so heavy, I could barely feel the weight in my chest, and slowly, as he periodically repeated his instruction, air trickled in. My head swam with sudden light-headedness, but I was breathing. He moved his hand to my shoulder, rubbing it up and down my arm as he continued to whisper, "Breathe in."

Eventually it became a habit again, something I didn't have to think about, and I closed my eyes against a blinding sense of shame. I'd never had a panic attack before, though I'd seen them plenty in others, and my own inability to do anything sensible was mortifying. More so, having someone else witness it. When I felt fifty percent sure I wouldn't fall flat on my face if I stood, I tried to push to my feet.

Desmond's arms tightened around me. Not painfully, but enough that I wasn't going anywhere without a fight. "I'm a coward," he said quietly. "And worse than that, I think I may be my father's son; but if I can help you this way, please let me."

If the little match girl had someone curled around her like this, someone warm and solid against her back, his own body wrapped around her, would she have survived?

Or would they have both frozen?

Shifting until his back hit the wall, Desmond gently tugged at me until I was almost sideways between his legs, my cheek pressed against his upper chest so I could nearly hear his heart beat. I timed my still-shaky breaths to that, feeling how it jumped and skipped whenever I moved. He didn't have his brother's stocky frame, the obvious threat of muscle, nor his father's wiry strength. He was slender like a runner, all lean angles and long planes. He hummed softly, something I didn't recognize and couldn't properly hear pressed against his chest, but his fingers brushed against my skin in the shape of piano chords.

We sat in the damp, dark cave in clothing soaked

from the waterfall, clinging to each other like children against a nightmare, but when I fell asleep, the nightmare would still be there. When I woke up, the nightmare would still be there. Every day for three and a half years, the night-mare would always, *always* be there, and there was no comfort against that.

For a few hours, though, I could pretend.

I could be the little match girl and strike my illusions against the wall, lost in the warmth until the glow faded and left me back in the Garden.

"They weren't just fellow captives, were they?" Victor asks after giving her a moment to collect herself. "They were your friends."

"Some of them are friends. All of them are family. I guess that's just what happens."

Sometimes it was hard to make yourself get to know other people. It would just hurt more when they died, or hurt them when you died. Some-times it was hard to believe it was worth that pain. At the heart of the Garden, though, was loneliness and the ever-present threat of shattering, and connecting with the others seemed the safer of two evils. Not the lesser, necessarily, but the safer.

So I knew that Nazira was even more worried about forgetting than Bliss. She was an artist, and she filled sketchbook after sketchbook with her family and friends. She drew outfits she'd loved, her home and school, the little swing set in the city park where she'd gotten her first kiss. She drew them over and over, and panicked if the details changed or got fuzzy.

There was Zara the Bitch, and when *Bliss* names you that, you know you're an unholy terror. Bliss was generally scathing and intolerant of bullshit; Zara's default setting was mean. I appreciated that she didn't buy into the illusion, but she made things hell for those who needed to cling to it. Like Nazira, who believed that as long as she didn't forget anything from before, she'd see it all again. Not a week went by that I didn't break up a fight between them, usually by dragging Zara to the stream and shoving her in until she cooled off. She wasn't a friend, but in quiet moments, I liked her. She loved books like I did.

Glenys ran and ran and ran, endless laps around the halls, until the Gardener ordered Lorraine to give her twice as much food as the rest of us. Ravenna was one of the few with an MP3 player and speaker, and she'd dance for hours. Ballet, hip-hop, waltz, tap without shoes, all the classes she must have taken for years, and if you walked by her, she'd grab your arm and pull you in to dance with her. Hailee loved doing everyone's hair, and could make the most fantastic arrangements, and Pia wanted to know how everything worked, and Marenka did gorgeous cross-stitch. She even had a tiny pair of super-sharp embroidery scissors that the Gardener required her to wear on a ribbon around her neck so no one could use them to hurt themselves. Adara wrote stories, and Eleni painted, and sometimes Adara would ask Eleni or Nazira to illustrate scenes for her.

And there was Sirvat. Sirvat was . . . Sirvat.

She was hard to know.

It wasn't just that she was standoffish, which she was, or quiet, which she was. It was that you never knew what the hell was going to come out of her mouth. She was Lyonette's final introduction. Lyonette asked me not to help with that one, because Sirvat was just that strange, and neither Lyonette nor I could guess what my reaction would be. So the first time I met her was after her wings were done. She was sprawled along the stream bank, face in the mud, with Lyonette staring at her in utter confusion.

"What are you doing?" I asked.

She didn't even look at me, half of her pale brown hair clumped with mud. "You can die from water more ways than drowning in it. Drinking too much is as lethal as not having any."

I glanced over at the perplexed Lyonette. "Is she actually suicidal?"

"I don't think so."

She wasn't, most of the time. We learned that was just Sirvat. She identified flowers we could theoretically eat to kill ourselves, but ate none herself. She knew a thousand different ways a person could die, and had a fascination for the girls in glass that none of us wanted to understand. She visited them almost as much as the Gardener did.

Sirvat was a queer duck. I honestly didn't spend much time with her, and she didn't even seem to notice, much less mind.

But most of us knew each other. Even when we chose not to share our lives from before the Garden, there was an intimacy to our company. For better or worse—almost always worse—we were Butterflies. Irrevocable common ground.

"And you mourned each other." It isn't a question.

Her mouth tilts. It isn't a smile, not even a grimace, just an acknowledgment that some kind of expression should be there. "Always. You never had to wait for someone to show up in the glass. You mourned them every single day, as they mourned you, because every day we were dying."

"Did Desmond get close to any of the other girls?"

"Yes and no. In time. It was . . ." She hesitates, eyes darting several times between Victor and her damaged hands, before sighing and clasping her hands in her lap, out of sight under the table. "Well, you have to know it was complicated."

He nods. "What did his father think?"

The day after Simone went into the glass—not that we saw her, with the walls still down—the

Gardener brought me back to his suite for a fancy private dinner. So far as I could tell without specifically asking, I was the only one he brought in there. I suppose it should have been flattering, but I only found it unsettling. The conversation stayed light. He didn't mention Simone at all, and I didn't bring her up because I didn't want to know the worst of it. The only mystery this place had left was *how* he killed us.

When dessert was finished, he told me to take a seat with a fresh glass of champagne and relax while he cleaned up. I chose the recliner rather than the couch, popping the footrest up and arranging my long skirt to cover even my feet. I could have presented at an award show in that dress, and I wondered just how much money he sank into the Garden and our upkeep. He had something classical playing on an old-fashioned record player, so I closed my eyes and rested my head back against the deep padding.

The thick carpeting in the suite muffled his footsteps, but I could still hear him return. He stood over me for a time, just watching. I knew he liked to watch us sleep sometimes, but it was somehow creepier when I was awake.

"Did Desmond upset you the other night?"

My eyes snapped open, which he seemed to take as his cue to perch on the arm of the chair. "Upset me?"

"I was looking over some of the footage and

saw you pushing him away. He followed you into the cave but there are no cameras in there. Did he upset or hurt you?"

"Oh. No."

"Maya."

I managed a small smile, for his sake or my own I wasn't sure. "I was upset, yes, but before Desmond arrived. I had a panic attack. I'd never had one before so I didn't know what to do, and I misconstrued his arrival at first. He helped me through it."

"A panic attack?"

"If after a year and a half, that's my strongest reaction, I don't think it's particularly alarming, do you?"

He returned the smile, warm and sincere. "And he helped you?"

"Yes, and stayed with me until I was calm."

He had stayed with me through the night, even when we heard two isolated doors open, when we heard his father walk the hallways with a sobbing Simone. Sometimes he liked a final fuck before killing a girl; better in her room than in those secret rooms, I guess. Des stayed with me until the morning, when all the doors lifted and the other girls filtered into the Garden to cling together against the painful loss that he didn't understand, because he didn't know she was or would soon be dead. Did he think she was just being kicked out? Or taken for an abortion?

"My younger son can be hard to know."

"Meaning you can't read his reaction to us."

He laughed and nodded, sliding down next to me in the chair. One arm came around my shoulders, arranging my head against his chest, and for a moment we could have been any two people cuddling together for a movie.

Except, if we had been any two people, my skin probably wouldn't have been crawling.

It certainly never crawled with Topher, or when we all piled onto Jason or Keg's couches, or any of the other boys from work. Intimacy with the Gardener was as much an illusion as the wings he carved into our backs; it didn't make anything real.

"He doesn't like talking about it with me."

"Given that we are a sort of harem, I don't imagine most young men would be comfortable discussing this with their fathers. You might ask your parents for tips on how to approach someone, or what to do for a first date, but the sex thing is usually verboten even when there isn't the question of willingness."

And it was another reminder that we weren't just any two people, because all he did was laugh and turn my head to kiss me. It occurred to me that I could go to his private kitchen en suite and pick up a knife to drive through his heart. I could have killed him then and there, but what stopped me was the thought that Avery would inherit the Garden.

"Avery was all excitement when I first introduced him to the Garden. He talked about it whenever we were alone. Perhaps a father doesn't need to know that many details about his son. But I can't see that Desmond has done anything more than look around."

"Does that disappoint you?" I asked neutrally.

"It puzzles me." His hand traveled up my arm to the back of my neck, where he tugged at the tie of my dress. The black silk pieces came loose in his fingers and he watched them slither down my collarbones to my waist, leaving my breasts bare. He lightly traced one nipple as he spoke. "He's a healthy young man surrounded by beautiful women, and I know he isn't a virgin, yet he doesn't avail himself of the opportunities."

"Perhaps he's still adjusting."

"Perhaps. Or perhaps variety isn't what appeals to him." He lifted me slightly in the chair so he could shift under me, giving himself better access to my breasts and pushing my dress over my hips to my thighs. "He looks for you when he comes, even if he doesn't find you."

"Apparently I'm a very direct sort of person," I said dryly, and he chuckled.

"Yes, I can see why he would put his questions to you. What would you do, if he came to you as I do?"

"I assumed that, as with you and Avery, we were to do whatever was asked of us. Was that incorrect?"

"So you would let him touch you?" He bent his head to my breast, lips moving against sensitive skin. "You would let him take his pleasure with you?"

Desmond wasn't his father.

But he was his father's son.

"Unless you tell me otherwise, I do what's asked of me."

He groaned and tugged the dress completely off, dropping it to pool in a black puddle by the chair, and as his mouth and hands turned my body traitor, not a word was said except for my name, over and over, harsh cries against the silence.

There are some qualities—some incorporate things, that have a double life . . . There is a two-fold Silence—sea and shore—body and soul. One dwells in lonely places.

He took me again and again that night, in the chair, on the carpet, in the king-sized bed, and I recited everything I could remember, even drink recipes, but long before the morning came, I'd run out of words and felt the poison seep through the cracks into my soul. I'd gotten used to the sick feeling that came with letting the Gardener fuck me, but I'd never get used to the nauseating pain that came of letting him believe he loved me.

When he finally escorted me back to my room, he sat on the edge of my narrow bed and settled the blanket around me, stroking the hair back from

258

my face and giving me a lingering kiss. "I hope Desmond comes to realize what an extraordinary young woman you are," he whispered against my lips. "You could be so good for him."

After he left, I got out of bed and stood in my shower, scrubbing at my skin until it was raw because I just wanted to pretend that I could slough away the feeling of his touch. Bliss found me there, and with unexpected tact, she didn't say a word. She helped me rinse off the last of the soap and conditioner and turned off the water, toweling my hair as I dried off the rest of me, and when my hair was brushed free of tangles and bound back in a neat braid, we curled together under the blankets.

For the first time, I understood why she'd think about jumping.

For the first time, those extra years didn't seem worth the negligible possibility of escape.

For the first time in a year and a half, I felt every drag of the needle across my skin as my prison was inked into my body. If I'd never been much for hope, neither had I been much for despair, but I could feel it choking me with every memory. I took a deep breath, listening to the echo of Desmond's voice in the cave, and let that remind me to keep breathing so that even Bliss, who saw me through things the others never even imagined I felt, wouldn't see just how fucking scared I was.

In terror she spoke, letting sink her wings till

they trailed in the dust—in agony sobbed, letting sink her plumes till they trailed in the dust— till they sorrowfully trailed in the dust.

But my wings couldn't move and I couldn't fly, and I couldn't even cry.

All that was left to me was the terror and the agony and the sorrow.

Victor leaves the room without a word.

A moment later, Yvonne steps into the hall from the observation room, handing him two bottles of water. "Ramirez called with an update," she reports. "The girls in more delicate condition are stabilizing. They still want to talk to Maya before answering too many questions. Senator Kingsley is starting to lean on Ramirez to get to Maya."

"Shit." He scrubs at his cheek. "Can Ramirez keep her leashed in the hospital?"

"For a little while. She's negotiating between the senator and her daughter. She figures she can get a few hours out of that with everything else going on."

"All right, thanks. Let Eddison know when he gets back?"

"Will do."

Politicians are like child services, he thinks. Ultimately useful, but a pain in the ass all the way there.

He returns to the interrogation room and hands Inara one of the bottles.

She accepts it with a nod, unscrewing the cap with her teeth rather than her tender hands. Half the bottle disappears before she puts it down, her eyes closed. One finger traces patterns on the metal surface of the table as she gathers herself for the next question.

He watches the motion, his gut clenching when he realizes that what he thought were nonsense symbols prove to be butterfly wings, traced again and again into the metal like a reminder of what brought her here. "I'm running out of time to protect you," he says finally.

She just looks at him.

"Powerful people want to know what happened. They're not going to have my patience with you, Inara, and I have been very patient."

"I know."

"You need to stop dancing around this. Tell me what I need to know."

For a while, the Gardener just had to continue being baffled by his younger son. Desmond came to the Garden regularly, but he didn't touch anyone past a hand to help them up.

And he brought his textbooks.

During the days, I stayed with the newest arrival, an exquisite creature of Japanese descent. During the nights, Danelle stayed with the sleeping girl and I sat up on the cliff, clinging to the illusion of space. Desmond frequently joined me there, and the first few times we sat in silence, each of us lost to our own reading. It had been a long time since I could sit with a male and not feel actively threatened. Not safe, precisely, but not threatened. We talked about his studies, sometimes. Never about the Garden. Never his father.

I hated him, I think, for refusing to put the pieces together, but I didn't show it. The Gardener was never going to let us go, and Avery was too dangerous to try to influence. I wasn't sure Desmond was hope, but he was the closest thing to it that I could see.

I wanted to live, and I wanted the other girls to live, and for the first time, I wanted that myth of the escaped Butterfly to be true. I wanted to believe I could get out without ending up in glass or the riverbank.

Then one night Desmond brought his violin.

The Gardener had told me his son was a musician, and I'd seen the way his fingers silently played chords against books, against rocks or knees or any available surface when he was thinking. It was like he translated his thoughts into music so they could make sense.

I was lying stomach-down on the rock with my book and an apple in front of me, keeping an eye on three of the girls down in the main Garden. They were neck deep in our small pond, splashing at each other as best they could, and I knew the sensors had to have alerted the Gardener that someone was in the water, but all they had to do was play long enough for him to get comfortable and move on to something else. He wasn't present in the Garden that night—he'd mentioned something about a charity function with his wife when I came to escort the new girl back to her room after the first tattoo session—but I didn't doubt he had a way to watch us if he wanted to. Eleni and Isra had been there three and four years respectively, generally past the point of foolishness, but Adara had arrived only two months or so before me. She mostly held up well, but every now and then she sank into severe bouts of depression that were nearly crippling. They were clinically based, and without her meds I was surprised they weren't more frequent, but we tried to make sure she wasn't left alone during these episodes. She was mostly through the latest of them, but her mood still teetered.

Desmond walked up the path, his case in hand, and stopped beside the rock. "Hi."

"Hello," I replied.

Normal was a variable thing in the Garden.

I eyed the case in his hand. Would asking him to play for me flatter his ego? Or would it make him feel like I owed him a favor? I was skilled at reading the Gardener and Avery; Desmond was more difficult. Unlike his father and brother, he didn't know what he wanted.

I was good at escaping people, not manipulating them. This was new ground.

"Play for me?" I asked eventually.

"You wouldn't mind? I have a proficiency tomorrow, and didn't want to wake up Mother. I was going to practice outside, but, uh . . ." He pointed up.

I didn't look. I could hear the rain against the glass. I missed the feeling of rain.

There was nearly always music playing in the apartment. Kathryn liked classical, but Whitney liked Swedish rap, and Noémie liked bluegrass, whereas Amber liked country, and in the end we had the most eclectic listening experience imaginable. Here some of the girls had radios or players in their rooms but for most of us, music was a rare thing anymore.

I closed the book and sat up as Desmond rosined his bow and stretched his fingers. It was fascinating to watch all the little rituals that went into warming up, but when he finally set the bow to the strings to play for real, I realized why his father called him a musician.

It was more than just playing. Though I was no expert, he seemed technically skilled, but he could make the notes weep or laugh across the strings. He infused each piece with emotion. Down in the pond, the trio stopped splashing and just floated so they could hear. I closed my eyes and let the music wrap around me.

Sometimes when Kathryn and I were sitting out on the fire escape or the roof at three or four in the morning after work, a guy from the next building over would come out onto his roof to practice the violin. He'd fumble his fingering and his bow work wasn't always to tempo, but sitting in the semi-darkness that was as close to true night as the city could get, it was like the violin was his lover. He never seemed to realize he had an audience, everything in him focused on the instrument and the sounds they made between them. It was pretty much the only thing Kathryn and I routinely did together. Even if we had the night off, we made sure we were awake to go outside and listen to that boy play.

Desmond was better.

He segued smoothly from song to song, and when he eventually let the bow swing down to his side, the last notes hovered expectantly.

"I don't think you'll have a problem passing your proficiency," I whispered.

"Thanks." He checked over the instrument, cradling it gently, and when he was satisfied all was as it should be, he put it away in the velvet-lined case. "When I was younger, I used to dream about being a professional musician."

"Used to?"

"My father took me to New York and arranged for me to spend a few days with a professional violinist, to see what it would be like. I hated it. It all felt . . . well, soulless, I guess. Like if I actually did that for a living, I'd grow to hate music. When I told my father I'd rather do something that still let me love music, he said he was proud of me."

"He seems frequently proud of you," I murmured, and he gave me a queer look.

"He talks to you about me?"

"A little."

"Um . . ."

"You're his son. He loves you."

"Yes, but . . ."

"But?"

"But it doesn't strike you a little weird that he talks about his son to his captives?"

I decided not to tell him the entirety of what his father had said about him. "More weird than him having captives at all?"

"True."

And here he was, finally able to call us captives, and unable to try anything to change that fact.

The stream that connected the waterfall and the pond was barely three feet deep, but Eleni managed to swim all the way up to the rocks before standing. "Maya, we're going in now. Do you need anything?"

"Not that I can think of, thanks."

Desmond shook his head. "Sometimes you seem like a house mother."

"What a twisted little sorority."

"Do you hate me?"

"What, for being your father's son?"

"I'm starting to realize just how much," he said quietly. He sat down next to me on the rock, draping his arms over his bent knees. "One of the girls in my Freud and Jung class has a butterfly tattoo on her shoulder. It's ugly and badly drawn, one of those butterfly-type fairies with a face that looks like a melted doll, but she was wearing a tube dress and I saw it and all I could think of for the rest of class was your wings and how beautiful they are. They're horrible, but they're beautiful, too."

"That's pretty much how we look at it," I replied neutrally, curious to see where he was going with this.

"I doubt the sight of your wings gets *you* off."

Oh.

Yes, definitely his father's son.

But unlike his father, ashamed of that fact.

"In one of my other classes, we were talking about hoarders and I thought of my father's story about *his* father's butterfly collection, but then of course I thought about my father's version of that, and suddenly I was thinking about you again and how you can be more dignified in nothing but ink and scars than most people can manage fully clothed. For weeks now, I've been having these . . . these *dreams,* and I wake up sweating and hard and I don't know if they're nightmares or not." He shoved his hair back from his face, hooking that hand behind his neck. "I don't want to believe I'm the type of person who could do this."

"Maybe you're not." I shrugged at his sideways look. "Going along with it is complicated, but it doesn't mean you'd ever do it yourself."

"It's still going along with it."

"Right and wrong doesn't mean there's an easy choice."

"Why *don't* you hate me?"

I'd been thinking about that a lot the past few weeks, and still wasn't sure I'd found the answer. "Maybe you're as trapped here as we are," I said slowly. Except I *did* hate him a bit, as much as but in a different way than his father and brother.

He turned that over for a while. In a flash of lightning, I tried to make out the emotions racing across his face. He had his father's eyes, but he was much more self-aware than the Gardener would ever be. The Gardener clung to his delusions. Desmond eventually confronted the hard truths, or at least the beginnings of them. He didn't know what to do with them, but he didn't try to make them less than they were.

"Why don't you try to escape?"

"Because girls before me did."

"Escaped?"

"Tried."

He winced.

"There is only one door that leads out of this space, and it is locked and coded at all times. You have to punch in your code for both entry and exit. When maintenance comes in, the rooms become soundproof. We could scream and pound all we wanted to and no one would ever hear us. We could stay out here when the walls come down for maintenance, but someone tried that about ten years ago and nothing happened except that she disappeared." And reappeared in glass and resin, but Desmond still hadn't seen those Butterflies. He seemed to forget what his father had said about keeping us after we die. "I'm not sure if your father hires incurious people or if he made it seem unexceptional, but no one came to the rescue. When it comes right down to it, though, we're afraid."

"Of freedom?"

"Of what happens if we *almost* get there." I looked up at the night beyond the glass panes. "Let's face it, he could kill all of us pretty quickly if he ever felt the need to. And if one of us made the attempt and failed, what's to say he wouldn't punish all of us for it?"

Or at least the one who made the attempt and me, because he thinks they tell me everything. How would I not know of such a plan?

"I'm sorry."

What an asinine thing to say, under the circumstances.

I shook my head. "I'm just sorry you ever came here."

269

Another sideways look, somewhere between hurt and amused. "Completely sorry?" he asked after a minute.

I studied his face in the moonlight. Twice he'd helped me through panic attacks, even if he only knew about one. He was fragile in a way his father and brother weren't, someone who wanted to be good, do good, and just didn't know how. "No," I said eventually. "Not completely." Not if I could figure out some way to lead him to usefulness.

"You're a very complicated person."

"And you're a complication."

He laughed and held his hand out between us, palm up, and I didn't hesitate to take it, lacing our fingers together. I leaned into him, resting my head on his shoulder, and found a comfortable silence between us. He reminded me of Topher a bit, if more complex, and just for a little while, I wanted to pretend this boy wasn't his father's son, that he was my friend.

I fell asleep that way, and when morning sunlight struck my eyes, I slowly sat up to find that we'd curled together through the night, his hand on my hip and his other arm cushioning my cheek from the stone. The new girl wouldn't be awake for a few hours yet, but Desmond had classes and at some point, a violin proficiency he'd pass without even trying.

Hesitantly, I reached out and stroked a comma

of dark hair back from his forehead. He stirred and unconsciously followed the gesture, and I couldn't help but smile. "Wake up."

"No," he mumbled, and grabbed my hand to shield his eyes.

"You have classes."

"Skip 'em."

"You have a proficiency."

"Mm proficient."

"You have finals next week."

He sighed but it turned into a face-splitting yawn, and he grudgingly sat up to rub the sleep from his eyes. "You're bossy, but nice to wake up to."

I looked away because I wasn't sure what was showing on my face. His fingertips, lightly callused from the strings, touched my chin and brought my face back to his, and the only thing there was a soft smile.

He leaned forward, then caught himself and started to pull back. I closed the distance between us, his lips soft against mine. The light touch on my chin moved back until his hand could cup my cheek and he deepened the kiss until my head was swimming. It had been so long since I'd actually kissed someone, rather than just allow them to force a kiss on me. The Gardener thought his son could love me, and I thought he might be right. I also thought love would prove a different motivation for the son than for the father. I hoped.

When Desmond moved away, he pressed a kiss against my cheek. "Can I come see you after classes?"

I nodded even as I silently acknowledged that my life had reached an entirely new level of fucked up.

"And the Gardener was happy about this?"

"Actually, he was. I mean, I'm sure there was a certain degree of self-interest in it—after all, if Desmond was emotionally attached to one or more of us, he was unlikely to risk anything happening to us. That had to be part of it, but I think most of it was that he genuinely enjoyed seeing his son happy."

Victor sighs. "Just when I think this story can't get more twisted."

"It can always get more twisted." She smiles as she says it, but he knows better than to trust it. It's not at all a nice smile, not something that should be so easily displayed on a girl her age. "That's life, right?"

"No," Victor says quietly. "It isn't. Or at least it shouldn't be."

"But that's not the same thing. *Is* and *shouldn't* are entirely different things."

He's starting to think Eddison isn't going to come back.

He can't really blame him.

If this is the twisted she's admitting to, how much worse is the twisted she's still hiding?

"How did things change after his finals?"

He was around more in the summer, except for an hour or so in the early afternoon when he walked with his parents in the outer greenhouse. If he came in the mornings, he stayed atop the cliff or in the library, respecting the privacy of my conversations with the other girls in the cave. Danelle had come to replace Lyonette as my balance in the more delicate of those conversations, just as she'd started taking the night shift with our new arrivals.

There wasn't much to the night shift, given that they were in a drugged sleep, but still. I appreciated being able to get some space.

And despite the wings that spread across her cheeks and forehead, Danelle could be trusted as a sensible option. I'd grown used to her double set of Red-Spotted Purples, with their contrasts of deep, rich color and bright pattern breaks. I won't say it suited her, any more than the ones on my back suited me, but she'd made them a part of her and learned from the experience. She and Marenka were the last to receive the wings on their faces; after that, they'd talked everyone else out of sucking up to that extent. There were some who came close, but they hadn't crossed the line yet.

I took the earliest conversations and she traded with me once the new girl showed signs of waking. Danelle held back on actually meeting the new girls until they were more or less settled, just like the others with the wings on their faces did.

After the first session, I was actually in the room whenever the Gardener worked on the new girl's tattoo. She hated needles, but if I read to her—and let her squeeze the ever-loving fuck out of my arm—she could lie still for it. It was by her request that I was there, rather than the Gardener's, though I think he was pleased by it. As I read aloud from *The Count of Monte Cristo* and wondered if that counted as irony, I watched the brilliant ice blue of a Spring Azure spread across her porcelain skin, broken by occasional veins or fringes of silver-white and one narrow band of midnight blue on the tips of the upper wings.

Bliss brought an ice pack with the lunch trays to put on my now-perpetually bruised arm.

The Gardener didn't touch me if Desmond was in the Garden, but his son's interest in me roused a corresponding excitement in him. It was no secret among the girls that he liked me best—honestly, I think they were relieved—but he'd gone from coming to me two or three times a week to damn near every day.

He still went to the other girls, of course, but when he was with anyone else, he didn't care if his younger son was in the Garden or not. And there was still Avery, but his fangs had been mostly pulled by the destruction of his playroom and the clear pride his father had in Desmond. With his younger brother as a strong example of how their father wanted us treated, it was hard for him to give in to the things he enjoyed.

I grew to hate lunch, because every single day, when Desmond went to share the meal and the early afternoon with his mother, the Gardener came to me with a need that made his hands shake. I started taking lunch in my room just so I wouldn't have to suffer the indignity of him coming to the dining room and calling my name across conversations. Even though he knew Desmond hadn't done any more than kiss me, just the thought that he could do more was enough to make the Gardener nearly mess his pants.

And dear fucking Christ, the possibility that he scoured the security footage hoping to see his son with me was enough to make my brain turn off completely.

At least those visits had a specific time limit, because he had to be up at the house by a quarter to two to meet his wife for their walk. While the family strolled along the square in the outer greenhouse, I spent the hour with the girl he rechristened Tereza. She was just shy of seventeen, the daughter of two litigators, and almost never spoke above a whisper. When she did, it was important, like her asking me to read to her while the Gardener inked her wings. She could also be drawn into conversation about music. She played piano, we learned, and wanted to be a professional pianist. She and Ravenna could talk for hours about ballet scores. She paid attention, noticed the undercurrents of any given situation, so she seemed to understand our precarious existence even before I showed her the display cases that first week.

For her sake, so she'd have a way to keep herself grounded, I asked the Gardener to give her a keyboard.

He installed an upright piano in one of the empty rooms, replacing the bed with a beautiful instrument and an entire wall of filing cabinets of sheet music. Except for meals, sleep, and putting up with her visits from the Gardener—numerous because she was new—she was in that room, playing the piano until her hands cramped.

Desmond met me in the hallway one afternoon, leaning against the Garden-side wall. His head was tilted to one side as he listened. "What happens if someone has a breakdown?" he asked quietly.

"In what way?"

He nodded in the direction of the doorway. "You can hear it in the music. She's disintegrating. She's getting choppy, changing the tempos, pounding at the keys . . . maybe she doesn't talk, but that doesn't mean she's adapting."

You never really forgot that he was a psych major.

"She'll either break or she won't. There's a limit to what I can do to prevent that."

"But what happens if she does?"

"You know what happens. You just don't want to admit it." He'd never asked why Simone hadn't returned. Tereza's arrival was greeted with consternation followed by an obvious, concerted effort to not think about it too deeply.

Desmond paled, but nodded to show he understood. Then he promptly changed the subject. If you don't look at the bad thing, the bad thing can't see you, right? "Bliss has some sort of project spread out over the rock. She told me if I sat on any of the clay, she'd shove it up my nose."

"What was she working on?"

"I have no idea; she was still softening the clays."

Summer afternoons were almost unbearably warm in the Garden, the heat soaking through the glass. Most girls spent the afternoons in the water or the shade to escape it, or in their rooms where they could actually feel the cooler air moving through the vents. I wasn't going to disturb Bliss if she was working on something, especially if she was doing it in the hottest part of the Garden, so I took Desmond's hand and led him down the hall. It was cooler in the back corner, where the base of the cliff stood directly against the hall glass and blocked the sunlight.

I turned in to my room and Desmond immediately began studying the shelf above my bed. He tapped the carousel to make it spin. "For some reason I don't really see you as a carousel person," he said, turning to look at me.

"I'm not."

"Then why—"

"Someone else was."

He looked back at the carousel and didn't say anything. He couldn't ask for more without hitting things he tried so hard not to think about.

"The gifts we give say as much about us as the gifts we get and keep," he murmured eventually. He touched the muzzle of the sad little dragon, which now had a tiny pajama-clad teddy bear to keep him company. "Is it the things that are important, or the people?"

"I thought classes were over for the summer."

He gave me a sheepish grin. "Habit?"

"Right."

My room had changed a bit from that first day. My sheets were a deep rose, the blanket a rich, brilliant purple, with stacks of pillows in a pale fawn-brown. My toilet and shower were both concealed by drapes of a matching brown, rose and purple sashes hanging loose against the walls in case I wanted to clip them back for any reason. There were two short bookcases along one wall with the various books the Gardener had given me personally, rather than adding into the library, and the knickknacks spilled over onto these shelves, the most important—or at least the most personal—staying on the shelf above the bed.

Other than the knickknacks, it was hard to say the room reflected anything about me, as I hadn't chosen anything about it. Even the trinkets were hard to pin down, really. Evita had once painted me a lovely chrysanthemum on a rock, but that showed her sunny personality, not mine. My keeping it just meant that *she* was important to me.

And then there was the thing that made me ever conscious of just how *not* mine the space was: the blinking red camera light above the door.

I sat on the bed, my back against the wall, and watched him bend sideways to read the spines of the books. "How many of these were my father's choice?"

"Maybe half."

"*The Brothers Karamazov*?"

"No, that one was mine."

"Really?" He grinned at me over his shoulder. "Dense, isn't it?"

"On the surface. It's fun to discuss."

I discussed a lot of books with Zara, but never the classics. That was something Noémie and I had done, dissecting them, getting into debates that could last for days or even weeks without ever fully being resolved. Rereading Dostoevsky kept Noémie fresh in my mind in a way that wasn't as painful as directly reminding myself of her and the others in New York. There was a book for each of the girls from the apartment. It was subtler than Nazira's drawings or Bliss's figures, but the same impulse.

"Why am I not surprised that you like books with layers?" He finished his perusal and stood next to the bed, hands in his pockets.

"You can sit on the bed, you know."

"I, uh . . . this is your space," he said awkwardly. "I don't want to presume."

"You can sit on the bed, you know."

He smiled this time and toed off his shoes, sitting next to me on top of the blankets. We'd kissed a few times since that first one, each one tentative and just a little overwhelming. His father, and to a lesser extent his brother, hovered between us whenever it seemed it might go a little further, and I wasn't sure how I felt about that.

Actually, I wasn't sure about much of anything when it came to Desmond.

We talked a bit about his friends, about his school, but even that was hard sometimes. I'd been in the Garden long enough that the outside world had become somewhat surreal, like a half-believed legend. Eventually, it was time for dinner, time for him to go back to the house for a while so his mother didn't wonder where he was all the time, and we walked down the hall hand in hand. If I walked him to the entrance, would he send me away before he punched his code into the lock? I wondered whether that precaution was one his father had drilled into him. If I ran through the door, would he take pity and let me go?

Could I get the police back here for the other girls before anything happened to them?

If I hadn't been absorbed with the problem of the door, I might have noticed right away, might have recognized how strange the silence was, but it took me a minute to realize we should have been hearing piano music down this entire stretch of hallway. I dropped his hand, not caring that he followed, and ran to the music room, terrified of what I might see.

Tereza was alive and uninjured.

But broken.

She sat on the piano bench, everything about her posture correct and perfect, and her hands were even on the keys, arched and poised. She looked like she could burst into music at any point.

Unless you looked at her face, at the tears that tracked silently down her cheeks, at the absolutely vacant look in her eyes, and understood that whatever made her Tereza wasn't there anymore. Sometimes it happened as quickly as a blink, as a heartbeat, as anything that should have been normal from one to the next.

I straddled the bench next to her, one hand against her back. Still staring straight ahead into nothing, she shuddered. "If you can come back, please try," I whispered. "I know it's bad, but after this there's nothing. Worse than nothing."

"Do you think we would make it worse by trying something?" Desmond asked carefully.

"Try what?"

"Here, come off the bench and hold her on the very edge." He sat down on the far end and carefully scooted over until he had the full range of keys. Tereza didn't fight or struggle when I took her hands away. Desmond took a deep breath and started to play, something soft and gentle and full of pain.

Tereza's breath hitched, the only sign that she heard.

I closed my eyes as the song continued, my chest tightening with tears I didn't know how to shed. He didn't just play, he effused, and the more he went on, the more Tereza shook in my arms, until finally she burst into heaving sobs and buried her face in my chest. Desmond kept playing, but now the song changed to something light and airy, not cheerful so much as comforting. Tereza wept, but she was *there,* still a little broken, with a few of the essential pieces missing, but responsive. I hugged her tightly, and for an agonizing moment I wondered if it would have been kinder to let her stay shattered. To let her die.

When we didn't show up at dinner or send for trays, Lorraine told the Gardener. We were still in the music room, coaxing Tereza to play something for us, when he appeared in the doorway. I noticed him there but didn't spare him much thought, too intent on the girl who was still shaking like a leaf. Desmond kept his voice soft, made no sudden movement, and finally she put her hands back on the keys, depressing a single note.

Desmond pressed a note lower down.

Tereza hit another one, which he answered, and gradually the notes became chords and progressions, until they were playing a duet I almost recognized. When it was done, she took a deep, slow breath, let it out, then took another.

"You get used to it," she whispered almost inaudibly.

I very carefully didn't look at the doorway. "Yes, you do."

She nodded, used her skirt to wipe off her face and throat, and started another song. "Thank you."

We listened to her for a couple of songs, until the Gardener stepped into the room to get my attention. He crooked his finger and I bit back a sigh, getting to my feet and joining him in the hallway. Desmond followed.

Desmond had saved her, but wouldn't admit to himself what he'd saved her from.

"Lorraine said you skipped dinner," he said quietly.

"Tereza was having a rough patch," I answered. "She was a little more important than dinner."

"Will she be all right?"

She had to be, or she'd be in glass. I glanced at Desmond, who took my hand with a light squeeze. "I don't think this will be the last rough patch she'll have, but I think this will be the worst. Delayed shock, I guess. Desmond got her playing again, though, so that's a good sign."

"Desmond?" The Gardener smiled, the concern replaced with pride, and he gripped his son's shoulder. "I'm glad to hear it. Is there anything I can do to help her?" I bit my lip and he actually shook his finger at me. "Maya, the truth now."

"It might be best if you didn't have sex with her for a little while," I sighed. "Spend time with her, fine, but I think sex is going to ask more of her than she can give right now."

He blinked at me, somewhat taken aback, but Desmond nodded. "And keep Avery away from her," he added. "He's always liked breaking things."

"How long?"

"Couple of weeks, maybe? Mostly we'll just need to keep an eye on her, see how she's doing."

Too aware of his son to give in to what was in his eyes, the Gardener pressed a kiss against my forehead. "You take such good care of them, Maya. Thank you."

I nodded because it seemed safer than talking.

He moved past us into the room and Tereza's song faltered, but gained strength when all he did was pull out a chair from the corner to listen to her play.

Desmond and I stood in the hallway for several songs, waiting to see if the choppiness would return, but she sounded like she was at a recital, all smooth grace and memorization. When there didn't seem to be an immediate threat of a new breakdown, he gently tugged on my hand to lead me down the hall. "Are you hungry?"

"I'm really not."

His father would have insisted on my eating anyway, because skipping meals wasn't healthy. His brother would have insisted on my eating because it would have amused him to watch me force the food past my nausea. But Desmond simply said, "Okay," and led the way to the cave.

It was empty, everyone else still in the dining room, and when we were in the center of the damp room, he stopped, turned, and put his arms around me, holding me close. "He's right about one thing," he said against my hair. "You do take good care of them."

The only reason I knew how was because of the apartment, because Sophia mothered us all in her slightly warped way. And Lyonette. Sophia took care of her girls, but Lyonette taught me how to tend Butterflies.

"It must be hard to adjust to a place like this, if you've been on the street," he said. "To be safe, but not allowed to leave."

We weren't from the street, and we weren't safe; I just didn't know how to make him understand that, with the girls in glass hidden away.

We eventually went to the kitchen, once the panic receded enough that my appetite could make itself known, and as we ate bananas and Nilla Wafers, Adara popped her head in and promised to stay with Tereza through the nights. Adara's depression gave her a different perspective than the rest of us, and she'd had to carefully piece herself back together several times before.

I kissed her cheek because I didn't have the words to thank her properly.

Danelle volunteered her time to the cause as well, inviting the Gardener back to her room like she used to do in the days when she'd earned the wings on her face. I don't think he was blind to the reasons for it, but I think he was touched by it nonetheless, because even if it wasn't for his sake, it was at least for Tereza's. Doing a good thing for another Butterfly was the same as doing it for him.

Desmond poured a glass of milk and perched next to me on the counter, passing the glass between us. "If I were to do something really pathetic, do you think you could pretend to like it to humor my ego?"

I looked at him warily. "I'd love to be supportive and say yes, but I can't promise that without knowing what it is."

He drained half the glass in one gulp. "Come on. I'll show you."

"Is it still being supportive if I say I'm scared but will come along anyway?"

"It'll do." He lifted me off the counter and took my hand as we walked out of the kitchen and into the Garden. It was still a little bit light out, twilight painting across the sky, and I watched the colors change. He ducked us behind the waterfall into the cave, then let go of my hand. "Wait here."

He came back less than a minute later. "Close your eyes."

When Desmond told me to do something—more to the point, when I actually did it—I didn't feel like I was merely obeying. I obeyed the Gardener, I obeyed Avery.

Desmond was more careful about what he asked me to do.

The waterfall drowned out the sound of his movements, but after a moment I heard music. Music I actually recognized. "Sway" was Sophia's favorite song, the one she danced to with her girls at the end of every visit, and she couldn't hear the last notes without crying. Desmond took my hands, placed one of them on his hip, and stepped in close. "Open your eyes."

An iPod and speaker sat on a safely dry portion of the floor near the hallway. He smiled at me, a little bit nervously, and gave a lopsided shrug. "Dance with me?"

"I've never . . . I don't . . ." I took a deep breath, and somehow his nervous smile was on my lips. "I don't know how to dance."

"That's okay. All I can do is waltz."

"You can waltz?"

"Mother's charity functions."

"Ah." He pulled me even closer, until my cheek rested against his shoulder, and he swayed us back and forth. He held our joined hands against his chest, his other hand sliding to the small of my back. Softly, almost inaudibly at first, he started singing along. I let him lead, burying my face in his shoulder to hide whatever my face was showing.

There's this moment when you know that suddenly, everything's changed. Most people have that moment many times in their lives.

I had it when I was three, and I realized my dad wasn't like the rest of his family.

I had it when I was six, and I sat on the fucking carousel as everyone walked away.

I had it when I had to take a taxi to my Gran's, when my Gran died, when Noémie poured me that first drink at the apartment.

I had it when I woke up in the Garden, when I got a new name that was supposed to eradicate everything I had been before.

And now, in the arms of this strange, unaccountable boy, I knew that even if nothing else changed, everything was different.

Maybe I could change him. Convince or trick or manipulate him into contributing to the freedom I wanted for all of us—but it wouldn't be without a price.

"Des . . ."

I could feel his grin against my temple. "Yes?"

"Right now I could hate you a little."

He didn't stop dancing, but the smile faded. "Why?"

"Because this is royally fucked up." I took a slow, deep breath, thought about what to say next. "And because this is going to break my heart."

"Does that mean you love me too?"

"My mother taught me to make sure the man always says it first."

He leaned back a little, just enough to see my face. "Did she really?"

"Yes."

I don't think he could tell if I was serious or not.

The song ended, rolling over to something I should probably have recognized, and he put some space between us. "Who am I saying it to? Because you may answer to Maya, but it's not who you are."

I shook my head. "I can't think like that. Not when I don't have any chance to be that person again."

His face fell, but honestly, what did he expect? Then he got down on one knee, holding both my hands, and smiled up at me. "I love you, Maya, and I swear, I will never hurt you."

I believed part of that.

I didn't want to feel guilty for it.

But I did, so I perched on his knee and kissed him, and he got so involved with kissing me back that he overbalanced and we both fell onto the damp stone. He laughed and kept kissing me and kissing me and I knew I could never believe the rest of it. Desmond wasn't good, no matter how much he wanted to be, and better than his family just wasn't enough. Every day he helped keep us here, he hurt me.

"I didn't recite Poe that time, in case you were wondering."

"No, for that I'm sure you were paying full attention," Victor agrees dryly. "So, were you serious?"

"What, me and Des?"

"Well, yes, but more specifically, what you said about your mother."

"Actually, yes."

He ponders that for a moment, tries to make sense of it.

He fails.

"Still want to find out who I am and where I came from?"

"Yes."

"Why?"

He sighs and shakes his head. "Because I can't put a fake person on the stand."

"I'm not a fake person; I'm carefully and genuinely handcrafted."

He shouldn't laugh. He really shouldn't laugh but he does and then he can't stop, and he's leaning against the table trying to at least muffle the sound. When he finally looks up, she's smiling at him, a real one this time, and he answers it gratefully.

"The real world intrudes, doesn't it?" she asks gently, and his laughter fades.

"Keeping me honest?"

"It hurts you to ask, and it hurts you to listen, even when so much of it you've heard before. I like you, Special Agent Victor Hanoverian. Your girls are lucky to have you. The story's almost over anyway. Then it can't hurt for a little while."

The end of the summer brought a shift in the Garden. Desmond had spent so much time with us he'd become a fixture, and even though I was the only one he touched, I wasn't the only one who got to know him. Tereza talked to him more than she talked to me, because music crossed the boundaries of our cage and made her forget, even if just for a while. Even Bliss seemed to like Desmond, though I wouldn't stake a wager on how much of that was for my sake.

Gradually, the girls felt comfortable with him

in a way they never would with his father and brother, because he was never going to ask anything of them. Most of them had given up hope of ever being rescued, so there wasn't even much bitterness as to why he didn't report anything.

And the Gardener was over the moon.

The very first time we talked about Des, he'd said "his mother's very proud of him." I had thought that meant that he wasn't, but I knew better now. He was always proud of Desmond, but when faced with a girl who knew only Avery, he had to acknowledge the son who openly shared the same fascination with keeping an unwilling harem. Now that Desmond was part of the Garden, his father's happiness was complete. Tereza's breakdown was the only one that summer. There were no accidents, no twenty-first birthdays, nothing to force us to remember that we couldn't have just a little bit of fun.

Well, except for the Gardener and Avery still raping at will. That put a damper on things.

But the Gardener shifted how he treated me. After Desmond and I had sex, the Gardener didn't touch me that way anymore. He treated me like a . . . well, like a housemother, I guess. Or a daughter. I wasn't like Lorraine, I wasn't being exiled from his affection, but somehow he decided that I was Desmond's now. With Avery he shared; with Desmond, he gave.

Fucked up, no?

But just for a while, I was willing to accept that without question. If I was going to have any hope of moving Desmond, it couldn't just be infatuation. I needed him to truly love me, to be willing to fight for me, and that wasn't going to happen if he was still sharing me with his father and brother.

The Gardener even disabled the camera in my room because Des asked him to, said it made him self-conscious to think that his father was watching him have sex, and couldn't he be trusted not to hurt me, when he loved me so dearly?

Okay, I'm sure the conversation was a bit more graceful and manly than that, but Bliss had the girls in stitches with her version of it.

Desmond was still his father's son, though. Whenever I tried to walk him to the door, he'd politely but firmly send me away so I couldn't see him put in his code. "It would destroy my mother," he said when I finally mentioned it. Taking direct action against his father would be complicated, I got that, but why not give us the chance to rescue ourselves? "My family's name, our reputation, our company . . . I can't be the one to destroy that."

Because a name means more than a life. Than all our lives.

The weekend before the fall semester started, we had a concert in the Garden. Desmond brought in better speakers and set them up on the cliff, and just for the evening, the Gardener gave us all bright colors and treats, and fuck, it was pathetic how happy we were that evening. We were still captives, we still had death sitting on our shoulders and counting down to our twenty-first birthdays, but that night was magical anyway. Everyone laughed and danced and sang, no matter how badly, and the Gardener and Desmond danced with us.

Avery sat off to one side and sulked, because the whole thing had been Desmond's idea.

After we cleaned everything up and the girls split off into the rooms for the night, Des brought the smallest speaker back to my room and we danced, swaying in place as we kissed. Intimacy with Des wasn't real, any more than with his father, but he didn't realize that. I'd never said it, but he thought I loved him too. He thought this was happiness, that this was somehow healthy and stable, the kind of thing you build a life around. He either missed or glossed over my frequent reminders that caged things have shorter lives.

Des wanted so badly to be good, to do good, but our circumstances hadn't changed, nor were they likely to.

When we finally tumbled onto the bed, I was almost dizzy from his kisses, and he couldn't stop laughing. His hands were everywhere, and he followed them with his mouth, his laughter tickling my skin. Sex with Des wasn't intimacy, but it was fun. He drove me crazy with his teasing, until I finally rolled us over and pinned him, biting my lip as I sank down onto him. He groaned and rolled his hips, then laughed when a really inappropriate song started playing. When I slapped his stomach, he sat up to kiss me dizzy again, then pushed me onto my back at the foot of the bed.

Which is when I saw Avery, standing in the doorway and scowling as he jacked himself off.

I yelped—not proud of that—and Desmond looked up to see what had alarmed me. "Avery! Get out!"

"I have as much right to her as you do," Avery growled.

"Get. Out!"

There was a small part of me that was about to die laughing. Fortunately, that part was mostly squashed in the general sense of fury and mortification. I thought about reaching for a blanket, but Avery had seen all of me before, and Desmond . . . well, his bits weren't exactly showing at the moment. I closed my eyes as they argued over my head because I didn't want to know if Avery still had himself in hand while he fought with his brother.

And because the laughter was threatening to win.

Enter the Gardener. Because of course. "Just what the hell is going on? Avery, put that away."

I opened my eyes to see Avery fastening his

pants and the Gardener trying to button his shirt. Oh, look, the whole family except for Eleanor. Swearing under his breath, Desmond pulled away from me and handed me my dress before reaching for his pants.

Sometimes it's the little things.

"Would you care to explain why your argument is carrying over the entire Garden?" the Gardener demanded, his voice low and dangerous.

The brothers started talking over each other but their father cut them off with a sharp gesture.

"Maya?"

"Des and I were having sex, and Avery decided to invite himself to the party. He was standing in the door and jacking it."

After a wince at my crudeness, the Gardener stared at his firstborn, the anger slowly joined by an appalled horror. "What were you thinking?"

"Why does he get to have her? He's never helped you bring anyone in, he's never gone out with you to find them, but you give her to him like a fucking bride and I'm not even allowed to touch her?"

It took a minute for the Gardener to find his voice. "Maya, would you please excuse us?"

"Of course," I answered politely. Because Courtesy is as much a bitch as Disdain. "Would you like me to leave?"

"Not at all, this is your room. Desmond, join us, please. Avery. Come."

I stayed on the bed until I couldn't hear their footsteps anymore, then pulled on my dress and raced down the hall to Bliss's room. She sat on her floor with a stack of clay beside her and what looked like a teddy bear massacre on cookie sheets in front of her.

"What was the fuss?"

I sprawled on her bed as I told her, and she giggled herself into near hysterics.

"How long do you think until he bans Avery completely?"

"I don't know if he would ever do that," I said regretfully. "Avery is hard enough to control when he's here; how much harder must it be out there?"

"We'll never find out."

"That's true."

She handed me a ball of clay to knead. "Can I ask you something personal?"

"Personal like how?"

"Do you love him?"

I almost asked which him—especially since we'd just been talking about Avery—but I realized what she meant half a second before I could make myself look like an idiot. I glanced up at the winking red light of the camera and slid off the bed so we were huddled together. "No."

"Then why are you doing all this?"

"Do you believe a Butterfly escaped?"

"No. Maybe. Sort of? Wait . . . well, fuck.

Suddenly the world makes sense again. Think it'll work?"

"I don't know," I sighed, kneading the ball of clay. "He's horrified of being his father's son, but he's also . . . proud? For the first time in his life, it's easy for him to see that his father is proud of him. That still means more to him than I do, and he's too scared to think of right and wrong."

"If there'd never been a Garden, if you'd met him at the library or something, do you think you'd love him?"

"Honestly? I don't think I know what that kind of love is. I've seen it in a few others, but for myself? Maybe I'm just not capable of it."

"I can't decide if that's sad or safe."

"I can't think of any reason it can't be both."

The couple across the street loved each other almost to distraction, and the arrival of their baby somehow made them more complete, rather than detracting from what they had between them. Rebekah, the lead hostess at the Evening Star, deeply loved her husband—who happened to be Guilian's nephew—and sometimes seeing them together was so sweet we all melted a little.

Even as we teased them, of course.

Taki and Karen had it, their daughter and her wife had it.

But each time I saw it, I knew I was in the presence of something extraordinary, something that not everyone found or was capable of recognizing and sustaining.

And I'm the first person to admit that I am one fucked-up individual.

"That's fair. And honest." She took the clay from me and handed me another, this one a bright fuchsia that left colored streaks all over my skin. "We never really thank you."

"What?"

"You take care of us," she said quietly, her brilliant blue eyes locked on the teddy bear forming in her hands. "It's not like you're maternal or anything, because really, fuck that, but you give the tough love and you listen and there's that interference you run with the Gardener in that private room of his."

"That's not something we need to talk about."

"All right. Give me the clay and go wash your hands."

Bemusedly, I did as she said, scrubbing the fuchsia streaks from my skin. She handed me a turquoise ball of clay. This time when I sat down beside her, I actually looked at all the pieces. Half the scattered teddy bear parts—heads, paws, and tails—were black, the other half white. Some of them had actually been assembled with uniforms, the black in shades of red and the white in shades of blue. Half of each color were slightly larger and their uniforms more ornate, and several of them seemed to be paired. "Are you making a chess set?"

"Nazira's twentieth birthday is in a couple of weeks."

And my eighteenth birthday was a few weeks after that, but birthdays weren't generally celebrated in the Garden. It felt a little too much like mockery, like we were celebrating how much closer we were to death. Other people got to look at a birthday and say, "Yay! One year older!" We met our birthdays with "Fuck. One year less."

"It's not a birthday gift," she continued sourly. "It's an 'I'm sorry your life sucks so fucking much' gift."

"Good gift."

"And shitty timing," she agreed. She rolled a tiny ball of gold clay into a rope, pinched it in half, twirled it together, and the red king got a shoulder braid for his uniform. "Do you hate him just a little too?"

"More than a little."

"He would be going against his family."

"Whereas now he's just going against common decency and the law," I sighed. I held out the softened clay and she handed me a ball of royal blue. I knew better than to ask to make one of the bears—my clay creations sucked. "Bliss, I guarantee you there isn't a side of this I haven't turned over in my head. It stopped making sense a long time ago, if it ever did."

"So just go with it and see what happens."

"Pretty much."

"He's coming."

Footsteps sounded down the hall, growing louder, and a moment later Desmond walked in and dropped to the floor beside me, handing each of us an orange. "Is that a chess set?"

Bliss rolled her eyes and didn't answer, so while she made teddy bear soldiers, I kneaded the clay and Desmond played with his iPod and travel speaker to continue the concert.

And that orange? First and only time I ever got the peel off in a perfect spiral.

Eddison finally returns holding two bags, one containing bottles of soda and water, the other with what proves to be meatball subs. When he gives one to the girl, he also pulls a small plastic bag from his pocket and sets it on the table before her.

She picks up the bag, then stares at the contents. "My little blue dragon!"

"I talked to the scene techs; they said your room was protected by the cliff." He sits down across from her, busying himself with unwrapping his sub. Out of courtesy, Victor pretends not to see his blush. "They'll box everything up for you once it's released, but they went ahead and gave me that one to pass on."

She opens the bag and cradles the small clay creature in her hands, one thumb rubbing over the tiny, pajama-clad teddy bear tucked into the crook of its arm. "Thank you," she whispers.

"You've been more forthcoming. Somewhat."

She smiles.

"Vic, the scene techs are looking through the house. They'll let us know if they find the pictures."

For a time, conversation stops as they eat, though the girl has to wrap her tender hands in napkins to hold the hot sandwich. When the meal is done and the debris thrown away, she picks up the sad little dragon and curls her hands around it.

Victor decides it's his turn to be brave. "What happened to Avery?"

"What do you mean?"

"Did his father punish him?"

"No, they just had a long talk about respecting each other's privacy, and that the Butterflies were not possessions to be passed around but individuals to be cherished. To hear Des tell it, there was also a pretty sharp reminder that Avery wasn't allowed to touch me anyway, given the whole branding thing. Well, 'given the prior incident,' and Des had never asked about the scar on my hip. If you don't ask, you can keep your head buried in the sand."

"So things went back to normal."

"Such as it was."

"But something had to change."

"Something did. Its name was Keely."

Or, more properly, its name was Avery, and its victim was Keely.

I saw a lot less of Desmond once the semester started. It was his senior year and he was carrying a full course load, but he came in the evenings and brought his textbooks so he could study, and just like I'd helped Whitney, Amber, and Noémie study once upon a time in the apartment, I helped him. Without booze. Bliss helped too, by making fun of him whenever he got something wrong.

Or even just not completely right.

Bliss seized on any opportunity to make fun of him, really.

Avery's mood went from foul to worse as he watched his brother be such a part of the Garden. Like I said, most of the Butterflies liked Desmond. He didn't ask anything of them. Well, he asked them questions, and left it to them whether or not to answer.

He asked their names sometimes, but it had somehow become a tradition in the Garden that you only gave your name as your goodbye. But we told him that Simone had once been Rachel Young, that Lyonette had been Cassidy Lawrence. Any of the ones we knew who couldn't be hurt by the reminder.

Desmond wasn't a threat to them.

Avery, on the other hand, savaged Zara so badly during sex that his father banned him for a full month, then had to drug him to avoid the hissy fit that tried to follow. Zara could barely walk after that, and every part of her was bruised. Someone stayed with her at all times just to help her with basic functions like showering, getting to the toilet, and eating.

Lorraine was a competent enough nurse—if hardly a compassionate one—but she wasn't a miracle worker.

Infection set into Zara's hip, and it was either take her to a hospital or put her in glass.

I think you can safely guess which one the Gardener chose.

For the first time, he told us that morning, so we could have a full day with her to make our goodbyes.

I gave him a sideways look when he told me that, which was met with a lopsided smile and a kiss to the temple. "Even when it's just a swift embrace and a stolen whisper, you share things with each other in those moments. If it can provide Zara—and the rest of you—any comfort, I'd like to see that you get it."

I said thank you because he seemed to expect it, but part of me wondered if it was better to just have it happen all at once, rather than dragging it out over the day.

Before he left for class, Desmond brought us a wheelbarrow so we could maneuver Zara through the Garden. He smiled when he brought it, smiled as he kissed my cheek and left for school, and Bliss swore so fluently that Tereza blushed.

"He doesn't know, does he?" she panted when she could speak a language other than Obscenity. "He really has no clue."

"He knows Zara is ill; he thinks he's doing something nice."

"That—that . . ."

Some things don't need a translator.

That afternoon, while the Gardener walked with his wife in that other greenhouse that was so much closer than it seemed, Zara pushed herself up to sitting on her bed, sweat matting her fiery orange hair. "Maya? Bliss? Can you wheel me around for a bit?"

We folded a blanket into the wheelbarrow and arranged a few pillows under and around her, stabilizing her hip as much as possible. It wasn't her only broken bone, but it was decidedly the most painful. "Just in a lap through the hallway," she instructed.

"Looking for real estate?" Bliss asked, and Zara nodded.

It was something you couldn't help but wonder about. When you died, which case would you be in? I was pretty sure I knew which one the Gardener had picked out for me; it was right beside Lyonette, and positioned in such a way that you could see it from the cave. Bliss thought she'd be on my other side, just the three of us, hanging out forever in the fucking wall for future generations of Butterflies to wonder about and fear.

We walked slowly through the hall, me pushing the barrow and Bliss doing her best to stabilize the front. Zara stopped us near the front entrance, where the scent of honeysuckle filled the air and mixed with a more chemical smell from one of the rooms we never, ever saw open. Like the tattoo room, Lorraine's room, and Avery's former playroom, the walls were opaque and solid, with a punch pad beside an honest-to-God door. We weren't supposed to be here.

And I'd still never seen Des put in his main door code.

"Do you think if I asked for this one, he'd give it to me?"

"For the honeysuckle?"

"No, because we all avoid this part. Then I wouldn't be seen as much."

"Ask him. Worst he can do at that point is say no."

"If I asked you right now to kill me, would you?"

I studied the empty glass case because I didn't want to see if she was serious or not. Zara could be cruel, mocking the other girls until they cried, but she didn't have much of a sense of humor. "I guess I'm not that good a friend," I said finally.

Bliss said nothing.

"Do you think it hurts?"

"He says it doesn't."

"And you believe him?"

"No," I sighed, leaning against the doorway into the plant life. "I don't think he knows one way or the other. I think he wants to believe there's no pain."

"What do you think she'll be like?"

"Who?"

"The next Butterfly." She craned her head back to stare at me, her brown eyes fever-bright. "He hasn't gone hunting in a long time. Not since Tereza. He's been so happy with Desmond here that he hasn't even looked for anyone else."

"He might not go look."

She snorted.

He didn't always, though. Sometimes a girl died and he didn't go hunting. Not until someone else died. Sometimes he brought back one girl, occasionally he brought back two, though he hadn't done that during my time here. Trying to understand why that man did anything the way he did was a worthless endeavor.

We were still standing there when Lorraine came out of her room to start dinner. She seemed startled at first, one hand flying to the dark chestnut hair, somewhat faded and heavily streaked with silver, that she still wore long and up, as the Gardener preferred. Even though he never looked at her, never commented on it, she still wore it that way. She glanced at the bandaged Zara, at how pale she was except for two bright blotches of red on her cheeks, then at the empty case.

Zara's eyes narrowed. "Wishing you were in there, Lorraine?"

"I don't have to put up with you," the woman retorted.

"I know how you can be."

Suspicion warred with hope in fading blue eyes. "You do?"

"Yeah. Magically become thirty years younger. I'm sure he'd love to kill and display you then."

Lorraine sniffed and stalked past us, slapping Zara's ankle on the way. The movement jarred the broken, infected hip and she bit back a scream.

Bliss's eyes followed the cook-nurse. "I'll send Danelle to help you back."

"Why, where are you—" I took a second look at her expression. "Right. Never mind. Danelle."

The gasping Zara and I watched her jog away. "What do you suppose she's doing?" she asked after a minute.

"I'm not asking and I don't want to know in advance," I said fervently. "Depending on what it is, I may not want to know after the fact either."

A few minutes later, not just Danelle but a very confused Marenka walked down the hall to join us. "Should I ask what Bliss is doing?"

"No," we answered together.

"So I shouldn't ask why she borrowed my scissors?" murmured Marenka, a hand to her throat where a ribbon usually held her tiny pair of embroidery scissors.

"Right."

Danelle thought about that, accepted it, and lightly touched the edge of the wheelbarrow. "Into the Garden? Or back to your room?"

"Room," groaned Zara. "I think I get to take another painkiller."

Between us, Danelle, Marenka, and I got her settled back into bed with a glass of water and a happy pill. Then Bliss walked in, hands held behind her back, and an eminently satisfied look on her face.

Oh, God, I didn't want to know.

"I have a present for you, Zara," she announced cheerfully.

"Avery's head on a platter?"

"Close." She tossed something onto the coverlet.

Zara lifted it up to stare at it, then burst out laughing. It dangled from her hand, the ends slowly releasing from their pattern. "Lorraine's braid?"

"Enjoy!"

"Think I could take it with me?"

Danelle rubbed the ends of the hair between her fingers. "We could probably rebraid part of it into a garter for you."

"Or braid it into your hair like extensions."

"A crown, definitely."

Everyone who came in through the afternoon and evening had another suggestion to make, and it was an indication of our universal contempt for Lorraine that no one expressed any sorrow or sympathy for our cook-nurse. When it was time for dinner, we all took our trays and crowded into Zara's room, all twenty-odd of us, knee to knee on the floor and even in the shower.

Adara lifted a glass of apple juice. "To Zara, who can spit seeds farther than anyone else."

We all laughed, even Zara, who raised her glass of water to return the toast.

Nazira stood next, and I think we were all a little apprehensive about that one; Nazira and Zara got along about as well as Avery and Desmond. "To Zara, who may be a right bitch, but she's our bitch."

Zara blew her a kiss.

It was sick. I don't think there's a person there who doubted that. It was sick and wrong and profoundly twisted, and yet somehow it made us feel a lot better. One by one, we all stood and made a toast to Zara, some mocking, some serious, and sure there were plenty of tears to be had, even if not by me, but maybe the Gardener was right, maybe this did help.

When it was my turn, I stood and lifted my

glass of water. "To Zara, who's leaving us too soon, but who we will remember in a non-creepy fashion for the rest of our lives."

"However short they may be," added Bliss.

How fucked up were we that we laughed?

When everyone had taken their turn, Zara raised her glass once more. "To Zara," she said quietly, "because when she dies, Felicity Farrington will finally rest in peace."

"To Zara," we all murmured together, and drained our glasses.

When the Gardener came, it was without a dress but with Desmond, and he smiled to see all of us together. "It's time, ladies."

Slowly, everyone kissed Zara, gathered their trays, and filed out of the room with the Gardener kissing each and every one of them on the cheek. I waited until the end, perching on the side of the bed so I could take her clammy hand. Lorraine's silver-streaked braid was pinned like a coronet around her double-twist. "Anything I can do?" I whispered.

She dug under her pillow and gave me a battered, dog-eared, highlighted, and notated-half-to-death copy of *A Midsummer Night's Dream*. "I was really into theatre in school," she said softly. "When I was taken from the park, I was supposed to be meeting my friends for a rehearsal. I've spent three years writing notes for a production I'll never do. Do you think you and Bliss could put together a reading for everyone? Just . . . something to remember me by?"

I took the book and held it against my heart. "I promise."

"Take care of the next girl, and try not to visit me too much, okay?"

"Okay."

She pulled me into a tight hug, her fingers digging into my shoulders. Despite how calm she seemed, I could see her shaking. I let her hold on as long as she wanted, and when she finally took a deep breath and pulled away, I kissed her cheek. "I only just met you, Felicity Farrington, but I love you, and I will remember you."

"I guess that's as much as I can ask," she half-laughed. "Thank you, really and truly, for everything. You've made it all easier than it could have been."

"I wish I could have done more."

"You do what's yours to do. The rest belongs to them." She jerked her head at the men in the doorway. "I guess you'll see me in a couple of days."

"By the honeysuckle, so we'll almost never see you at all," I agreed, almost inaudibly. I kissed her again and walked out of the room, holding the book so tightly my knuckles popped.

The Gardener glanced at the braid that very obviously wasn't Zara's, then back at me.

"Lorraine's been crying," he murmured. "She says Bliss attacked her."

"It's just hair." I looked him square in the eyes. "She isn't you or your sons. We don't have to tolerate her hurting us."

"I'll speak with her." He kissed my cheek and went to Zara, but Desmond held back with a puzzled, slightly worried frown.

"Is there something I'm missing?" he asked me quietly.

"Too much."

"I know you'll miss her, but we'll get her taken care of. She'll be fine."

"Don't."

"Maya—"

"No. You don't know. You should, you've seen enough—well. I do know. You don't get to tell me she'll be fine. Right now you don't get to tell me anything."

Avery was the Gardener's firstborn, but in the ways that mattered Desmond was his heir.

And before long, we'd find out just how much his father's son he was.

I looked back at Zara, but the Gardener was in the way. Ignoring Desmond's hurt gaze, I walked away.

Returning my tray to the kitchen—and taking a spiteful glee in Lorraine's sniffles and her mere inch and a half of ragged hair—I declined an offer from several of the girls to join them and went

313

back to my room alone. After maybe half an hour, the walls came down. Zara was too injured for a final tryst, after all, and Desmond was there with them. I curled up on my bed with the play, read all the notes in the margins, and got to know Felicity Farrington a little.

Around three in the morning, the wall that blocked me from the hallway lifted. Only that wall—the ones to either side that looked through display cases and, if you squinted, into Marenka's and Isra's rooms, stayed in place. They'd been there for weeks, and it was a strange breed of lovely to not see dead bodies every time I opened my eyes. I closed the book on my finger, steeling myself to see the Gardener in the doorway, one hand at his belt and his eyes full of excitement.

But it was Desmond, his pale green eyes haunted and bruised in a way I hadn't seen in months. He clutched the glass wall to keep himself standing, his knees buckling and swaying with every attempt to support his weight.

I closed the book properly, slid it onto the shelf, and sat up on the bed.

He took a few wobbly steps into the room and fell hard to his knees. He buried his face in his hands, then flinched violently, staring at his hands like they'd somehow become separate from the rest of him. A sickly sour chemical smell wafted around him, the same scent I noticed any time I went near the honeysuckles at the front door. His entire body shook as he doubled over, pressing his forehead against the cool metal floor.

Almost ten minutes passed before he said a word, and even then his voice was hoarse and broken. "He promised we would take care of her."

"He did."

"But he . . . he . . ."

"Put her out of pain, and prevented her from decay," I said neutrally.

". . . murdered her."

Not entirely his father's son then.

I pulled off my clothing and knelt down in front of him, unbuttoning his shirt. He gave me a sick look and batted my hands away. "I'm putting you in the shower—you reek."

"Formaldehyde," he muttered. This time he let me undress him, and stumbled along behind me as I pulled him across the room to sit in the shower. A twist of my wrist sent warm water pouring over him.

There was nothing sexual about what happened next. It was like bathing Sophia's girls when they were half-asleep. When I told him to lean forward or lift his arm or close his eyes, he obeyed, but numbly, like it didn't entirely make sense. My shampoo and body wash were both fruity as hell, but I washed him head to toe until the only remaining chemical smell was his clothing.

I draped him in towels and used one of his shoes to push the clothing out into the hallway, then returned to dry both of us off. I had to keep wiping his face—unseen in the shower, a constant stream of tears ran down his cheeks.

"He injected something to make her sleep," he whispered. "I thought we were going to carry her out to the car, but he opened a room I'd never seen before." A shudder wracked his body. "Once she fell asleep, he put her in this orange and yellow dress and laid her out on an embalming table, and then he . . . he hooked up . . ."

"Please don't tell me," I said quietly.

"No, I have to, because he's going to do that to you someday, isn't he? That's how he, how he *keeps* you, by embalming you while you're still alive." Another shudder, a sob that fractured his voice, but he continued. "He stood there *explaining* all the steps to me. So I could do it on my own someday, he said. Love was more than just the pleasure, he said; we had to be willing to do the hard things too, he said. He said . . . he said . . ."

"Come on, you're still shivering."

He let me lead him to the bed and pull the covers up over him, and I sat beside him, atop the blanket, hands in my lap. "He said if I really loved you, I wouldn't let any hand other than my own take care of you."

"Des . . ."

"He showed me some of the others. I thought . . . I thought he just left them back on the streets! I didn't realize . . ." He broke down completely, weeping with an intensity that damn near shook the bed. I rubbed circles on his back as he choked on the sobs, unable to give him more comfort than that because he still didn't know the full truth. Zara had the bone infection, and he thought all broken people killed themselves or let themselves go so completely that they died. He didn't know about attitudes and ages.

And at that moment, when he was so close to broken himself, I couldn't bring myself to tell him. I couldn't use him broken. I needed him brave.

I didn't think he ever would be.

"She picked out her case," he managed a few minutes later. "He made me carry her there, showed me how to pose her, how to close the glass completely to pour the resin in. Before he closed the glass, he . . . he . . ."

"Kissed her goodbye?"

He gave a jerky nod, hiccupping with the force of his sobs. "He told her he loved her!"

"As he understands it, he does."

"How can you even stand to be around me?"

"Sometimes I can't," I admitted. "I keep telling myself that you don't know the whole of it, that you're still ignorant of so much of what your father and brother do, and some days that's the only way I can even look at you. But you . . ."

"Please tell me."

"But you're a coward," I sighed. "You know that keeping us here is wrong. You know it's against the law, you know he rapes us, and now you know he kills us. Some of these girls might even have families looking for them. You know this is wrong, but you don't report it. You said you were going to learn how to be braver for me, but you haven't. And I honestly don't know if you can."

"Finding out about this . . . having it all come out . . . it would kill my mother."

I shrugged. "Give it enough time and it'll kill me too. Cowardice may be our natural state but it's still a choice. Every day you know about the Garden and don't call the police or let us go, you're making that same choice again and again. It is what it is, Desmond. You just don't get to pretend anymore."

He started weeping again, or maybe it was weeping still, all one massive shock that just kept compounding past his ability to bear it.

He spent the rest of that dark morning lying silently on my bed, and when sunlight came to the Garden, he gathered up his formaldehyde-scented clothing and walked away.

He didn't talk to me for weeks, and only came into the Garden once: to see Zara after the resin solidified and the wall came away from her case. All the walls lifted then, and the reality that had blurred over the summer crashed back down with resounding force. We were Butterflies, and our short lives would end in glass.

"Wait, I thought you said things changed with Keely," Eddison says.

"I did, yes. I'm getting there."

"Oh."

She rubs her thumbs against the blue dragon's neck and takes a deep breath. "Keely arrived four days ago."

It took time to keep my promise to Zara. The Gardener readily agreed to get us a full set of *A Midsummer Night's Dream* when I told him what it was for, but he wanted the affair "done right." He ordered up all sorts of costumes and gave Bliss a box of clays that weighed as much as she did to make us flower crowns. We assigned parts and coached girls through the language. Some of them had read a play or two in English, but most didn't have much in the way of real exposure.

I'd lived for almost two years with Noémie, who walked around the apartment in her underwear reading aloud soliloquies as she brushed her teeth.

Yes, brushed her teeth, which for that very reason took forfuckingever.

When the evening arrived, the Gardener had Lorraine arrange a feast in the Garden itself, spread on both sides of the little stream. We had these strange chairs somewhere between an ottoman and a beanbag, all in bright colors, and each of us had semi-sheer silk gowns in beautiful colors that for once had nothing to do with the wings inked on our backs. I was reading for Helena and the Gardener had given me a gown of forest and moss greens, with a single layer of deep rose. That was the color Bliss matched for my crown of clay roses.

Most of us wore our hair down under the crowns, simply because for that one night we *could*.

There was a sharp edge to the laughter as we all prepared. We were doing this for Zara, but the Gardener had made it into a fancy. Even knowing our reason for it, I'm sure he was convinced that it was a measure of how happy we were under his loving care that we wanted to put on an entertainment for him. That man had an astonishing talent for seeing what he wanted to see.

He hadn't even noticed that Lorraine had bought a wig so she could still seem to have long, well-maintained hair for him to want to play with, the sick bitch.

And he persuaded Desmond to attend.

He was thrown, I think, by his son's reaction to Zara's death. Des was his father's son, but he didn't have his perspective. Desmond couldn't see it as anything but murder, yet it didn't push him into action.

At the end of the first week of silence and absence from his son, the Gardener came to my room before breakfast. "Desmond seems very out of sorts," he announced as soon as I was marginally awake. "Did you two argue?"

I yawned. "He's having trouble processing what happened to Zara."

"But Zara's fine. She's out of pain." He honestly seemed confused.

"When you said you were going to take care of her, he thought you meant take her to a hospital."

"That would have been foolish; there would have been questions asked."

"All I'm doing is translating."

"Yes, of course. Thank you, Maya."

I'm sure there were a number of father-son conversations in the intervening weeks to which I wasn't privy, but Desmond showed up for the reading looking like he hadn't slept for shit. He must have had a presentation in class that day, because he was wearing a dress shirt and tie with his khakis. Granted, the shirt was open at the collar, the tie loose, and the sleeves rolled back, but it was still dressier than usual, and I was somewhat disgusted with myself for the fleeting thought that the sea-foam green shirt looked very good with his eyes.

He had a hard time looking directly at any of us, especially me. I'd told Bliss the gist of our last discussion over a night of making fake chocolate chip cookies with which to trick Lorraine. She'd shrugged and said I was kinder than she would have been.

Seeing as the clay cookies were her idea, I didn't argue.

The reading started really well. Until Zara's notes, I'd never paid much attention to the words—once you hear "to be or not to be" mangled by toothpaste, it gets a little hard to care—but this was a really funny play, and we amped it up wherever we could. Bliss played Hermia, and during one of the scenes where we argued, she actually pounced on me from across the stream, startling a belly laugh from the Gardener.

In the middle of one of Marenka's speeches as Puck, the front door slammed open to frame Avery, a tiny bundle over one shoulder. Marenka stopped and looked to me, her eyes wide within her mask of a White Peacock. I stood and went to her side, watching Avery jog into the Garden. After a moment, the Gardener and Desmond stood beside us.

"I brought us a new one!" Avery announced, his face wreathed in smiles. He shrugged off his burden, letting it drop to the sand. "I found her, I got her. Look, Father! See what I found for us!"

The Gardener was too busy staring at his older son, so I knelt down and twitched aside the wrapped blanket with shaking hands. A few of the girls screamed. Oh fuck oh fuck oh fucking shit.

The girl inside hadn't even hit puberty yet. Blood crusted one side of her face in streaks from her temple, the fair skin there already starting to bruise, and other bruises, scratches, and impressions could be seen through tears in her clothing as I pulled away the rest of the blanket. More blood soaked her thighs and the fabric around it. Shit, her underwear was covered with pink and purple cursive *Saturday*s, the kind of thing you just know they don't make in big girl sizes. A really inappropriate part of my brain noted that it was only Thursday.

She was small, with gangly limbs and the impression of growth, like suddenly she'd shoot up. Pretty, in a preteen kind of way, with a ruined ponytail of almost copper hair, but very, very young. I wrapped the blanket back around her to hide the blood and held her close, utterly speechless.

"Avery," whispered the shocked Gardener. "What the hell have you done?"

I absolutely did not want to be a part of that conversation. Danelle helped me stand with the girl in my arms, supporting her head. "Bliss, your dress with the back, can we have that?"

She nodded and raced away to her room.

Danelle and I walked quickly to my room, where we stripped the girl, threw her ruined clothing in the laundry chute, and washed her. I had to wash the blood from her thighs and gently squirt more water into her to flush the fluids and bits of torn tissue; Danelle was busy retching into the toilet. She came back, wiping a shaky hand across her mouth. "She doesn't even have any hair down there yet," she whispered.

No hair on her crotch or underarms, no breasts, no hips, this was definitely still a child.

Danelle held her up so I could wash her hair. By then Bliss was there with her dress—the only thing that was likely to fit her and keep her fully covered, even if it was a bit loose—so we got her dried off, clothed, and tucked into my bed.

"Now that she's here, do you think . . ." Not even Bliss could finish that thought.

I shook my head, inspecting the girl's hand where several nails had torn short. She must have fought. "They're not touching her."

"Maya—"

"They're *not* touching her."

A pained bellow ripped through the Garden and we flinched.

But it wasn't from a female, so we didn't move.

Other girls fled from the sound, crowding into my room, until I finally had to tell most of them to leave. We had no idea when this child was going to wake up, and she was going to be terrified and in pain and really didn't need twenty-something people staring at her. Only

Danelle and Bliss stayed, Danelle keeping herself behind the girl so her face wouldn't be seen right away.

Except the bookshelf on my right wall didn't entirely hide Lyonette.

Bliss tugged the curtain for my toilet as far as it could go, lifting the bottom and tucking it between several of the books to anchor it. If you knew something was there you could still see her hair, the curve of her spine, but not at a casual glance.

And we waited.

Bliss made a quick errand to fetch bottles of water, as well as bullying a few aspirin out of the cowed Lorraine. Aspirin wasn't going to do much in the long run—it was great against headaches from the drugs, but that wasn't what she had— but it was something anyway.

Then the Gardener appeared in my doorway. He glanced at the wall and the arrangement of the curtain, then to the girl on the bed, and nodded, reaching into his pocket. He pulled out a small control, and after a minute or so of fiddling with it, the walls came down on either side, leaving the front open. "How is she?"

"Unconscious," I said shortly. "She's been raped, she's been hit very hard in the head, and she'll have a world of other hurts."

"Was there anything to show her name? Or where she came from?"

"No." I gave her hand to Bliss so I could walk across the room, standing right next to the pale, suddenly worn-looking man. "No one touches her."

"Maya—"

"No, no one touches her. No wings, no sex, nothing. She is a *child*."

To my shock, he actually nodded. "I'm giving her to your care."

Danelle cleared her throat. "Sir? She hasn't actually woken up yet; couldn't she be taken somewhere? Left at a hospital or something? She wouldn't know anything."

"I can't trust that she didn't see Avery," he said heavily. "She has to stay."

Danelle bit her lip and looked away, her hands stroking the girl's hair.

"I think it best if you leave," I told him evenly. "We don't know when she's going to wake up. It would be best to not have any males present."

"Of course, yes. You'll tell me if . . . if she needs anything?"

"She needs her mother and her virginity," snapped Bliss. "She needs to be safely at home."

"Bliss."

She snorted, but fell silent at his warning tone.

"You'll tell me," he said again, and I nodded. I didn't bother to watch him leave.

He wasn't gone long before Desmond came, that bruised look even stronger in his eyes. "Will she be all right?"

"No," I said stiffly. "But I think she'll live."

"That yell? Father caned Avery."

"Yes, because that will make her feel so much better," Bliss snarled. "Go fuck yourself."

"What did he do to her?"

"What do you think he did to her? Shook her hand?"

"Desmond." I didn't continue until he was finally looking at me, meeting my eye. "This is what your brother is, but it's what all three of you do, so right now you need to not be here. I know you're all full of self-pity and loathing right now, but I will not have any males around this child. You need to go."

"I'm not the one who hurt her!"

"Yes, you are," I snapped. "You could have prevented this! If you had just gone to the police, or let one of us go so *we* could go to the police, Avery wouldn't have been free to kidnap her, to savage her, to rape her, to bring her here where it will happen to her again and again and again until she's dead too young. You allowed this to happen, Desmond, actively allowed it, so yes, you are the one who hurt her. If you're not going to do anything to help her, you need to get the hell away from her."

He stared at me, his face pale and shocked. Then he turned and walked away.

How could a child be worth less than a name? How could all our lives be worth less than a reputation?

327

Bliss looked after him, then reached out to touch my hand. "Do you think he'll come back?"

"I don't care."

It was even mostly true. I was tired in a way that went deeper than my bones. I simply did not have the energy to think about Desmond's continued uselessness.

The girl finally regained consciousness around two in the morning, groaning as she started to feel all the various aches and pains. I sat on the bed and gave her hand a gentle squeeze. "Keep your eyes closed," I said softly, pitching my voice low and comforting as Lyonette had taught me. I'd pretty much never done it before, but this girl needed me to be softer to her, fiercer for her. Sophia, I thought, would have recognized that distinction. "I'm going to put a damp cloth over your face to help take away some of that pain."

Danelle wrung out the washcloth and handed it to me.

"Where—what?"

"We'll get to that in a bit, I promise. Can you swallow pills?"

She started crying. "Please don't drug me! I'll be good, I promise, I won't fight anymore!"

"It's aspirin, nothing more. I promise you that. It's only to help the pain a little."

She let me sit her up enough to put the pills on her tongue and drink some water. "Who are you?"

"My name is Maya. I was taken by the same

people who took you, but I'm not going to let them hurt you anymore. They won't be able to touch you."

"I want to go home."

"I know," I whispered, adjusting the cloth over her eyes. "I know you do. I'm so sorry."

"I don't want to be blind anymore, please let me see!"

I shielded her eyes and slid away the cloth, watching her blink against even that much light. Her eyes were different colors, one blue and one grey, and the blue one had two freckles in the iris. I angled my hand so she could see my face without staring directly into the overhead light. "Better?"

"I hurt," she whimpered. Tears spilled from the corner of her eyes into her hair.

"I know you do, sweetheart. I know."

She rolled over and pressed her face into my lap, her skinny arms wrapping around my hips. "I want my mom!"

"I know, sweetheart." I curled over her, my hair spilling around her like that was any kind of shield, and held her as tightly as I could without causing pain. "I'm sorry." Sophia's Jillie would be eleven by now; this girl seemed around the same age, maybe a year older. But thinking of Jillie hurt just then. This child just looked so young and fragile, so broken. I didn't want to think of bold little Jillie like that.

She cried herself back to sleep, and when she woke again a few hours later, Bliss brought us all fruit. "Lorraine didn't make breakfast," she whispered to me and Danelle. "She's been sitting in the kitchen staring at the wall all night, according to Zulema and Willa."

I nodded and took one of the bananas, taking my seat next to the child. "Here, you must be hungry."

"Not really," she said miserably.

"Part of that is shock, but try to eat anyway. The potassium will help your muscles, help them not be so tight and painful."

She gave a quivering sigh, but took the banana and bit into it.

"This is Bliss," I said, pointing to my tiny friend. "And this is Danelle. Can you tell us your name?"

"Keely Rudolph," she answered. "I live in Sharpsburg, Maryland."

Forever and a half ago, Guilian had said something about Maryland.

"Keely, do you think you can be brave for me?"

Tears welled up in her eyes again, but God love her, she nodded.

"Keely, this place is called the Garden. There's a man and his two sons who take us and keep us here. They make sure we have food and clothing, that we have what we need, but they don't let us go. I am so sorry that you were kidnapped and brought here, but I can't change that. I can't promise that you'll ever see your home or family again."

She sniffled and I slid my arm around her shoulders, hugging her against my side.

"I know it's hard. I'm not just saying that, I really do know. But I promise you that I will take care of you. I won't let them hurt you. Those of us who are kept here form a kind of family. We argue sometimes, and we don't always like each other, but we're a family, and family looks out for each other."

Bliss gave me a crooked smile; even though she didn't know much, she knew that wasn't how I'd been raised.

But I'd gotten a taste of that in the apartment, and I'd learned the rest of it here. We were a fucked-up family, but a family nonetheless.

Keely looked at Danelle and shrank against me. "Why does she have a tattoo on her face?" she whispered.

Danelle knelt down in front of the bed, taking both of Keely's hands in hers. "This is another thing you have to be brave for," she said gently. "Do you want to hear it now, or do you want to wait for a little bit?"

Biting her lip, the child gave me an uncertain look.

"It's your choice," I told her. "Now or later, you can choose. If it makes it easier, I promise that it's not going to happen to you."

With a deep, shaky breath, she nodded. "Now then."

"The man who keeps us? We call him the Gardener," Danelle said simply. "He likes to think of us as Butterflies in his Garden, and he tattoos wings on our backs because it helps him pretend. When I was first brought here, I thought that if I made him like me more than anyone else, he'd let me go and I could go home. I was wrong, but I didn't learn that quickly enough, and he did the wings on my face to show others that he thought I was happy with what he did."

Keely looked up at me again. "You have wings too?"

"On my back, yes."

Her eyes flicked over to Bliss, who nodded. "But you won't let him do that to me?"

"I won't let him touch you at all."

We took her out into the Garden in the early afternoon, Bliss going ahead of us to warn the other girls. Normally most of the others stayed away from the new girl until she was settled. Keely was different. Singly or in pairs, as nonthreateningly as possible, every girl but Sirvat came to say hello, to introduce herself, and, maybe most importantly, to promise that they'd help protect her. I was okay with Sirvat absenting herself from that.

Marenka knelt down and let Keely trace the white, browns, and black of the wings on her face so she wouldn't be scared anymore. "I'm going to move my things so you'll be right next to Maya," she told her. "That way if you get scared or don't want to be alone, you won't have to worry about getting lost. You'll be right next to her."

"Th-thank you," she managed.

Lorraine roused herself enough to put together a cold lunch for us, though she was crying the entire time. I wanted to believe that maybe she'd finally realized just what the Gardener was, that she was horrified that a child so young had been taken, that she was mortified over how she'd been mooning and jealous of dead girls. I really wanted to believe that little bit of good of her. I didn't, though. I didn't know why she was so shocked and upset, but I didn't think it was for anyone's situation but hers. Maybe buying the wig—or, more likely, Bliss not getting in trouble for the attack—finally made her realize that the Gardener was never going to love her again.

We took our lunches up on the cliff, where the sun was warm and the space around us open. Keely still didn't have much of an appetite, but she ate to humor us. Then she saw Desmond walking up the path and she buried herself against me. Bliss and Danelle moved in close, as well, protecting her from all sides.

Desmond wasn't the threat, but he was a male. I understood the impulse.

He stopped a safe distance away, kneeling down

on the rock and spreading his arms wide. "I'm not going to hurt you," he said quietly. "I'm not going to touch you, or even come any closer than this."

I shook my head. "Why are you here?"

"To ask her name and where she came from, so I can do what's right."

I started to scoot off the rock, but Keely's arms tightened around my waist. "It's okay," I whispered, hugging her close. "I'm just going to go talk to him. You can stay right here with Bliss and Danelle."

"What if he hurts you?" she whimpered.

"He won't. This one doesn't. I'll be right back. You'll see me the whole time."

She slowly released me to transfer her grip to Danelle. Bliss was soft and curvy, but she was not cuddly.

I walked past Desmond to the very edge of the cliff and, after a moment, he followed me. He stood a foot or so away, shoving his hands deep in his pockets. "What are you doing?"

"What's right," he answered. "I'm calling the police, but I need to know her name. There's got to be an AMBER Alert out for her."

"Why now? You've known about the Garden for six months now."

"How old is she?"

I glanced back at her over my shoulder. "She and her friends were hanging out at the mall to celebrate her twelfth birthday."

He swore and studied his feet, the toes of his shoes a little over the edge of the rock. "I've been trying so hard to convince myself that my father is telling the truth, that even if you're not here by choice you at least came from something he could rescue you from."

And still, in the face of this twelve-year-old girl, he was deluding himself.

"The streets, maybe, or bad families," he continued. "Something that made this just a little bit better, but I can't . . . I know it was Avery who took her, not Father, but this has to stop. You're right: I *am* a coward. And I am selfish, because I don't want to hurt my family, and I don't want to go to jail, but that girl is . . ." He stopped, panting with the force of his words and the tangle of emotion behind them. "I kept telling myself that I needed to learn to be braver, and Jesus, what a stupid thing to think. You don't learn to be brave. You just have to do what's right, even if it scares you. So I'm calling the police with as many names as I know and telling them about the Garden."

"You're really calling?" I asked.

He flashed me an angry look.

"Yes, I'm asking, because I can't go tell that girl that help is on the way if you're going to back out or bury your head back in the sand. Are you really doing this?"

He took a deep breath. "Yes. I'm really doing this."

I reached out and lightly touched his cheek to bring his eyes to mine. "Her name is Keely Rudolph, and she lives in Sharpsburg."

"Thank you." He turned to walk away, then stopped, walked back, and pulled me into a searing kiss.

And then walked away without another word.

I returned to the rock. "We need to stay in my room for the rest of today," I told the girls. "Go ahead without me, I'm just going to tell everyone else."

"Do you really think he's going to do it?" Bliss asked.

"I think he's finally going to try, and God help him if it doesn't work. Go, quickly."

It was like the ultimate game of hide-and-seek, tracking down each girl and telling her to stay in her room. I didn't care if they were in their own rooms, just that they were out of the Garden proper, because as soon as the Gardener learned about that call the walls were coming down, and I didn't even want to think about what would happen to any girl he found outside of them. Every word was whispered because I didn't know how strong the mics were and didn't know if the Gardener had already heard what his son intended.

I found Eleni and Isra in the cave, Tereza in the music room, Marenka in the room that would no longer be hers, with Ravenna and Nazira helping her pack all of her embroidery stuff. Willa and Zulema were in the kitchen watching Lorraine cry hard enough to set her wig askew, Pia was at the pond studying the sensors for the water level. One by one I found them and passed the news along, and they walked quickly away.

Sirvat was the last one I found, her entire front pressed against the glass of Zara's display case. The intricate black, white, and orange-yellow wings of a Pearl Crescent filled her back, and her eyes were closed as she stood motionless.

"Sirvat, what the fuck are you doing?"

She opened one eye to look at me. "Trying to imagine what it's like in there."

"Seeing as she's dead, I don't think she can help you with that. She doesn't know either."

"Can you smell it?"

"The honeysuckle?"

She shook her head and backed away from the glass. "The formaldehyde. My biology teacher used it to preserve specimens for dissection. They must have a ton of it in that room, because the smell is so strong here."

"It's where he prepares us for the cases," I sighed. "Sirvat, we need to stay in the rooms. The shit's hitting the fan."

"Because of Keely?"

"And Desmond."

She touched the locked door, protected by its lock code. "We always had to be really careful with the formaldehyde. Even diluted in alcohol, it's not always stable."

I never felt bad for not being closer to Sirvat. She was a strange duck.

But she let me pull her away and toss her into her room. I ran back up onto the cliff and up one of the trees to try and see if anything was going on, but I couldn't even see the house, much less the front of the property. The Gardener had plenty of money and plenty of space, a bad combination when it comes to psychopathic tendencies.

The lights flickered violently and I hurled myself over the edge of the cliff, scraping and banging as I clambered down the rough holds and through the waterfall to get to my room before the walls came down.

Bliss handed me a towel. "It occurs to me, half an hour too late, that we might have been better off all getting together in one place in the Garden. If Desmond tells the cops that we're in the inner greenhouse, they'd insist on checking it out, right? If we were out there, they'd see us."

"Believe it or not, I thought of that." I stripped off my soaked dress and pulled on the dress I'd been given at Desmond's arrival, the one with the back. It wasn't one of the Gardener's favorites because it obscured the wings, but at the moment I didn't care. I wanted to be running, to be fighting, to be doing almost anything but sit in that tiny room and wait. "If he's able to talk the police out of investigating, or if he was able to convince Desmond not to make the call, what do you suppose he'll do to anyone who disobeyed the room call?"

"Dammit."

"Bliss . . . I'm scared," I whispered. I sank down onto the bed and reached for Keely's hand. She took it and curled into me, seeking comfort. "I hate not being able to hear anything."

Marenka and I had once experimented with shrieking at the top of our lungs during a maintenance session. Our rooms were right next to each other's and we couldn't hear a thing. Even the vents closed when the walls came down.

Hours passed before the walls went up. We stayed in the rooms at first, too scared to move, for all we'd hated sitting still. Then we couldn't stand it anymore and walked out into the Garden to see how our world had changed.

Maybe, finally, it was for the better.

"Was it?" Eddison asks when it's clear she's not going to continue.

"No."

III

Inara rubs her thumbs against the sad little dragon, one of her scabs catching on the brow ridge and tearing away.

Victor trades a look with his partner. "Grab the coat," he says, pushing back from the table.

"What?"

"We're going to take a little ride."

"We're doing what?" Eddison mutters.

The girl doesn't ask any questions, simply takes his jacket and shrugs into it. The little blue dragon stays in one hand.

He leads them down into the garage, opening the front passenger door for the girl. She looks at the car for a moment, her mouth crooked in an expression he can't really call a smile. "Something wrong?"

"Except for coming here and to the hospital, and presumably from New York to the Garden, I haven't been in a car since the taxi heading to my Gran's."

"Then you'll understand if I don't offer to let you drive."

Her lips twitch. The easy laughter and comfortable atmosphere they'd finally achieved in the room is gone, vanished in the face of what they've been working toward all along.

"Is there a reason I have to sit in the back?" Eddison complains.

"Would you like me to invent one?"

"Fine, but I get to pick the music."

"No."

The girl arches an eyebrow, and Victor grimaces.

"He likes country."

"Please don't let him pick," she says pleasantly as she slides into the seat.

Chuckling, he waits for her legs to be clear before he closes the door.

"Where are we going on our little field trip?" Eddison asks as the men cross to the other side of the car.

"First stop is coffee, then we're going to the hospital."

"So she can check on the girls?"

"That too."

Rolling his eyes, Eddison lets it go and settles into the backseat.

When they arrive at the hospital, coffees in hand—tea, for Inara—the entire building is surrounded with news vans and gawkers. The part of him that's been doing this job for too long wonders if every parent who's ever lost a girl between sixteen and eighteen is out there with a candle and a blown-up picture, hoping for the best, or maybe even hoping for the worst so long as the nightmare of not knowing is finally over. Some stare at their cell phones, waiting for a call that, for many, will never come.

"Are the rooms blocked off for the girls?" she asks, angling her face away from the passenger window and letting her hair fall forward to hide her further.

"Yes, with guards at the doors." He squints ahead at the emergency entrance to see if he can get away with bringing her in through there, but four ambulances fill the bay with a flurry of activity around them.

"I can walk past a few reporters if I need to. They can't honestly expect me to talk about it."

"Did you ever watch the news in the city?"

"We caught it every now and then at Taki's when we were getting food," she answers with a shrug. "We didn't have a TV, and most of the people we hung out with only had their sets hooked into game platforms or DVD players. Why?"

"Because they do expect you to talk about it, even when they know you're not allowed to. They will shove their microphones in your face and ask you personal questions with no sensitivity and they'll share your answers with anyone who cares to listen."

"So . . . they're like the FBI?"

"First Hitler, now reporters," Eddison says. "I'm thrilled you have such a high opinion of us."

"I clearly don't know enough about reporters to find them offensive, so I don't know that it's too terrible."

"If you don't mind wading through them, we can head in," Victor says before either of them can add anything else. He parks the car and walks around to open the door for her. "They're going to be yelling," he cautions her. "They'll be loud and in your face, and there will be cameras flashing everywhere. There will be parents asking questions about their girls, wanting to know if you've seen them. And there'll be people insulting you."

"Insulting me?"

"There are always some people who feel that the victim must have deserved it," he explains. "They're idiots, but they're often vocal. Of course you don't deserve it, no one *deserves* to get kidnapped or raped or murdered, but they'll say it anyway because they believe it or because they want a few seconds of attention, and because we protect free speech, we can't do anything about it."

"I guess I grew so used to the horrors of the Garden, I forgot how awful Outside could be."

He'd give anything to tell her that it isn't true.

But it is, so he stays silent.

They walk out of the garage to the main

entrance, the agents flanking the girl protectively, and the lights and sounds rise to a fever pitch. The girl ignores them with grave dignity, staring straight ahead, refusing to even listen to the questions, much less answer them. There are barricades to keep everyone back from the path to the hospital, with local police manning them. They're almost to the doors when one enterprising woman crawls under the barricade and between an officer's legs, her microphone cord trailing behind her.

"What is your name? Are you one of the victims?" she demands, waving her mic in front of her.

The girl doesn't answer, doesn't even look at her, and Victor signals for the officer to take the woman away.

"With a tragedy such as this, you owe the public the full story!"

Her thumb still rubs thoughtfully against the little blue dragon, but she turns to look at the reporter, who struggles against the officer's grip on her arms. "I think if you actually knew anything about the case you're claiming to report," she says softly, "you'd have better sense than to suggest I owe *anyone* a thing." She nods to the officer and resumes her progress to the sliding doors. Cries follow her, those closest to the door asking after missing girls, but everything fades to a dull roar when the doors hiss shut behind them.

Eddison actually grins at the girl. "I was expecting you to tell her to fuck off."

"I thought about it," she admits. "Then I remembered that you two were likely to be in the frame, and I didn't want Hanoverian's mother to wash his ears out for hearing such filthy language."

"Yeah, yeah, come on, children."

For a hospital, there's a significant police presence, even in the main lobby. FBI, local police, representatives from other police departments, child services, all of them talking on phones or clicking away on laptops or tablets. Those not tied into the technology are dealing with something far more difficult: the families.

As Eddison drops their empty cups into the bin by the doors, Victor waves to the third member of their team, seated beside a couple in their mid-thirties. Ramirez nods but doesn't take her arm from around the shoulders of the exhausted woman next to her. "Inara, this is—"

"Agent Ramirez," Inara finishes for him. "We met before I got taken away. She promised to keep the doctors from being assholes."

Victor winces.

Ramirez smiles. "Overbearing," she corrects. "I promised to *try* to keep them from being *overbearing*. Though I think you were Maya then."

"I was. Am." She shakes her head. "It's complicated."

"These are Keely's parents," says Ramirez, gesturing to the couple.

"She keeps asking for you," says Keely's father. He's pale and red-eyed but he offers his hand to shake. She holds up her burned, gashed hands in silent apology. "I understand you helped protect her once she was there?"

"I tried," she hedges. "Not that she's lucky to have been there, but it's fortunate she wasn't there long."

"We were going to have her moved to a private room," his wife adds through a sniffle. She clutches a Hello Kitty backpack and a handful of tissues. "She's so young, and the questions the doctors are asking are so personal." She trails off into her tissues, and her husband picks up the thread.

"She panicked, said if she couldn't have you, she wanted to stay with . . . with . . ."

"Danelle and Bliss?"

"Yes. I don't . . . I don't understand why she would . . ."

"This is all an awful lot to take in," Inara tells them gently. "It's frightening. Keely wasn't in there long, but for those couple of days, she wasn't alone. The three of us were with her the entire time, and often some of the other girls as well. It's comforting to be with people who know exactly what you've gone through. It'll get better." She glances down at the dragon in her hand. "It's not that she's not over the moon to see you; she is. She missed you terribly. But being alone in a room right now is . . . likely to cause her panic. Just be patient with her."

"What did they do to our little girl?"

"She'll tell you that as she can. Just be patient with her," she repeats. "And I'm sorry, I know you must have a million questions and concerns, but I really need to go check on the others, including Keely."

"Right, right, of course." Keely's father clears his throat several times. "Thank you for helping her."

His wife stands and embraces the startled girl, who throws a wary look at the grinning Victor. When he makes no move to help, she grimaces and gently pulls away from the woman's arms. "How many other parents are here?" she mutters as they walk away.

"About half of the survivors, with a few more on the way," Ramirez answers, jogging to catch up with them by the elevators. "They haven't notified any of the parents of the dead girls yet; they want to be absolutely sure it's them."

"That would be good, yes."

"Agent Ramirez!" calls a strident voice, followed by the swift clicks of heels on tile.

Victor groans. They were so close to passing unnoticed.

But he turns, along with his partners, to face the

approaching woman. Inara just keeps looking at the screen above the elevator, watching the numbers descend.

Senator Kingsley is an elegant woman in her fifties, her black hair arranged around her face to give an impression of softness that her severe expression counteracts. She still looks fresh despite having been at the hospital since last night. Her crisp red suit is striking against her dark skin, the small American flag pin on her lapel nearly drowned by the color. "This is her, then?" she demands, stopping in front of them. "This is the girl you've been hiding?"

"We've been interviewing her, Senator, not hiding her," Victor says mildly. He reaches out to grip Inara's shoulder, gently but firmly turning her around.

Inara's eyes flick over the woman. She musters a smile so obviously fake it makes him wince. "You must be Ravenna's mother."

"Her name," the senator says tightly, "is Patrice."

"It was," Inara agrees. "And it will be. Right now it's still Ravenna. Outside isn't real yet."

"And just what the hell does that mean?"

The smile disappears. Inara's thumb rubs against the sad dragon. After a moment, she straightens and looks the woman in the eye. "It means you're too real for her to handle yet. The past two days have been too much. We've spent

349

so long living in someone else's terrible fantasy that we don't know how to be real anymore. It'll come, in time, but your real is very . . ." She glances at the knot of aides and staff members hovering a respectful distance away. "Very public," she says finally. "If you can get rid of the entourage, maybe it'll be easier for her."

"We're just trying to get to the bottom of this."

"Isn't that the FBI's job?"

The senator stares at her. "She's my daughter. I'm not just going to sit by and watch—"

"Like every other parent?"

Victor winces again.

"You stand for the law, Senator. Sometimes that means standing back to let it work."

Eddison spins to hit the call button for the elevator again. Victor can see his shoulders shaking.

But Inara isn't done yet. "Sometimes it means being mother *or* senator, not both. I think she'd like to see her mother, but with what she's been through, the adjustments she'll have to make, I don't think she can handle the senator. Now, if you'll please excuse us, we need to check in on Ravenna and the others." The elevator dings and she steps through as soon as the doors open. Ramirez and Eddison join her.

Victor waves them up. The senator may be speechless for the moment, but that never seems to last long.

And it doesn't. "I've been informed that that woman, Lorraine, was complicit in what was done to my daughter. I promise you, Agent, if I hear even the slightest hint that that girl is part of this, I will bring the full weight—"

"Senator. Let us do our job. If you want to know what happened to your daughter, if you want to get to the truth, you have to let us do our job." He reaches out to touch her elbow. "I have a daughter only a little younger than Patrice. I promise you, this is not something I take lightly. They are incredibly strong young women who have been through hell, and I will honor them by giving them my best, but you have to take a step away."

"Could you?" she asks shrewdly.

"I hope I never find out."

"God help you, Agent, if this blows up in your face."

Victor watches her walk away, then hits the Up button. As he waits for the elevator, he can see her rejoin her knot of people, giving orders and asking questions, her younger staff members scrambling to respond. The older ones are steadier, less overwhelmed.

He rides up to the fourth floor and steps out into a noticeable hush, so different from the crammed and frantic lobby. The others have waited for him. A cluster of doctors and nurses talk at the nurses' station, but the presence of armed guards at the doors keeps the volume down.

One of the nurses waves at Ramirez. "Need to talk to the girls again?"

"We have someone else who needs to see them." She points to the girl and the nurse follows her gesture with an easy smile.

"Ah, yes, I remember you. How are your hands doing?"

She holds them up for the nurse's inspection.

"The stitches are clean, and there's no swelling," she murmurs. "That's a good thing. Are you picking at the scabs from the smaller wounds?"

"A little?"

"Well, don't do it anymore. You want these to heal. Let's get some bandages on these just in case."

Within minutes, her hands are once again wrapped in gauze that's carefully taped around her fingers to allow for some mobility. As long as the nurse has her stationary anyway, she does a quick check of the smaller injuries on her side and arm.

"You look good, sweetie," the woman concludes, one hand on her shoulder. "Agent, you can take her now."

The girl salutes, making the nurse wave her off with a smile.

As they come to the first of the doors, Inara takes a slow breath, pulling the little blue dragon back out for comfort. "I can't guess what the dynamic is going to be," she confesses.

Victor pats her shoulder. "Go and find out."

The local officer standing guard awkwardly shifts his weight. "They're all two doors down."

"All?" Eddison asks sharply.

"They insisted."

"They being the traumatized young women?"

"Yes, sir." He pulls off his hat to scratch at his flyaway blond hair. "One of them taught me a few phrases I've never heard even on drug busts."

"Probably Bliss," murmurs the girl. Rather than argue with the man, she simply walks down another two doors, followed belatedly by the trio of agents, and nods to the officer at that post. "May I go in?"

He glances to the agents, who all nod. "Yes, ma'am."

Though individual words and voices are indistinct, they can hear the sound of conversation through the wall. It stops as soon as the door swings open, then peaks when the inhabitants of the room see the girl.

"Maya!" A black and white bare-assed blur flies across the room and into the girl's arms. "Where the fuck have you been?"

"Hello, Bliss." Patting the smaller girl's messy black curls, she looks around the room. Somehow the two-bed room has four beds in it. All of the walking wounded are clustered on the beds of the more seriously injured, holding hands or sitting with arms around shoulders or waists. A

353

few of the braver parents sit on hard chairs beside the beds, but most of them are clustered against the far wall talking amongst themselves while still keeping an eye on their daughters.

Victor leans against the wall with a smile, watching the smallest shadow creep between two of the beds to work her way between the two young women. It's a joy to see the girl's gentle smile, how tightly she holds the child against her.

"Hello, Keely. I met your parents."

"I think I hurt them," whispers Keely, but Inara shakes her head.

"They're just scared. Be patient with them, and be patient with yourself."

Victor and his partners hover near the door for nearly an hour, watching the young women laugh and toss jokes and insults back and forth, as they comfort the occasional breakdown or tears. Despite her obvious distaste for it, the girl allows herself to be introduced to the parents. She listens to them patiently as they tell her all about their searches for their daughters, how they never gave up hope, and the only sign of her cynicism is the cocked eyebrow that sends Danelle into giggles strong enough to set off her heart monitor.

Ravenna he can identify—she looks like a younger version of her mother—and he watches their short conversation intently, wishing he could hear any of it. The senator's daughter has bandages wrapped around most of one leg.

Ravenna's the dancer, he remembers. As Inara gently touches the bandages, he wonders how this will affect that.

He can name some of the other Butterflies from her stories. For others he has to listen for the names they toss around, try to pin them to their owners. With the exception of Keely, never renamed, none of them use their original names. It's still the names from the Garden on their tongues, on their minds, and he can see the parents cringe every time. Inara said that sometimes it was easier to forget; for the first time, he wonders if any of them did. Or perhaps she's right, and they're not ready for this to be real yet.

It's tempting to stay there longer, to bask in the sight to push back some of the horrors of the past few days, but Victor can't relax into it completely. There's more she has to see, and more she has yet to tell them.

More they need to know.

He lifts his wrist to check his watch and immediately Inara's eyes are on him, a question that doesn't need words. He nods. She sighs, closing her eyes for a moment to collect herself, then starts the process of reassuring everyone she'll be back. She's almost back to the door when Bliss catches her hand.

"How much have you told them?" she asks bluntly.

"Most of what's important."

"And what have they told you?"

"Avery's dead. The Gardener is likely to survive to stand trial."

"So we'll all have to talk."

"It's time, and look at it this way: maybe the FBI will be easier to tell than your parents."

Bliss grimaces.

"Her parents are on their way," Ramirez whispers to Victor, "flying over the Atlantic from her father's new teaching position in Paris. It's hard to tell whether they gave up looking for her, or if they simply had to do what was best for the children they still had."

From her expression, it's clear Bliss isn't inclined to give them the benefit of the doubt.

With a last hug for Keely, Inara leaves the room with Victor and Eddison; Ramirez remains behind to talk with the parents. They pass a string of empty rooms with guards at the doors, all the rooms the girls are supposed to be in but aren't, then a run of unoccupied rooms that form a buffer between the girls and the rooms at the far end of the hall, with their own guards.

When they stop, Eddison glances in the door's small window and shoots his partner a curious look. Victor simply nods. "I'll wait out here," the younger man says.

Victor opens the door, ushers the girl through, and closes it carefully behind them.

The man on the bed is hooked into an

unbelievable array of machines, all beeping softly with their own sounds and rhythms. A nasal cannula feeds oxygen into his system, but an intubation kit stands nearby for the very real possibility of being needed. Dressings obscure much of what the blanket doesn't cover, some of them bandages, some of them glistening salves and synthetic materials to draw the heat out of the burns and prevent infection. The burns extend to one side of his scalp, a bubbling mess of discolored, blistered skin.

The girl stares at him with wide eyes, her feet rooted barely a yard inside the room.

"His name is Geoffrey MacIntosh," Victor tells her gently. "He isn't the Gardener anymore. He has a name and a host of disfiguring injuries, and he isn't the god of the Garden anymore. He never will be again. His name is Geoffrey MacIntosh, and he'll be brought to trial for everything he's done. This man *cannot hurt you anymore.*"

"What about Eleanor? His wife?" she whispers.

"She's in the next room so they can monitor her heart; she collapsed at the house. As far as we can tell, she never knew about any of this."

"And Lorraine?"

"A few doors down. She's being questioned to determine the extent to which she can be charged for her part in all of this. There will be a number of psychological evaluations before that's decided."

He can see the name take shape on her lips, but she doesn't ask. She sinks down into one of the hard chairs against the wall, leaning forward against her knees to study the unconscious man in the hospital bed. "None of us had ever seen him so angry," she says in a tiny voice. "Not even for all the harm that Avery caused. He was *furious*."

He offers her his hand and tries to hide his surprise when she actually takes it, the gauze rubbing against his skin.

"None of us had ever seen him like that."

The three of them stood at the far end of the Garden, closest to the door, and the Gardener had clearly flipped his shit. He was screaming at Desmond, and there was Avery, looking smug as hell. I guess he figured his father wasn't too upset about Keely anymore.

Rather than move closer, I inspected what I could see of the Garden. There had been people there, that much was clear. Boot prints were visible in the sand and some of the plants were trampled. Someone had even left a gum wrapper on the stream bank. Had the officers just been incurious? Had the Gardener given them an explanation that made sense?

"The dimensions," whispered Bliss. "If he brought down *all* the walls, they may not have realized there were hallways. There are tracks on both sides of the main doorway."

So maybe they had looked, and just couldn't find us.

Desmond had actually made the call.

My heart hurt because I wanted to be proud of him, but really, all I could think was it's about fucking time. Knowing we were kidnapped, violated, murdered, and displayed wasn't enough, but at least the raped and brutalized twelve-year-old finally was.

"This is wrong!" he cried when his father finally took a breath. "Taking them is wrong, keeping them is wrong, and killing them is wrong!"

"That is not your decision to make!"

"Yes, it is! Because it's against the law!"

His father slapped him so hard he stumbled back and fell. "This is my home, and my garden. Here, I am the law, and you went against that."

Laughing like a little boy at Christmas, Avery disappeared and came back only moments later with a bamboo cane, probably the same one that had been used on him the day before. Seriously, a cane. Who the fuck canes their grown children? Actually, who canes their children at any age? But Avery handed the cane to his father and tackled his younger brother, tearing at his clothing until his back and part of his ass were bare.

"This is for your own good, Desmond," the Gardener said as he rolled up his sleeves. Desmond struggled, but Avery tucked him into a headlock.

With Keely's face pressed to my stomach so she couldn't see, we stood and watched as the Gardener beat his son with the cane. It left bright red marks that quickly swelled into welts and Avery, the sick fuck, cheered with every impact. Desmond continued to struggle but didn't cry out, despite how much it had to hurt. The Gardener counted them out, and after twenty blows, he tossed the bamboo away from him.

Avery's cheers stopped. "That's it?" he demanded. "You gave me that many for branding the bitch!"

I pressed a hand against my hip and felt the thick scar tissue left from that brand. Were twenty blows of a cane equivalent?

"Avery, stay out of this."

"No! He could have put us both in prison, on death row even, and you let him off with twenty?" He dropped his brother to the sandy path and got back to his feet. "He nearly destroyed everything you've been working toward for thirty years. He turned his back on what it means to be your son. He turned his back on you!"

"Avery, I told you—"

Avery pulled something from the back of his belt, and suddenly it didn't matter what his father had told him. Avery had the room.

A gun will do that.

"You gave him everything!" he yelled, pointing the gun at his brother. "Your precious Desmond, who never did a thing to help you stock the Garden, and you were so damn proud of him. 'The Butterflies like him.' 'He doesn't hurt them.' 'He understands them better.' Who gives a shit? I'm your son too, your firstborn. I'm the one you're supposed to be proud of."

His father held his hands up, staring at the gun. "Avery, I was always proud of you—"

"No, you were scared of me. Even I know the difference in that, Father."

"Avery, please put the gun down. There's no place for that here."

"There's no place for that here," he echoed with a sneer. "That's what you've always said about anything I wanted!"

With a deep, pained groan, Desmond rolled onto his back and propped himself up on his elbows.

The gun went off.

Desmond fell back to the path with a cry, blood blooming across the breast of his tattered shirt. The Gardener lurched forward with a sob and the gun went off again, and the Gardener fell to his knees, clutching his side.

I thrust Keely at Danelle and shoved them both down behind a boulder. "Stay here," I hissed.

Bliss grabbed my hand. "Is he worth it?"

"Probably not," I admitted. "But he did call."

With a sad shake of her head, she let go, and I raced forward from the clutch of girls. I was almost to Desmond when Avery grabbed me by the hair and yanked me off my feet.

"And here's the bitch herself, the little queen of the Garden." He pistol-whipped me so hard my ears rang, and part of the gun sliced my cheek with the impact. Dropping the gun, he kicked me onto my knees and fumbled at his belt. "Well I'm the king of the Garden now, so you'd better learn to show me some respect."

"You put that near my mouth and I'll bite it off," I snarled, and from behind the boulder, Bliss cheered.

He hit me again, and again, and raised his hand to do it once more when Nazira's voice stopped him.

"I can hear sirens!"

I couldn't hear anything but the bells going off inside my skull, but some of the other girls said they could hear them too. I wasn't sure if they were trying to distract him or if the sirens were real.

Avery dropped me and ran through the Garden to take the path up the cliff to see for himself. I crawled to Desmond, who was trying to keep pressure on his chest with one hand. I moved his hands away and did it myself, his blood warm and sticky as it pumped against my palm. "Please don't die," I whispered.

He weakly squeezed my hand, but otherwise didn't try to answer.

The Gardener groaned and pulled himself to his son's other side. "Desmond? Desmond, answer me!"

The pale green eyes—his father's eyes—fluttered open. "The only way to protect them from him is to let them go," he panted. Sweat beaded his face. "He'll kill them all, and they'll be in pain at every moment."

"Just stay awake, Desmond," his father pleaded. "We'll get you to the hospital and we'll figure this out. Maya, keep pressure on it!"

I hadn't stopped.

But now I could hear the sirens.

Avery jumped and swore atop the cliff, and the girls raced forward to surround us, probably figuring the Gardener and Desmond were a safer bet than Avery-off-the-deep-end. Even Lorraine was clustered with us, and no one tried to brush her away. Bliss picked up the gun with shaking hands, but she kept her eyes trained on Avery.

And the sirens got louder.

"I can't figure out why they came back," she whispers, clutching his hand for dear life. "They didn't find anything the first time, right? Or the Gardener wouldn't have lifted the walls."

"One of the officers who stayed at the station ran the names Desmond gave over the phone. Keely's name they recognized because she was so recently missing, but when he ran some of the others, FBI flags came up on the search. His supervisor contacted us and we met them back out there. Cassidy Lawrence, for example. She went missing almost seven years ago from Connecticut. There's no reason to say her name with Keely's unless there's actually a connection between them."

"So Lyonette was part of why we were finally found?" she asks with a faint smile.

"Yes, she was."

They sit in silence for a few minutes, watching the man on the bed breathe in and out.

"Inara . . ."

"The rest of it."

"Hopefully this is the last difficult thing I'll have to ask of you."

"Until you ask me to take the stand," she sighs.

"I'm sorry, I truly am, but what happened next?"

Fucking Sirvat.

The Gardener pulled the remote control thing out of his pocket and punched a series of numbers into the tiny pad on it. "Sirvat, please go into the room right by the door and get some towels and rubber tubing."

"The one by Zara?" she asked.

"Yes, that's the one."

A slow smile spread across her face and she

spun away with a laugh. Sirvat had been there about a year and a half, and as long as I'd known her she'd been solitary and just . . . odd.

The Gardener adjusted his belt to put pressure on the wound in his side and stroked his son's hair, telling him to stay awake, asking him questions and begging him to respond. Des squeezed my hand in response to some things and he was still breathing, but he didn't try to talk, which I thought was probably for the better.

"When we get the towels tied on him, will you let us take him out the front?" I asked.

The Gardener just looked at me, nearly through me, seemingly weighing his Butterflies against his son, even now. Finally, he nodded.

Then I smelled it and froze.

Danelle was the next to smell it, her nose wrinkling. "What is that?"

"Formaldehyde," I hissed. "We need to get away from that room."

"What room?"

The Gardener paled even more. "No questions now, ladies, come."

We had to drag Desmond across the sand, the Gardener stumbling and swaying after us. We splashed through the waterfall—anyone who tried to go behind it and stay dry got pushed in by Bliss—and crowded into the cave.

Over the sound of the waterfall, we heard Sirvat laughing, and then . . .

She shakes her head. "I don't know how to describe the explosion," she tells him. "It was just massive, all this sound and heat. A few of the rocks came down from the top of the cliff, but the cave didn't collapse like I was half afraid it would. There were flames and glass everywhere and all these stupid little sprinklers misting straight into steam. Air poured in from the shattered roof and the flames leaped toward them. Smoke poured out, along with the real butterflies, but even with that, the smoke was so thick we could hardly breathe. We had to get out of there."

"You went through the stream?"

"Until we reached the pond. Our feet got cut up pretty badly from the glass, but the flames were spreading and the water seemed like a better option. The front half of the Garden was just this huge blaze. I asked the Gardener . . ." She swallows hard, looks at the man in the bed. "I asked Mister MacIntosh if there was an emergency exit, any other way to get out, but he said . . . he never thought anything would happen."

She twists her hand in his grip until her other hand can reach underneath the bandages to touch the scabs. He gently pushes it away.

The flames were spreading so fast. Panes of glass shattered overhead, raining down on us in chunks and shards. Willa dodged one but stepped directly into another that cut her head almost in half. We could see the flames beyond the glass, eating into the outer greenhouse.

The Gardener shook his head, leaning on Hailee for support. "If it reaches the room with the fertilizers, there will be a second explosion," he said, coughing.

By now, most of the girls were crying.

I tried to think of any possible way we weren't trapped and fucked. "The cliff," I said. "If we break some of the glass on the wall, we could go out onto the roof of the halls."

"And what, slide down the breaking or broken panes of glass for the outer greenhouse?" muttered Bliss. "And still probably break ankles, legs, *spines* when we land?"

"Fine. Your turn."

"No fucking clue. Your turn."

Desmond chuckled, then groaned.

Pia screamed and we spun around to see Avery behind her, his burned and blistered forearm across her throat. A chunk of glass quivered in his shoulder, soot and gashes streaking down his cheeks. He laughed and bit her neck as she struggled against him.

"Avery, let her go," the Gardener moaned.

Despite the roar of the flames, we heard her neck snap.

He threw her body to the side and then jerked back from a sharp crack. I turned to see Bliss with the gun up, her feet planted, and she shot him again. He bellowed with pain and threw himself forward, and she squeezed off two more shots until he finally fell face-first in the flowers.

One of the larger trees, all its branches aflame, snapped near its roots and crashed into the wall with a terrific groan. Glass shattered, metal panes snapping under its weight, and the black roof that ran between the two sections of greenhouse collapsed beneath it. We could see the outer greenhouse through the dancing flames.

"I still have nothing," Bliss said, and choked on the smoke. "Really, it's still your turn to think of something."

"Fuck off," I muttered, and she gave me a weak grin.

I hooked my ankle around Ravenna's knee and pulled her to take my place pressing against Desmond's chest. With how much we were moving him I didn't think it would do any good, but I couldn't bear not to at least try. He'd tried, even if he hadn't succeeded. We could try.

And I didn't want him to die. Not when he'd finally given us a chance to live.

I ran to the fallen tree, tugging away the larger chunks of glass and the more jagged branches. Pain seared through my hands, but if there was even the chance of this being the way out, I had to try. Then Glenys and Marenka were helping me, and then Isra joined us, and we tried to dig a way around the trunk. We were able to clear one side of it, and with all four of us pushing and straining from the other side, we managed to push the trunk just far enough into the outer greenhouse.

Marenka tugged a piece of glass from my arm and flicked it away. "I think I know a way to carry him through."

"Let's try it."

She lifted Desmond by the shoulders, hooking her hands under his armpits. I stood between his legs and hooked my hands under his knees. It wasn't graceful, and it certainly wasn't easy, but we were more or less single file.

Bliss led the way through, Danelle and Keely close behind her. Isra stayed back, pushing aside more debris as it fell, the Gardener beside her. Not helping, because he couldn't, really, but getting the more frightened—or frozen—girls to follow us. The smoke was getting worse, getting thicker, and we were all choking on it. Figures moved beyond the outer greenhouse and suddenly a great crack ran along one of the six-foot panes that butted the floor. Someone was swinging an ax at it. We held back, waiting to see if they would get through, and after a few more hits, the center of the pane shattered. Using the ax head, a fireman knocked the rest of the glass out of the pane and threw down a heavy folded tarp over the chunks.

"Come on," he—she?—yelled through the mask. Other firemen followed, and two of them took Desmond from us. It wasn't particularly fresh, but we got the first free air we'd had in forever, and the few girls who weren't crying already started as they stepped onto crisp autumn grass and felt the cold air wrap around us. Some of them fell to their knees in shock and had to be dragged away.

I was trying to count heads after they took Desmond, and I could see Isra doing the same thing in the outer greenhouse, both of us trying to figure out how many we'd lost before we reached this point. Then there was this . . . this . . . *whump* and another explosion billowed out from one of the rooms and the last I saw of Isra, she was flying sideways in a ball of fire, three of the others still clinging to her, the Gardener on the ground with flames dancing over him. I tried to run to the girls, but one of the firemen grabbed my wrist and yanked me away.

"And then the ambulances, and the hospital, and the room where I met you," she sighs. "And that's it. The whole story."

"Not quite."

She closes her eyes, bringing the hand with the little blue dragon to her cheek. "My name."

"The Gardener has his name now. Is yours really so terrible?"

She doesn't answer.

He stands and brings her to his feet. "Come on. One more thing to see."

She follows him out the door, passing by a frowning Eddison talking to a scene tech in a windbreaker, and into the door across the hall. This time he takes her all the way to the bedside before she can see who it is, and when she does her breath hitches.

Desmond's eyes open slowly, unfocused from drugs, but when he sees her, a faint smile curves his lips. "Hey," he whispers.

She has to shape the word several times before her voice catches up to the impulse. "Hey."

"I'm sorry."

"No . . . no, you . . . you did the right thing."

"But I should have done it a lot sooner." His hand moves atop the blanket, plastic tubing curling under the tape keeping the needle under his skin.

She moves as if to take his hand, but her fingers clench into a fist before they touch him. She stares at him, mouth slightly open, her lower lip quivering with shock.

His eyes slowly close as he falls still. Asleep or unconscious is anyone's guess.

"He's still weak," Victor says quietly. "He has a long recovery ahead of him, but the doctors say he's probably out of the woods."

"He's going to make it?" she whispers. Her eyes

gleam wetly, but no tears fall. Clutching the little blue dragon in one hand, she folds her arms across her stomach, a sense of protection she shouldn't need anymore. "He'll be tried as complicit," she says eventually.

"That isn't up to us. There may be a deal of some sort for him, but—"

"But he should have called six months earlier, and soon everyone will know it."

Victor scratches at his scalp. "I admit, I thought you'd be more relieved to see him alive."

"I am. It's just . . ."

"Complicated?"

She nods. "It might have been kinder to leave him without the consequences of his cowardice. It was far too little and far too late, but he finally did the right thing, and now he'll be punished for taking so long. Maybe he could have died brave, but he'll live a coward."

"So it never became real?"

"Real enough to leave scars. So not very real at all. How could it have been more?"

"He'll very likely stand trial to some degree. You will probably be called to testify against him."

Still looking at the young man in the bed, she doesn't answer.

He's not sure there's anything to say. "Inara—"

"Inara!" calls a female voice from the hall. "*Ina*—yes, I see your badge, you arrogant bastard, but that's my family in there! Inara!" There are sounds of a scuffle, then the door slams open to frame a woman of average height and maybe thirty years old or so, faded auburn hair threatening to tumble from a scraped-together bun.

Inara freezes partway through turning to the intruder, her eyes impossibly wide. Her voice creeps out as little more than a breath. "Sophia?"

Sophia runs into the room, but Inara meets her halfway, and the two of them cling to each other with white-knuckled grips. They sway from side to side from the force of the embrace.

The Sophia? The apartment mother? How did she even know Inara was here?

A thunder-faced Eddison stalks into the room, glaring at the woman as he passes. He thrusts a plain black scrapbook, thick with pages, into Victor's hands. "It was in a locked, hidden drawer in his office desk. The techs were running the names when they found something interesting."

Victor almost doesn't want to know, but this is his job. Tearing his eyes away from the two women, he sees a green sticky note fluttering from the edge about two-thirds of the way through. He opens to a few pages before it.

A young woman with terrified, tearful eyes stares back at him from a photo, shoulders hunched and hands partly raised as if caught in the process of trying to hide her naked breasts from the camera. Beside it, a picture from behind, showing fresh wings. Beneath it, those same wings in a fresh display case, the crisp edges of the wings blurred by the glass and colorless resin. In the empty space, there are two names—Lydia Anderson, on top, and below, Siobhan—in a firm masculine hand, followed by "Gulf Fritillary" and dates four years apart.

The next page has a different girl, and the one after, the one with the sticky, has only two pictures. And only one date. Beneath the picture of an auburn-haired beauty with wary hazel eyes, the writing says—

"Sophia Madsen," Victor reads aloud, stunned.

The woman looks at him over Inara's shoulder. She says the next line for him. "Lara."

"How—"

"No one would have talked of a Butterfly escaping if one never had," Inara mumbles into Sophia's hair. "It would have hurt too badly."

"The escape was real. You . . . you escaped?"

They both nod.

Eddison scowls. "The tech analysts typed in the name and it hit against our list of Evening Star employees. They sent someone to the restaurant and both listed residences, but she wasn't there."

"Of course I wasn't," retorts Sophia. "How could I be there when I was already on my way here?" She pulls back from Inara. Doesn't let go, just steps back enough to take all of her in. Sophia's shirt is worn and overlarge, the gaping neck sliding down one shoulder to reveal a bra strap and the edge of a faded wingtip, stretched with gained weight. "Taki saw you on the news, being brought into the hospital, and he ran to the apartment to get everyone. They called me, and oh, Inara!"

Inara wheezes in Sophia's renewed embrace, but doesn't ask her to let go.

"Are you all right?" asks Sophia.

"I will be," Inara replies quietly, almost shyly. "My hands are the worst, but if I'm careful, they should heal."

"That's not all I'm asking, and I *am* asking. I have my own place now, I can break the apartment rules."

Inara's face lights up, all the uncertainty and shock vanishing. "You got your girls back!"

"I did, and they'll be so glad to see you. They've missed you as much as the rest of us. They say no one reads to them as well as you do."

Eddison doesn't quite manage to turn his laugh into a cough.

Inara gives him a sour look.

For his part, Victor's almost relieved to see her sidestep the more probing question. At least she does it with everyone. He clears his throat to get their attention. "I'm sorry to interrupt, but I have to insist on an explanation."

"He usually does," Inara mutters.

Sophia just smiles. "It's pretty much his job.

375

But perhaps . . ." She glances over at the boy in the bed, Victor's eyes following. Desmond hasn't so much as twitched in all the noise. "Elsewhere?"

Victor nods and leads them out of the room. In the hallway, he can see Senator Kingsley standing alone in front of the door to the Butterflies' room, taking deep breaths. She should look softer in just the blouse and skirt; instead, she just looks scared. Victor wonders if her suit is like Inara's lip gloss, a way to armor up against the rest of the world.

"Do you think she'll go in?" Inara asks.

"Eventually," he answers. "Once she realizes this isn't something she can be ready for."

He takes them into a room in the buffer zone between the Butterflies and the MacIntosh family. It's private, at any rate, and one of the guards shifts down to make sure they're not disturbed. Inara and Sophia settle side by side on one of the stripped beds, facing the door and anyone who might try to enter. Victor sits on the opposite bed. He's unsurprised that Eddison decides to pace, rather than sit.

"Ms. Madsen?" Victor prompts. "If you please?"

"You do like to get right down to it, don't you?" Sophia shakes her head. "I'm sorry, but no, not yet. I've been waiting longer than you have."

Victor blinks, but nods.

Taking Inara's hand, Sophia wraps both of hers around it, holding tight. "We thought something from before had caught up with you," she says. "We thought you ran."

"It was a logical assumption," Inara tells her gently.

"But all your clothes—"

"Are just clothes."

Sophia shakes her head again. "If you were going to run, you would have taken your money. Whitney and I started an account for you, by the way. We didn't feel comfortable with that much cash sitting around."

"Sophia, if you're trying to find a way this is somehow your fault, you're not going to find it from me. We were all running from something. We all knew that. We all knew not to question it if someone disappeared."

"We should have. And the timing . . ."

"There was no way to know."

"The timing?" Victor asks.

"The event that the Gardener—Mister MacIntosh—"

Sophia gives a startled laugh. "He has a name. I mean, of course he does, but . . . how bizarre."

"The event at the Evening Star," Inara continues. "I didn't say anything about Mister MacIntosh being creepy, just about the run-in with Avery. But then we came home with all those costume butterfly wings."

"I drank myself damn near insensible," Sophia says grimly. "It was like being back in hell."

"I took her out to the fire escape to get some fresh air, and she ended up telling me all about the Garden."

"I'd never really told anyone before."

"Why not?" Victor asks. From the corner of his eye, he sees Eddison's pacing stop.

"At first, there didn't seem to be anything to say. I didn't know his name, I'd been so panicked on leaving that I didn't pay any attention to what was around me. I didn't know where the estate was. All I had was a tattoo and a growing fetus and a crazy story. I thought if I went to the police, they'd be just like my parents: assume I was drunk or high or screwing around and lying to avoid consequences."

"You went back to your parents?"

She makes a face. "They kicked me out. Said I was an embarrassment. I didn't have anywhere to go. I was nineteen and pregnant and didn't have anyone to help me."

Eddison perches on the very end of Victor's bed. "So Jillie is the Gardener's?"

"Jillie is *mine,*" she retorts, baring her teeth at him.

Eddison holds up both hands in a placating gesture. "But he is the father."

Sophia deflates, and Inara leans against her for comfort. "That was the other reason not to say anything. If he'd found out about her, I could have lost her. No court in the world would have let her stay with a heroin-addicted hooker when she could live with a wealthy, well-respected family. At least when social services took my girls, I could work to get them back. If he'd taken Jillie, I would never have seen her again, and I don't think Lotte would ever have gotten over it. They're my girls. I had to protect them."

Victor looks at Inara. "Isn't that what Desmond was doing? Protecting his family? You didn't think very well of him for it."

"It's not the same."

"Isn't it?"

"You know it isn't," she says dryly. "Sophia was protecting her children. Innocent children who don't deserve to suffer for what happened. Desmond was protecting criminals. Murderers."

"How did you escape?" asks Eddison.

"I was going to have to take a pregnancy test," Sophia replies. "I'd been gaining weight, and I was sick sometimes after lunch. Lor—our nurse brought the test to me, but got called away to deal with an injury before she could watch me take it. I just panicked. I ran around looking for any way out I might have missed in the past two and a half years. And I saw Avery."

"Avery was already in the Garden."

"He'd discovered it just a few weeks before. His father gave him a code but he had trouble remembering it. He was very slow when he put it in. That day I hid in the honeysuckle and watched him fumble through it. He even said the numbers while he pushed the buttons. I waited for a bit, then punched it in myself. I'd almost forgotten that doors could open normally."

Victor rubs at his cheek. "Did you tell any of the others?"

She starts to bristle, but then her shoulders slump. "I guess I can see why that's a question," she admits. "After all, by not going to the police, I left them there to die, didn't I? But I did try." She meets his eyes firmly. "I swear to you, I did try. They were just too scared to go. I was too scared to stay."

"Scared?"

"What happens if you only almost escape?" asks Inara, but it feels more like a reminder than a question.

"It had been less than a month since a girl named Emiline stayed out during maintenance," Sophia says. "She tried to tell the gardeners what was going on, but the Gardener must have smoothed it over somehow. The next time we saw her, she was in glass. Escape is a hard thing to attempt when you see it punished like that. But you blame me for leaving them behind."

"No." Victor shakes his head. "You gave them the chance. You can't save someone against her will."

"Speaking of which, Lorraine is here."

Sophia turns to Inara with dismay. "Oh no. Still?"

Inara nods.

"That poor woman," she murmurs. Inara gives her a sideways look but says nothing. "I was on the street with other whores longer than I was in the Garden, but I've never seen a woman so thoroughly broken as Lorraine. He loved her and then he didn't and it was never any fault of hers. Hate her if you have to, but I just feel sorry for her. More than the rest of us, maybe, she never had a chance."

"She's never going to be in glass now."

"She was never going to be in glass back when I knew her. Does it change anything?"

"Inara?" They all turn to look at Eddison; as far as Victor can remember, it's the first time Eddison has called the girl by name. "Did you get kidnapped on purpose? Is that what you've been hiding?"

"On *purpose?*" gasps Sophia, shoving off the bed.

"No, I—"

"You did this on purpose?"

"No! I—"

Victor tunes out Sophia's rather impressive lecture, turning sideways to look at his partner. "How did you get from complicit to getting caught on purpose?" he asks, mind racing. If Eddison is right, this could change everything.

There'd be no saving her from the senator, or the courts. To go to such lengths without going to the police? To be deliberate in the middle of such dangers is one thing, but to choose to go there? To knowingly endanger herself and, perhaps, those other girls?

"If she wasn't hiding that she was part of it, what was she hiding?"

"I was hiding Sophia!" snaps Inara, grabbing her friend's arm and tugging sharply. With a startled "oomph," Sophia falls back onto the bed. "On purpose, really, do I look that stupid?"

"Do you want me to answer that?" Eddison asks with a grin.

She glowers at him. "I was hiding Sophia," Inara repeats more softly. She glances at Victor. "I appreciate that my word may not be worth particularly much, but I swear to you, that's the truth. I knew if Sophia's name came up, so would the truth about Jillie, and I couldn't . . . Sophia worked so hard to get her life back together. I couldn't be the thing that turned that upside down. I couldn't be the reason she lost her girls. I needed time to think."

"About what?" Victor asks.

She shrugs. "I needed to see if there was a way to avoid tying her back to the Garden. Hiding the book would have been the easiest, but that . . . well. So then I thought, if I could just delay long enough, I could call her, warn her, but she . . ."

382

"You didn't expect her to come."

Inara shakes her head.

"But you knew about the Garden," Eddison insists.

"Not that it was them." Inara cradles the sad little dragon in both hands. "When her memories of the Garden started bleeding, it was at the sight of the costume wings, nothing more. None of us who worked that night said what the clients looked like; why would we? And they were fundraising for *Madame Butterfly*, the theme made sense. I didn't know."

Victor nods slowly. "You knew about the Garden, though, so when you woke up there, you didn't panic."

"Exactly. I tried to watch for Avery's codes, but he was more careful. Well, it had been ten years, after all. I looked everywhere but I couldn't find another way out. I even tried breaking the glass up by the trees. Didn't even crack."

"And then Desmond."

"Desmond?" asks Sophia.

"The Gardener's younger son. I tried . . ." Inara shakes her head, shoving her hair out of her face. "You know how Hope can get the guys she's fucking to do anything for her? Like they'd walk through a burning building if she mentioned her favorite necklace was in there?"

"Yes . . ."

"I tried that."

"Oh dear." Sophia bumps her shoulder into Inara's, a smile lighting up her tired features. "You being you, I can't imagine that going well."

"It really didn't."

"He did make the call," Victor reminds her.

"I don't think that was because of anything I did," she confesses. "I think that was mostly Avery."

"Wait, what now?"

"They couldn't co-exist in the Garden. Maybe not ever, but especially not there, and not with their father's pride at stake. They were competing for his love. Avery did something drastic, and Desmond did something drastic in response. They both lost."

"But you won."

"I don't think anyone won," she says. "Two days ago, there were twenty-three of us, including Keely. Now there are thirteen. How many do you think can actually adjust to Outside?"

"You think there will be suicides?"

"I think a trauma doesn't stop just because you've been rescued."

Eddison stands and takes the scrapbook from Victor. "I need to get this back to the scene techs," he tells him. "Need anything while I'm out there?"

"Check and see if anyone has gotten in touch with the MacIntosh family lawyer. Geoffrey and Desmond aren't in any condition to need one yet, but Eleanor should have counsel. Check on

Lorraine, too. See if the psychologists have made a preliminary determination."

"Roger." He nods to Inara and leaves the room.

Inara quirks an eyebrow. "You know, a few more days of being trapped in a tiny room with him, I might even start to think of him as a friend." She smiles at Victor, sweet and somewhat insincere but still real. It quickly fades. "So what happens next?"

"There'll be more interviews. Many more interviews. You'll be included in those, Ms. Madsen."

"I figured. I brought a suitcase for each of us."

"Suitcase?" echoes Inara.

"It's in the trunk; I borrowed Guilian's car." She smiles and gives Inara a small shake. "Did you think I was going to give up on you? We kept all your things and your bed is still there. I told you Whitney and I started an account with the ridiculous amount of money you had lying around. It should have some decent interest in it. And Guilian says you're welcome back at the restaurant."

"You . . . you kept my stuff?" she asks weakly.

Sophia gently tweaks Inara's nose. "You're one of my girls too."

Inara blinks rapidly, her eyes bright, but then tears spill over her lashes and down her cheeks. She touches a fingertip to the damp skin with astonishment.

Victor clears his throat. "The carousel's over now," he tells her quietly. "This time your family is waiting for you."

Inara sucks in a deep, shuddering breath, trying to collect herself, but Sophia's arms wrap around her, carefully easing her down to her lap. She dissolves into silent weeping. Only the tremors wracking her body and her uneven breathing give her away. Sophia doesn't stroke the dark, glossy hair. That's too much like the Gardener, Victor imagines. Instead, she runs one finger along the curve of Inara's ear, over and over again, until Inara gives a watery laugh and pushes herself back to sitting.

Victor holds his handkerchief across the space between the beds. She takes it and mops at her face. "People come back?" he suggests.

Her voice is soft with wonder. "And other people expect them to."

"You know there's one more thing."

Her thumb rubs against the sad, little blue dragon. "You have to understand, she isn't real. She never was. I wasn't a real person until I became Inara."

"And Inara can be the real person. You're eighteen now, if you were telling the truth."

She gives him a wry look.

He smiles, then continues. "You can legally change your name to Inara Morrissey, but only if we have your current legal name."

"You survived the Gardener and his sons," Sophia points out. "Even if your parents do come calling, you don't owe them anything. Your family is here in the hospital, and in New York. Your parents are nothing."

The girl takes a slow breath, lets it out even more slowly, then does it again. "Samira," she says eventually, her voice shaking. "The name on my birth certificate was Samira Grantaire."

He extends his hand. She looks at it for a moment, then rests the clay dragon on her thigh so she can lean out and accept the grip. Sophia has her other hand. "Thank you, Samira Grantaire. Thank you for telling us the truth. Thank you for taking care of those girls. Thank you for being so incredibly brave."

"And so incredibly stubborn," adds Sophia.

The girl laughs, her face bright and open and tear-streaked, and Victor decides this is a good day. He's not naïve enough to think that all is well. There will still be pain and trauma, all the wounds of the investigation and trial. There are dead girls to mourn, and living girls who will struggle for years to adjust to life outside the Garden, if they even can.

He still counts this as a good day.

Acknowledgments

Sometimes I think this part is harder than writing the whole rest of the book.

But there are so many people to whom I am deeply indebted for the existence of this book. To Mom and Deb, for answering disturbing and bizarre medical questions for research, and thus saving me from getting put on Lists for asking Google terrifying things. To Dad and my brothers, for continuing to support this strange, difficult dream of mine. To Sandy, for not giving up on the quiet, creepy little monster that didn't seem to have a home. To Isabel and Chelsea, for being early readers and having a reaction other than "What the hell is wrong with you?" To Tessa, for having the patience and talent to talk me off the ledges I keep finding myself on. To Alison and JoVon, for taking a chance on it, and Caitlin, for asking so many fantastic questions and herding me—however hysterical I got—into finding ways to better this book.

To the friends who've forgiven me for being profoundly antisocial while working on this, and the coworkers who are probably sick of hearing me talk about it, and the managers who are so excited to get it in.

To you, for sticking with me this long.

About the Author

Dot Hutchison is the author of *A Wounded Name*, a young adult novel based on Shakespeare's *Hamlet*, and the adult thriller *The Butterfly Garden*. With past experience working at a Boy Scout camp, a craft store, a bookstore, and the Renaissance Faire (as a human combat chess piece), Hutchison prides herself on remaining delightfully in tune with her inner young adult. She loves thunderstorms, mythology, history, and movies that can and should be watched on repeat. For more information on her current projects, visit www.dothutchison.com or check her out on Tumblr (www.dothutchison.tumblr.com), Twitter (@DotHutchison), or Facebook (www.facebook .com/DotHutchison).

Center Point Large Print
600 Brooks Road / PO Box 1
Thorndike, ME 04986-0001 USA

(207) 568-3717

US & Canada:
1 800 929-9108
www.centerpointlargeprint.com